Praise for the work of

Sex and the Psychic Witch

"Sassy, sexy, and sizzling!"

"A great addition to any paranormal romance reader's collection!"
—*Paranormal Romance Writers*

"Ms. Blair's humor and wit is evident in many ways . . . *Sex and the Psychic Witch* is . . . a delight [that] will bring chuckles."
—*Romance Reviews Today*

"A sexy, hilarious, romantic tale with fun characters, snappy writing, and some super-spooky moments. I've looked forward to this story since the introduction of the triplets in *The Scot, the Witch and the Wardrobe*, and it was well worth the wait!" —*Fresh Fiction*

"Plenty of paranormal activity and lots of sexual tension . . . You'll love this heroine and absolutely great hero . . . A delightfully magical read."
—*Romantic Times*

"Hot scenes . . . spine chills . . . outrageous stunts . . . [and] a witchy climax that will warm your very soul. I can hardly wait until the next Cartwright triplet spins her spell. Out-Freaking-Standing!"
—*Huntress Reviews*

The Scot, the Witch and the Wardrobe

"Sassy dialogue, rich sexual tension, and plenty of laughs make this an immensely satisfying return to Blair's world of witchcraft. Fans will welcome back familiar characters in supporting roles, but newcomers will take to it just as well." —*Publishers Weekly*

"Snappy dialogue can't disguise the characters' true insecurities, giving depth to Blair's otherwise breezy, lighthearted tale." —*Booklist*

continued . . .

My Favorite Witch

"Sexy."
—*Booklist*

"Annette Blair will make your blood sizzle with this magical tale . . . A terrific way to start the new year!"
—*Huntress Reviews*

"This warmhearted story is a delight, filled with highly appealing characters sure to touch your heart. The magic in the air spotlights the humor that's intrinsic to the story. A definite charmer!"
—*Romantic Times*

"Annette Blair writes with wit and humor . . . Mixed with the fun, Ms. Blair shares the beauty of unconditional love . . . A great story."
—*Romance Reviews Today*

"Lighthearted comedy, a touch of magic . . . unexpected twists . . . a romance that sizzles . . . A great story sure to be placed on the prized keeper shelf!"
—*The Romance Readers Connection*

"Sparkles with wit, romance, and a love so grand, no magic could ever hope to create it. It's from the heart, the truest magic of all."
—*Fallen Angel Reviews*

"A fabulous read! Kira and Jason are made for one another and their witty, teasing, sexy banter is laugh-out-loud fun. Ms. Blair has a gift for layering her characters and revealing them gently, cleverly, allowing readers to get to know them on a deeper level."
—*Fresh Fiction*

"Annette Blair charms her readers with the amusing *My Favorite Witch* . . . An enchanting pairing . . . Bewitching."
—*The Best Reviews*

"*My Favorite Witch* is magically delicious! The chemistry between Annette's characters is incredible. A terrific contemporary romance, told with passion and verve, this book proves magic makes sex even sexier!"
—*Romance Junkies*

The Kitchen Witch

"Blair has crafted a fun and sexy romp."
—*Booklist*

"Magic. *The Kitchen Witch* sizzles. Ms. Blair's writing is as smooth as a fine Kentucky bourbon. Sexy, fun, top-notch entertainment."
—*Romance Reader*

"Bewitching! Full of charm, humor, sensuality . . . An easy-reading, reader-pleasing story that makes you feel good all over."
—*Reader to Reader*

An Unmistakable Rogue

"*An Unmistakable Rogue* brings to mind the best of Teresa Medeiros or Loretta Chase: funny, passionate, exquisitely lyrical." —Eloisa James

"An innovative mix of family frolic and period gothic . . . fast-paced romance . . . plenty of sexual tension. Wonderful." —*Romantic Times*

"Humorous . . . Emotional . . . Delectable." —*Reader to Reader*

"What this story is filled with is love." —*Romance and Friends*

An Unforgettable Rogue

"Never has a hero submitted to such sweet seduction while making it clear that he is still very much a man in charge . . . Spicy sensuality is the hallmark of this unforgettable story." —*The Romance Readers Connection*

" 'Knight In Shining Silver' Award for KISSable heroes. Bryceson 'Hawk' Wakefield is most definitely *An Unforgettable Rogue*."
—*Romantic Times*

"I recommend *An Unforgettable Rogue* as an entertaining book in its own right, even more as part of the must-read Rogues Club series."
—*Romance Reviews Today*

An Undeniable Rogue

"A love story that is pure joy, enchanting characters who steal your heart, a fast pace and great storytelling." —*Romantic Times*

"An utterly charming and heartwarming marriage of convenience story. I highly recommend it to all lovers of romance." —*Romance Reviews Today*

"Awesome! To call this story incredible would be an understatement . . . Do not miss this title." —*Huntress Reviews*

"Annette Blair skillfully pens an exhilarating, humorous, and easy to read historical romance. You don't want to miss *An Undeniable Rogue*."
—Jan Springer

Gone with the Witch

Annette Blair

BERKLEY SENSATION, NEW YORK

THE BERKLEY PUBLISHING GROUP
Published by the Penguin Group
Penguin Group (USA) Inc.
375 Hudson Street, New York, New York 10014, USA

Penguin Group (Canada), 90 Eglinton Avenue East, Suite 700, Toronto, Ontario M4P 2Y3, Canada
(a division of Pearson Penguin Canada Inc.)
Penguin Books Ltd., 80 Strand, London WC2R 0RL, England
Penguin Group Ireland, 25 St. Stephen's Green, Dublin 2, Ireland (a division of Penguin Books Ltd.)
Penguin Group (Australia), 250 Camberwell Road, Camberwell, Victoria 3124, Australia
(a division of Pearson Australia Group Pty. Ltd.)
Penguin Books India Pvt. Ltd., 11 Community Centre, Panchsheel Park, New Delhi—110 017, India
Penguin Group (NZ), 67 Apollo Drive, Rosedale, North Shore 0632, New Zealand
(a division of Pearson New Zealand Ltd.)
Penguin Books (South Africa) (Pty.) Ltd., 24 Sturdee Avenue, Rosebank, Johannesburg 2196,
South Africa

Penguin Books Ltd., Registered Offices: 80 Strand, London WC2R 0RL, England

GONE WITH THE WITCH

A Berkley Sensation Book / published by arrangement with the author

PRINTING HISTORY
Berkley Sensation mass-market edition / May 2008

ISBN: 978-0-425-22121-1

BERKLEY® SENSATION
Berkley Sensation Books are published by The Berkley Publishing Group,
a division of Penguin Group (USA) Inc.,
375 Hudson Street, New York, New York 10014.
BERKLEY SENSATION and the "B" design are trademarks of Penguin Group (USA) Inc.

PRINTED IN THE UNITED STATES OF AMERICA

10 9 8 7 6 5 4 3 2 1

Chapter One

BENEATH a rare blue moon in June, Storm Cartwright, bridesmaid, her black hair streaked blue to match her gown, stood with Aiden McCloud, best man, the scruffy stud muffin she planned to kidnap after her sister's wedding, unless he decided to cooperate. In which case, hell was bound to freeze over before midnight.

"I know you hate tailcoats, Scruffleupagus, but, dragon's blood, you clean up good for an outlaw biker."

"I'll only feel good when I can take it *off*," he said.

She certainly hoped so. "This is your last chance," she warned him. "We both have two weeks off. Come with me to find the baby I hear crying in my mind when I'm near you."

Aiden raised a brow as dark as his hair, the quirk of his sculpted lips beguiling. "In your mind," he repeated thoughtfully. "Those words strike fear in my heart. I have saner things to do than chase the voices in *your* head, thank you very much."

"Do I scare you?" A sense of power fired Storm's confidence.

"You'd think so, wouldn't you?" Aiden shook his head as if he should know better.

A sea breeze tossed his thick, wavy hair so one lazy lock landed on his brow, giving a hint of the bad boy look she loved, even without the scruffy hair and five o'clock shadow. She grabbed her wildflower coronet to keep the wind from tossing that as well, and Aiden's gaze kept pace with the rise of her breasts as her arm went up.

Since meeting him—a case of electromagnetic attraction at first sight—Storm's clairvoyance and clairaudience had kicked into overdrive. Near him—heard only by her—a crying baby's psychic plea put all her senses on high alert, because if the baby *wasn't* connected to him, she wouldn't hear it cry around him. Her plan to follow the sound and find the child—his child, she believed, and he denied—meant taking him on a journey with no destination, a concept he found ludicrous at best.

And who could blame him? If she couldn't hear the cry so clearly, *she* wouldn't have believed it.

They regarded each other in a kind of silent face-off filled with electric currents.

Aiden stroked the soft flesh of her wrist with his thumb, sending a shiver all the way to her marrow, as fragrant peach rose petals drifted past. His smiling Irish eyes fired sparks of green her way as he assessed her with his hungry gaze, touching her in places that ached for his tactile attention.

One hot look, and he could turn her to jelly.

"Drop the agenda," he whispered, his rough, suggestive voice stroking more tender nerve endings, "and it's a hot date road trip in a luxury motor coach that could pamper you prissy."

"Hah. Me, prissy? In your dreams, Biker Boy." Maybe she should accept the hot date road trip and let the sound of the crying baby direct them without telling him. She already planned to hijack his motor home along with him.

"Forget it," Aiden said, reclaiming his hand. "No road trip, and no wands or spells to get your way. Your body language makes me twitch. Maybe I'll stay in Salem. I've never explored the Witch City. You could give me a"—he leaned close—"personal tour." He eyed the triquetra tattoo low on one breast as it peeked from the plunging neckline of her vintage royal blue gown, then he forcefully shifted his hungry gaze to her mouth. "I could make a meal of those luscious blackberry lips of yours."

Translation: He could screw her senseless.

Storm sighed in satisfaction. The stage was set: a horny hunk, a full moon, a wedding beneath the stars, music wafting over the island, waves breaking against the shore, fairy-lit trees, rose-scented air, and a wedding reception made for seduction.

Whether he knew it or not, Aiden McCloud was going to steal her away to his home on wheels later, and she was going to let him.

For three weeks, they'd been playing a sexual version of chicken, a bit like juggling fireballs, almost hoping to get burned. As far as she was concerned, this was more than her sister's wedding. It was an opportunity for some pre-foreplay foreplay culminating in a premeditated coed inferno, which might . . . or might not . . . take the top spot on her agenda at the end of the day.

She'd make it happen, and she didn't need magick to pull it off. She had a plan: a choreographed seduction . . . and celibacy . . . three weeks' worth. Yes, abstinence, amazingly enough, as in the lack of, as in they'd never had sex . . . with each other . . . a rather mystically mutual state of affairs that fit her scheme so well, she hadn't questioned it, though perhaps she should have.

Too late to worry about that now.

After the reception, if her allies played their parts, she and Aiden would drive off alone together on a psychic quest with sex as a bonus. Multiple bonuses, and multiple multiples . . . she hoped.

The search for his child felt to her like a spiritual directive, and answering that child's cry became her psychic mandate . . . a matter of need meeting destiny.

Secure in the altruistic excellence of her goal, Storm beamed.

Judging by Aiden's quick physical response to her grin, her anticipation hit him square in the libido.

Oh yeah, they were on the same wavelength, all right, both hot as lightning bolts and ready to strike.

Between them, they had sexual chemistry stockpiled in gigawatts.

"Cut that out," Aiden whispered, turning his back on the wedding guests to face her and hide his physical reaction. "We're standing, literally, in the spotlight. People are watching."

"Dragon's blood," Storm whispered in return, glancing down at him. "You're certainly giving them something to see. *You* cut it out. This is the bride's day. Don't you go shortchanging my sister."

Storm made sure her scowl matched Aiden's, but inside, she was rubbing her hands together in glee with a warm, tingly, sex berry gel.

Judging by his insta-boner, the role of seducer was "up" for grabs.

Aiden leaned in, his nearness tickling her skin and invading her senses like whipped cream and peach blossoms. "I'm gonna get you for this," he promised.

Dragon's blood, he looked hot. "Finally," she quipped, tossing the proverbial gauntlet to speed her plan on its merry way. "You'll excuse me if I have my doubts about your libido going the distance?"

Aiden straightened in indignation. "Are you kidding me?" he snapped, forgetting they weren't alone, disbelief in the set of his square jaw, the echo of his words causing whispers.

Storm shushed him as the strains of "Blue Moon," rather than the wedding march, wafted from the orchestra. She stepped forward to take the arm of the groomsman Morgan Jarvis, and Aiden stepped back to escort her sister Destiny, the maid of honor, for the trek down the garden path. At the gazebo, Aiden went to the groom's side and

Storm to the bride's, to witness the marriage of Aiden's best friend, King, to her sister Harmony.

Now climbing the gazebo steps to meet her groom, Harmony wore the impeccably restored gold linen day gown that had led her to King Paxton in the first place, a vintage blond lace cathedral veil trailing behind her.

When the music stopped, the bride as high priestess cast a ritual circle that encompassed the bridal couple, the wedding party, the justice of the peace, and four cats.

In addition to Destiny and Storm, the bride's two clone attendants, Harmony had also chosen her future step-daughter, Reggie, and her pregnant half sister, Vickie, who positively glowed.

Standing up for King were his three-year-old grandson as ring bearer, his two best friends, and the Scot who'd knocked up Harmony's half sister and married her shortly afterward.

Capping a wedding ceremony melding Celtic and traditional elements, Harmony and King kissed as husband and wife for the first time. Applause and a hearty rendition of "By the Light of the Silvery Moon" followed them into Paxton Castle for the wedding reception.

The constellations winked, and the moon smiled wide as Storm anticipated seducing Badass McCloud throughout the reception and into the night, then taking him prisoner . . . likely in shackles.

And somewhere down the road—once he willingly joined her quest—she anticipated having her very wicked way with him.

Chapter Two

LET the seduction begin, her ass!

Storm paced the length of the upper gallery overlooking the great hall. She hadn't so much as touched Aiden since before the ceremony, and that hardly counted with a hundred wedding guests watching their every move.

With the videographer at the bottom of the stairs and the photographer at the top, she had been forced to stay on Morgan's arm as they formed part of a formal procession, gliding up the stairs in their wedding finery to the balcony. There, an Austrian crystal chandelier cast prismatic lights like moonbeams on the restored gold damask walls, giving the Victorian castle a quixotic ambience all its own. And there, the photographer and videographer got busy.

Storm failed to remain patient through the photo shoot as she watched Aiden partnering Destiny. Okay, so the maid of honor and best man were well-chosen, and she wasn't one of them. Fine. That wasn't the point. The point was that her seduction hadn't yet begun, and the evening was marching on. At least she'd get to sit with Aiden at supper and dance with him afterward.

All things being equal, the photographer took great shots. Storm's personal favorite—this one—with King bending Harmony low over his arm and kissing her senseless . . . forever.

When the bride and groom finally came up for air, Storm stepped up to Aiden and tapped him on the shoulder. "My turn," she said, having caught the photographer's eye, and with a promising wink, she bent Aiden over her arm and kissed her favorite stud muffin senseless.

The photographer's chuckle and multiple shutter clicks were all the encouragement Storm needed, though at some point during the stunt, both cameras and onlookers ceased to exist.

Coming up for air, Storm faced the wedding party—some smiling, some not, but who cared? She'd taken her first step. "My bad," she said and grinned.

Looking more dazed than annoyed or embarrassed, Aiden straightened his tailcoat and tugged on his French cuffs.

Storm fanned herself. Score one for the kidnapper.

"Tasteful, Sis," Destiny said. "Upstaging the bride on her wedding day." A stunner in her turn-of-the-century mulberry gown, Des was doing some upstaging of her own.

Harmony slipped her arms around them both while the photographer and videographer kept shooting. "Don't worry about it," she told Destiny. "This bride is used to Storm warnings. I'm betting that particular picture will be one of my favorites. I do believe the photographer caught every step of Aiden's shock . . . and surrender."

Aiden swore beneath his breath, but Storm pretended not to hear.

"Now, a posed picture of the triplets," the photographer said, catching them off guard. "Please?" he begged when they hesitated, as they always did, about posing as a three-pack.

"It's not as if we're dressed alike," Harmony said, which meant she wanted the picture as a memento of her wedding day.

The photographer beamed with satisfaction. "Bride in gold in the middle, bridesmaid in blue on one side, maid of honor in pink on the other. Triplet bombshells," he said, giddy behind his camera. He climbed the top riser to take a shot looking down toward the opulent castle great hall, men in black tie and women in vintage gowns sipping cocktails below.

The photographer then rearranged them and seated them on the risers with their bouquets on assorted antique tables behind them. "This time, blue hair in the middle," he said, overlapping their skirts to hide the risers and posing them with their heads together.

"I always liked the three musketeers shot," Storm quipped.

The photographer stood back, cleared his throat, and took the picture. "I could have won an award for that picture, young lady, if your hair was blonde like it should be."

An unexpected hand fell on Storm's shoulder as she shot to her feet and kept her from going for the guy's jugular. "Buddy," Aiden told the jerk, "if I hadn't stopped her, you'd be singing soprano right now. Storm is unique. Gorgeous. Dazzling. We like her the way she is. Apologize, or deal with me."

"Aye, and me, too, you bletherin' fool," Rory, her Scot brother-in-law, said, bringing the rest of the wedding party to her defense.

After the photographer apologized, Aiden took her hand and led her from the balcony. "You're a nut, you know that? What were you gonna do, coldcock him?"

Storm huffed. "Why are you yelling at *me*?"

"Because I can't hit *him*."

"I was thinking along the lines of castration. Got a problem with that?"

"Yeah, it makes me wanna puke." Aiden slid his hand to her nape and brought her brow to his. "You smell like . . . berries . . . or wildflowers." He inhaled, sighed, and stepped quickly back. "I must be allergic."

"Your allergy reeks of commitment phobia."

"My aftershave is called Independence. If anything reeks, it's that. I wear it as an expression of strength and fortitude, and I wear it proudly, make no mistake."

Storm nuzzled his cheek and down to his neck to wallow in the scent. "I like it." Okay, so she'd caught his attention, too. *She* wouldn't let a little thing like a declaration of independence stop her. "My perfume is billed as passionate, impulsive, and electric," she said. "It's black currant and lily of the valley, a floral-fruity scent."

"Like you," he said, still up close and personal.

She raised her head. "You think I'm electric?"

"No, I think you're a fruit."

Before Storm could react, Destiny hooked an arm through Aiden's and whisked him down the stairs. Storm took Morgan's arm and followed.

Each couple entered the great hall to formal introductions and applause and went to the wedding supper table to stand before their place cards.

After King and Harmony sat down, the wedding party did, too, and Storm leaned forward to see the far end of the table, on the opposite side of the bride and groom, where Aiden sat with Destiny.

"Spell me! How am I supposed to seduce him from here?"

"He's not going anywhere," Morgan said.

"Did I say that out loud?"

"Afraid so."

"Keep my secret?"

"It's no secret, Blue Hair."

Storm wilted. "Am I that obvious?"

Morgan covered his mouth with a knuckle for a minute, as if he were trying not to smile. "Obvious?" he asked. "You've got 'I'm hot for Aiden' tattooed on your forehead. Be warned. The more you chase, the faster he'll go."

Morgan had a great smile. Who knew? And a sense of humor, too. Storm relaxed. "It's not what you think."

"Right. It's his crying baby you're after," Morgan added. "Here's a clue: The thought of that kid doesn't scare Aiden half as much as you do."

"Don't judge me, Morgan. I'm not the only one around here with a tattoo. Yours says, 'I need to get laid by Destiny.'"

"See, that's where you're wrong. I don't need to get laid at all." Morgan's eyes twinkled for a minute before he erupted in a full-bodied laugh, open and guileless. "How about we get to know each other better over supper?" he suggested.

"Sure. What do you wanna talk about?"

"You tell me Destiny's secrets, and I'll tell you Aiden's?"

"Deal."

Wild stories about Aiden and Destiny kept them entertained through dinner.

"Do you realize," Morgan asked, "that every time we laugh, Aiden leans forward to frown at us?"

"Perfect," Storm said, surprised that the time for the ritual cake cutting came so fast. Soon, she was biting into a decadent piece of red velvet wedding cake with icing seashells that matched their gowns.

"The wedding party dance," Morgan said. "Shall we?"

Storm got up, but duh, Aiden was taking Destiny in his arms. "Well this bites," she said, stepping into Morgan's arms.

"I like dancing with you, too."

"I didn't mean—"

"Sure you did, but give me a minute, until the guests start joining in, and we'll switch partners. I'll take full responsibility."

"You're an okay guy, you know that?"

"Tell your sister," Morgan said as they closed in on Destiny and Aiden.

I will, Storm thought, but Destiny would never believe her.

Morgan tapped Aiden's shoulder, and when Aiden stepped aside, Storm stepped into his arms. "Surprise," she said.

Chapter Three

INDEPENDENT, his ass! He'd felt nothing but ... incomplete ... since he'd met the storm witch. Effin' A. He'd been impatient to get back to her ever since the ceremony. He loved having her in his arms. He hated that he loved having her in his arms.

He needed a straitjacket.

Aiden tried not to reveal his need by dancing with Storm as if she were a department store dummy ... until she went limp and tripped him up.

He caught his balance. "What was that about?"

"Treat me like a blow-up doll, I deflate. Any woman would. Are you trying to avoid me?"

"Of course not."

While King and Harmony were speaking their vows, he'd had a moment of clarity. The safest bet for Storm would be for him to stay as far away from her as possible ... for the rest of the evening ... the rest of their two-week vacation ... then for the rest of their lives ... which Aiden feared could only happen if an earthquake parted the continent, and he and Storm stood on opposite sides at the time.

He needed to get through this reception, this very long—pun intended—evening, without letting down his guard and giving in to his raging hormones, so he could do whatever it took to protect her from his fly-by-night lifestyle and no-commitment rule.

In addition to protecting her, he believed that his reasonably safe and sane world could use some protecting as well. Situation in point: "Are you trying to seduce me?" he asked.

Her thigh stroked his groin. "You couldn't tell?"

Wonderful. Over the last three weeks, they'd worked themselves into a sexual frenzy, a high-powered attraction that threatened to expose his utter stupidity. "Well, cut it out," he said. "We're in public here."

Storm's skeptical chuckle raised his blood pressure—as if there wasn't enough being raised around here. "Screw you," she said.

"Screw you."

"Please do."

He wished to hell he could. "We may have reacted to lust at first sight, Storm, but it's time to be practical." He would not be seduced into lowering his guard . . . or his pants.

"We may have reacted to it, but we never acted on it," she pointed out. "We've been practical by doing everything that could be done . . . without consummation. I say it's time to be impractical . . . and take out the big gun."

Big and getting bigger, yet he couldn't walk away, because, one: he'd embarrass the hell out of himself with this boner, and two: being a best man required manners during the bridal waltz.

"Behave yourself," Aiden said as he did the exact opposite and pulled her close, despite his determination to keep as much of a physical distance as an emotional one. But his man brain, as Storm called it, knew only too well where it wanted to go, and without his other brain's consent, he and Storm melded as if they'd been formed in the opposite halves of the same mold.

She sighed and rested her head on his shoulder.

Aiden closed his eyes and savored. Inhaling the honey-suckle scent of her hair, he about died happy. Having her in his arms again made him feel as if he'd . . . come home.

No, damn it! He hated the thought of home.

He didn't want home. He wanted wheels. Freedom. Independence. The life of a wanderer. A happy wanderer. No commitments . . . well, no more than his inheritance saddled him with. But love? Never.

Here he was waltzing with the greatest single threat to his lifestyle since . . . the woman who'd dumped him, and later died, while he was focused on screwing up his life—to prove he could.

Storm would be better off without him. Storm the goth bridesmaid—hair spikes tame for the occasion—had nearly seduced him in public before the wedding ceremony. A red flag if ever he'd succumbed to one.

No wonder he was shaking in his Italian wedding shoes.

Today in particular, Storm seemed focused on seduction, and wasn't she a huge success, holding him in thrall against his will.

No easy task, walking away from a sorceress weaving a sex spell, but she would be better off without him. And he . . . needed to make his own way in the world, his own choices and decisions . . . alone. That's who he was. A loner. A wanderer. He should tell her that he'd decided to leave tonight, rather than hang around Salem for the next two weeks, but the minute she trailed one long blue fingernail with white glitter hearts down his chest, Aiden lost the power of speech.

Just as well. If he told her he was leaving town, she might try to seduce him into staying and revealing . . . all.

Were secrets even possible around the scintillating psychic? "Are you the triplet who senses the past or the future?" he asked her. Please, God, let it be the future.

"I'm the triplet with the psychic power no one understands." Storm sighed. "I hear and see the present, of all things. Like the crying baby attached to you, who smells of baby powder and apricots, and makes me crave Froot Loops with chocolate milk. Like the fact that you really don't *want* to be with me at all."

Aiden scoffed, rather than admit how much he did want her and how bad he'd be for her. "I want . . . to be your friend."

Storm rolled her eyes. "Moving on. I know that you're as attracted to me as I am to you, which everybody knows, by the way, except they're sure we're sleeping together. Foolish them."

Aiden pulled the stunner against him and let his body ride the rhythm of hers, and after a few dazed minutes, he came to his senses. "Why would we go and ruin a great friendship by sleeping together?"

"Exquisite pleasure," she whispered, her answer warming his ear as she bit his lobe, making him shiver, standing his every nerve on end, and diverting his blood from his brain to points south. "Satisfaction," she purred.

Aiden's mouth went dry. His mind went blank. What were they talking about? Oh yeah, sleeping together, but why . . . because they were most certainly *not* sleeping together . . . un-freaking-fortunately. How stupid was he?

"I think people confuse sex with romance," he said. "They want romance, but they think of it in sexual terms. It's romance we need. Bantering is romantic, especially with someone who loves and knows how to banter, like you. And teasing . . . I'm an inveterate tease, and I *can* do romance. I just can't get involved."

"You couldn't be romantic if it came up and bit you in the butt."

"Thank you," he said. "I needed that splash of cold water."

"You're pissin' me off, McCloud. You're lucky I didn't throw crushed ice and that you didn't need it for your balls." She stomped on his foot with a spiked heel.

Aiden groaned, winced, and danced faster to keep his feet and her heels apart. "Trading insults," he said, "challenging each other, saying things you wouldn't say to anyone else, that's romance. Women need men, and men need women. They need romance. Dancing is a form of romance." God he sounded like a babbling idiot.

"You didn't *want* to dance with me, and as Destiny would say, 'There's dancing, and there's . . . dancing.'" Storm raised an arm, pressed a breast against his tailcoat over the racing beat of his heart, and toyed with the hair at his nape, a move that never failed to arouse. Good thing they were as close as two pieces of an X-rated puzzle.

"Storm, you're the best friend I've ever had. Let's not ruin it with—"

"Yep, it was friendship at first sight for us," she said, wit dry, sarcasm palpable, and still he fell into the sensual pull of her gaze.

With determination and difficulty, he withdrew from her spell. "We're great friends," he reiterated.

"Well, friend, in that tux you look lip-smacking, chocolate-dipping delicious, and I could eat you up with a spoon."

"I don't think spooning is allowed between friends."

"Neither is poking a friend on the dance floor with the steel cattle prod in one's pants."

Chapter Four

LEAVING his thinking to his insane man brain, Aiden about died of bliss as Storm continued to thigh-stroke him with wicked intent, taking him dangerously close to breaking his vow of celibate independence.

To distract himself, he scrutinized her with the eye of an artist examining a fine painting, but he found only perfection in the artwork of her creator, and more pleasure with every brush of her thigh.

She'd gone traditional for her sister's wedding, or as traditional as a goth could get. Easy on the eye makeup, four aquamarine studs in each ear—rather than cow bells or wind chimes—and her normally spiked, multicolored hair was now more blue than black and tamed to an under curl at her shoulders.

The ultimate kicky seducer—two thin blue strands of hair on each side of her face—skimmed her cheeks and curled beneath her chin to form an inverted heart. Turned him on like crazy.

Incredibly beautiful . . . and sexy as sin. Like a sex storm in a prizewinning package and all his to unwrap at will. Effin' A. He might have a heart attack thinking about it, never mind denying himself.

As if she understood his determination to keep his distance—big witchy twitchy surprise—Storm pulled out all the stops by allowing her innate sexuality free rein. She stopped trying to control her body and let it control her . . . Hell, she let it control them both.

She blew in his ear and sent shivery warmth to every warning signal in his highly revved libido.

"Come away with me," she cajoled, her throaty whisper enough to make him ready, which meant he should get in his motor coach and drive for two weeks straight, put thousands of miles between them, fifty states—yes, he'd have to drive all the way to Alaska to get the sex storm out of his system.

When she slid her hand slow and low down his back, his body turned traitor, and his cock took over his thinking big time. Getting away would be nothing short of self-preservation, like swimming for his life from the jaws of a shark—big, mean, hungry, fangs sharp.

Did sharks have fangs? Storm did.

He had to get the hell out of Dodge. He'd leave right after the reception, if not sooner.

As they swayed to the music, her curves caressed her gown in a play of sensual movement—smokin' hot and working it—no cares or inhibitions . . . except for that quick upward glance to see if she'd amply tested his self-imposed celibacy.

Not that she knew about the celibacy, or the how and why of it, she just—

Ah hell, she was *psychic*. She probably did know.

Well, if she did, and she hadn't killed him yet, he guessed that was a good sign. If she didn't know, no wonder she'd questioned his libido.

Which alternative was worse? Letting her think he was a dud? Or letting her in on his dumb ass declaration of independence.

Dud.

He *wanted* to prove his staying power—did he ever—but he couldn't afford to pay the price.

The dance ended. He kissed her hand. "Thank you for the most memorable dance of my life," he said and handed her off to the nearest breathing male.

Aiden headed for the bar and the kind of courage that came from a bottle.

Another mark against her. She was driving him to drink. "I'll have a scotch," he told the bartender.

"Ignoring her isn't working, is it?" Morgan asked, suddenly beside him.

"Who died and made you psychic? How can you ignore a walking orgasm in the shape of a goddess with magick laughter and satin skin? I'm hooked."

"By the saints," Morgan said. "You're *not* hooked."

"Damn straight I'm not."

Morgan chuckled. "She's already taken you off her hook. Now you're buttered, battered, and trembling in hot grease."

"Damn it, Morgan! Screw you."

"I wish somebody would." Morgan downed his champagne. "You gonna go on that trip she's got planned for the two of you?"

"Hell no. Do I look crazy to you?"

"You look like you need to get laid."

"Well, that makes two of us. Schmuck and Schmuck Incorporated."

Morgan ordered a scotch. "The difference between us is that I don't have an engraved invitation from the woman of my wet dreams to end my suffering. You do."

"You wouldn't take an invitation if you had one." Aiden picked up his scotch. "But if you did take it, you'd have nothing to lose."

"They're witches, psychics, everything I deny. I'd have my belief system to lose."

"You lost that years ago. You just haven't figured it out yet."

"Thanks for the heads-up, but we were talking about

your problem." Morgan looked over at Storm. "How can you say no to that?"

"Easy. I'll steer clear of her for the rest of the night and leave right after the bride and groom. I'll be in Alaska before Storm knows I'm gone. I don't even have to talk to her again tonight, if I don't want to."

"That's the problem, friend. You want to."

"Smart ass!" Aiden finished his scotch, slammed his glass on the bar, and ordered a cup of coffee. "But I'm a man with a great deal of *practiced* self-control."

"Yeah, yeah," Morgan said. "I've done a lot of practicing myself."

King joined them. "Aiden, the photographer wants a couple more shots of you and Storm."

"Why?" Aiden ignored Morgan's chuckle.

"To follow up on that kiss for a magazine article about wedding reception romances."

"Hooked, cooked, and topped with a *hot* lemon butter sauce," Morgan said, lifting his glass. "To schmucks who need to get laid."

Aiden confiscated the glass and emptied it. "*Two* schmucks." He slammed it on the bar. "Morgan, what if I turn the tables on her, make her think I'm taking her up on her offer, and scare her into running long enough for me to get away?"

"You get far enough to scare that one, and you won't have the willpower to run. What the hell makes you think she'll resist?"

"I can be resistible."

"I don't bloody doubt it, but that one's got a homing chip in her panties, and you're the mother ship."

Chapter Five

STORM, her sisters, and their magick cats stepped outside for a spell . . . or three. Des took her arm. "It looked like Aiden couldn't get away from you fast enough after that last set of pictures."

"Tell me about it." Storm clipped a sprig of climbing ivy off the castle's stone wall. "This should help me skirt obstacles and protect my psychic venture with speed and tenacity." She sighed. "But since Aiden's the obstacle, I should maybe take another sprig."

Destiny clipped two. "Here. Try the power of three. He's running like a cat with firecrackers tied to his tail."

Storm took the extra sprigs. "I'd like to tie firecrackers to his tailcoat."

Destiny winked. "He'd run faster, goth girl, but you know what they say about protesting too much."

"He wants to go? You know that, because you see the future, right?" Storm asked, not expecting an answer. "I'll weave the ivy sprigs into a triquetra and bind it to the nature of triplicities, so in addition to protecting my psychic mandate to find the crying baby, it'll help overcome any difficulties we encounter along the way."

"Difficulties you *will* encounter," Harmony said, "because you'll have the stubborn Aiden with you . . . if you're lucky."

"I plan to make my own luck. My psychic sense is strong, here. Finding that baby is my destiny. I'm getting scents, snapshots, too, and I know they're connected, though I can't make out the pictures yet. I'll find the child clinging to Aiden, whatever it takes."

"Go for it," Destiny said, "whatever the universe sets in your path."

"Destiny Cartwright, you know something about what I'm facing, don't you?"

"Only that you have rough roads to travel. We're too close for me to see more. You know that."

"I do know," Storm said. "But if you see roads, at least I'll be traveling."

Harmony caught the train of her veil over her arm. "Storm, I'm proud that you feel so strongly about this. Goddess knows you've heard enough babies crying in your psychic career. It's time you went out and rescued at least one of them."

Storm's chin came up. "It *is* a rescue. Thanks, Sis. A rescue. Who can argue with a rescue?" She wilted. "Aiden can. But I was never one to back down from an argument, and I won't start now. Not with a child at stake. Aiden may be stubborn but he's not heartless. My mind is made up. I'm doing this, and he'll thank me for it."

"Then we're behind you," Destiny said, each of her sisters nodding in agreement. "Speaking of consequences, did you tell King *why* we were coming out here, Harmony?"

"I told him that we wanted to say our witchy good-byes before he and I left on our honeymoon." She smiled like a sleepy kitten with a bellyful of cream.

Storm nudged her. "What did he say?"

The bride blushed. "He suggested that we spell it fast, because he was getting the bends waiting for his witchy hello."

"Like you haven't already been introduced." Storm scoffed.

"Be nice," Vickie said.

"Spell you, Glinda. You may be admitting you're a witch these days, but you're still a Goody Two-Shoes."

"And you're still the prickly goth with attitude that I wanted to kick out the door the first time I met you." Vickie kissed her cheek. "Most of the time, I'm glad I kept you."

"Aw stop it," Storm said. "I'm getting all misty-eyed."

"Well, you should," Harmony said. "Look around. Open your senses. A fairy-lit gazebo, orchestra music, and rose-scented night air, the sea shushing against the shore. The garden looks like a cathedral created by the Goddess, her-self."

"It does. It's incredible," Vickie said, her voice crack-ing. "The perfect setting for our task."

"You're *not* crying," Storm said, instantly sorry, because Vickie *had* gotten emotional with her pregnancy. "Hey, c'mon, Vic, the last time you cried, you flooded Salem. Cut it out."

Okay, Storm thought, impatience wasn't the way to deal with her sister's emotion.

Vickie sniffed. "I'm touched that you're letting me do the spell to protect the baby you're looking for."

Storm chafed. "Did you bring the bay leaves, or what?"

"What," Vickie said.

"Spell me, Vic, I told you—"

"I have them." Vickie chuckled. "I was trying to cheer you up by letting you be comfortably grumpy instead of uncomfortably . . . you."

"Another freaking Hallmark moment," Storm muttered.

Harmony, the peacemaker, put her arm around Vickie. "You're the perfect choice, little mother. Don't let our prickly Storm keep you from enjoying a good cry when you need it."

"Barf," Storm said, trying to chill. "Vic, I'm quite shocked that your rule-abiding Scot knocked you up before he made you legal . . . but I'm incredibly proud that you let him."

Vickie chuckled. "I'm pretty sure you knew when it happened. I heard you tell Harm and Des to leave us alone the afternoon I conceived. We were locked in my attic bedroom, remember?"

Destiny gasped. "The day we left Chinese food at your bedroom door?"

"Um-hmm."

Storm winced. "Spell me; I'll never be able to look at Chinese food the same way again."

"While I now find the thought of Chinese food sexually stimulating," Vickie said.

"Me, too," Harmony agreed.

"Well, you're about to go on your honeymoon," Storm pointed out, "so you would. I'm the one about to take a journey fraught with problems."

"Since King and I will also be journeying, I'd like you to end our ritual on the beach with the spiral spell for a journey of discovery, Storm. It'll be good for both our travels."

"Destiny," Storm asked, "what spell did you bring?"

Des raised a chalice. "A sprig of rosemary in wine to toast your adventure and spell you luck."

"Perfect," Storm said. "Let's make us some blue moon magick."

Chapter Six

IN the gazebo, they surrounded the Oak King altar from the wedding. Harmony cast a ritual circle with the silver, sheathed athame hidden in the chatelaine pocket of her wedding dress.

The four sisters held hands to work their magick with the power of four as one, while Storm chanted:

> *"Mother Goddess, moon of blue,*
> *Accept my goal; make it true.*
> *Lace the child's call through the man.*
> *Help the man to understand."*

She placed the triquetra of ivy sprigs in the center of the altar, before she continued.

> *"Send the babe's cry loud*
> *Enfold me like a shroud.*
> *Signs point to a path true*
> *Open my mind, Aiden's, too."*

Vickie let a handful of bay leaves float to the oaken altar and recited the spell she'd written to protect the crying child.

> *"Bay leaves nine, the child entwine.*
> *Goddess speed this psychic race;*
> *Defeat all bounds of time and space.*
> *Protect and bless the weeping one,*
> *With a loving dad, a loss undone."*

Destiny placed the chalice of wine with its sprig of rosemary in the center of the altar.

> *"We drink for luck*
> *To a journey struck*
> *With hope and love,*
> *And the peace of a dove.*
> *With every mile, a kiss*
> *With every moment, bliss."*

Destiny raised the chalice. "Storm, I give you this wine to sip as we join in your rescue. Luck and safe journey."

Storm sipped. "Harmony, I give you this wine to sip as we give you into your love's keeping. A life's journey in bliss."

Harmony sipped. "Vickie, I give you this wine to sip, barely, to keep your child, and the child Storm seeks, safe and secure."

Vickie sipped, barely. "Destiny, I give you this wine to sip as I ask for your goddess namesake to see us through our two weeks' separation and reunite us here together. May luck and safe journey be your destiny."

Destiny sipped. "God and Goddess, I leave this wine on the altar as an offering to you, to thank you for guiding us, apart and together, and for bringing our travelers home safe again."

Harmony opened the ritual circle, and they moved to the beach, each of their kittens following to lend their magickal essence to the spells. "Envision a circle of light," Harmony said as she took a stick and drew a clockwise spiral in the sand, five rows deep. Walking clockwise also, the sisters placed five smooth beach stones at regular intervals on the outer circle.

"The symbol of five signifies the four of us, and Vickie's little Rory, safe in her womb, with us in body, heart, and spirit, who represents for us, tonight, the child Storm is seeking. Imagine a line of light coming from the pebbles and meeting in the center, and then watch it spin and gain speed. Now step into the center and send your positive wishes spinning into the universe . . . for the crying child, for each separate journey, and for Aiden's collaboration."

A group hug ensued, with tears, life wishes, and a bit of Stormy sarcasm. "Now get the heck out of my circle."

She composed herself and looked to the moon for guidance.

> *"Understand my behest.*
> *A love bond is not my quest.*
> *I like freedom, so does he;*
> *Two rebels, wild and free.*
> *My quest is pure,*
> *The child, unsure,*
> *Into its father's arms, I lure,*
> *And trust your wisdom to ensure*
> *Whatever my price,*
> *I embrace the deed thrice."*

The four sisters chanted the final words that would seal each individual spell:

> *"This we will as one*
> *With harm to none,*
> *So mote it be done."*

They walked back to the castle, across the beach, lawn, and garden, arm in arm, bound in blood, spirit, hope, and love.

Back in the castle, the sisters headed for the ladies' lounge, Storm gathering the rest of the evening's players along the way. Once inside, she paced. "All of us, including Aiden, have to go back to the Salem dock together later. In order to begin my psychic journey, I need to get into his motor home *alone* with him. Does everybody know their parts?"

"I know mine," King's daughter, Reggie, said. "I can't stay. I have to get Jake to bed. He's only three, and this has been a long day. Night night."

"I know my part, too," Jake said with pride. "I get to pretend I'm asleep in Mama's arms, right?"

Storm ruffled Jake's hair. "I still can't believe my sister married a grandfather."

"A young grandfather, believe me." Harmony grinned.

"Show-off," Destiny said. "I know my part, and Morgan will play along if I have to spell-smack him."

Storm sat by Vickie. "I'm glad you and Rory are looking forward to castle-sitting, but I'm sorry you'll miss the fun on the dock, tonight, Big Sister."

"Hey, don't call me big. I'm sensitive about my size." Vickie grinned and covered her stomach. "He's kicking again. Feel."

"How did he get in there?" Jake asked.

"Love, Jake," Reggie told her son. "Love put that baby inside Vickie's belly."

"Oh," Jake said. "I thought she swallowed him."

"Holy monkshood," Destiny said. "I just realized that if your plan works, Storm, Morgan will be walking me home. How am I supposed to get rid of the pain in the—" She looked at Jake. "The pain in the patootie, when he gets me there?"

"That's up to you, but try practicing your womanly wiles."

"After I get Jake to bed," Reggie said, "right?"

"Practice on Morgan? Are you nuts?"

"If you and Morgan would stop arguing long enough, you might discover an attraction sparking your anger,"

Storm said. "You haven't given him so much as a glance, except for the wedding dance—a move he choreographed—which is a little like the way Aiden's been treating me, come to think of it."

Destiny huffed. "Morgan, lest you forget, is a paranormal debunker . . . trying to debunk our personal magick and psychic abilities."

"Okay, so you'll invite him into the house to debunk you."

"What's debunk?" Jake asked.

"Jake," Reggie said. "Let's go see Grampa before he leaves on his honeymoon."

"Aw, Mom, you never let me hear the good answers."

Storm noticed the pensive way Destiny was regarding her in the mirror, her expression signifying a glimpse into the future. She nodded. "You did tell Aiden that you think the crying baby is his, right, Storm?" Destiny asked, the kind of probing question usually reserved for a situation in which the present might segue *awkwardly* into the future.

Storm shivered. "*That's* what's making him skittish. Did you see him dancing with me tonight? Only when I tricked him into it."

"Why is he skittish?"

"He says he can't possibly have a baby." Storm scoffed. "How weird is that for a man who raises the bar on the standards governing hot studs the world over? He's like magick in a good, badass sort of way. My kind of way."

"McCloud is a lot of women's kind of good/bad," Vickie said.

"Right! So, of course, he could have a baby somewhere . . . whether he knows it or not."

Destiny touched a finger to her lips, her look thoughtful. "The romance isn't cooling between you and Biker Boy?"

"Hell no. It's sizzling, but I don't think he's ready to catch fire. No, snuff the fire bit. If I didn't know better, I'd think he was scared."

"Seriously?" Destiny smiled to hide her concern. "Aiden, the romantic who loves women, is afraid of catching fire?

He doesn't strike me as the kind to back away from a little sexual heat."

"A lot of sexual heat, actually. Okay, a freaking inferno," Storm admitted.

"Wow," Vickie said.

Destiny raised a speaking brow. "Since you and Aiden are both in rebellion, in hiding, and in denial, and neither of you has met the real you yet, I think you're more likely to kill each other than catch fire . . . but that's just me."

Chapter Seven

AIDEN watched Storm dazzle yet another dance partner. When the music ended and the guy chuckled and swooped in for a kiss, Aiden set down his coffee cup and ordered another scotch.

You'd think he could stay out of trouble on the opposite side of the room, but he guessed he was as safe as anybody could be on the same planet as a psychic witch with attitude who turned him on like fireworks on the Fourth.

When Storm didn't have a dance partner, which was rare, she'd stand on the dance floor alone and sway to the music while capturing his gaze, like she was doing now, so seductive that he had to direct his attention to the restoration work around him to stay in control.

Normally a source of pride, the impeccably restored century-old crown molding was, at the moment, a less than effective distraction.

Aiden feared that nothing could distract him where Storm was concerned, except turning the tables on her. He screwed up his courage and walked up to her. "I believe this is my seduction," he said. Lifting her and throwing her over his shoulder, he carried her off the dance floor.

She shrieked once and kicked twice but quieted when she realized everyone was watching ... until the two of them rounded the corner and he carried her up the stairs to his temporary quarters.

"What the blazes are you doing?" she asked when he set her down. "That was embarrassing."

"Less embarrassing than you chasing me all day? For you, maybe."

"What's this about?" she asked as she checked out his bed. "First you ignore me, then you treat me like a sack of doggy nuggets?"

"Take off your clothes," he said, "or I'll take them off for you."

"Why?"

"So I can succumb to your seduction. That is what you've been doing all evening," he said, pushing her gently back on the bed and following her down. "Seducing me?"

"Did you have a personality-change operation while I was dancing?" Storm asked, scrambling up against the headboard as he followed her, trapping her.

The next thing Aiden knew, something hit him in the chest like a sledgehammer and sent him flying backward. He landed flat on his back on the floor, and when he raised his head, he saw the footboard, until Storm peeked over the edge and looked down at him. "You okay?"

"How did you do that? I didn't see you move a muscle."

"Faster than a speeding bullet?"

Aiden shook his head to stop the ringing. "Remind me not to cross you."

"Don't cross me."

Determined not to show her how shaken he was, Aiden rose and spread his macho male feathers like an effin' peacock. She bought his act, thank the stars, because while he pointedly removed his tailcoat, she rolled off the opposite side of the bed to stand a safe distance away, or so she thought. "Do you want to undress yourself, or do you want me to undress you?" he asked, stalking her.

"Are you nuts? You've been like . . . celibate for three weeks and suddenly you're getting naked?"

"I'm tired of pretending to be a gentleman."

"You were never a gentleman," she countered. "If . . . we get naked, I'll need you to be fast."

"Fast?" Aiden tried to keep a straight face. Anybody as horny as him would likely come *while* she got naked. "*If* we get naked? Do you doubt my intentions?"

She looked down at his boner. "Well, no, they're a little . . . hard . . . to disguise, but . . ."

"But?"

"Well . . . I . . . I think this is rather bad timing, deserting my sister during her wedding reception."

Aiden skulked toward her, confusing her, he hoped, enjoying the proactive side of the seduction table, or bed, as the case may be. He had to give it to her; she didn't back away. When his body came up against hers, he cupped her bottom in one hand and began to insidiously raise her skirt, inch by decadent inch, with the other, and she didn't even flinch.

Her breathing became irregular. For that matter, so did his, not to mention the change in his other eager parts.

Aiden slipped his palm up Storm's thigh and found a garter. Farther upward, he found naked skin between her thigh-high stockings and panties. Very tiny panties. Effin' A, he was gonna pop his trousers. He stroked the edge of the panties and then slowly slipped a finger beneath the silky fabric to stroke the tender skin of her womanhood.

Horny witch alert. Hot and wet cauldron on the boil.

Storm let her head fall back against his arm, and Aiden's cock shot forward, only to come up against the finest French-seamed tuxedo pants money could buy.

He opened his mouth over hers to devour her while he separated her folds.

She urged him on and gave him access, and at some point, her words became a throaty pant.

He was gonna come just watching her, never mind touching her, and he didn't care.

Every stroke felt like satin, slick as a flower covered in morning dew. Like a rosebud, she opened for him. "That's my eager girl," Aiden said. "Let me in."

Two minutes with this woman could make him forget his name, never mind his resolve.

She arched into him as he found her sweet spot, and from her reaction, he knew he'd made her spiral.

"Aiden," she whispered. "Aiden, we . . . shouldn't—oh, sweet sassafras tea," she said. "I'm gonna, I'm gonna—"

"Come," he said. "Let yourself come."

And she did, two slowly rising times, but he wouldn't let her rest, not all the way. He made her come again, and again, reveling in his power, wishing they could go on like this forever. He even thought . . . for a minute . . . that she just might be the one woman who could . . .

Effin' A. His dick was hard as tempered steel, and she wasn't paying it the least attention. Again, she came. This was all for her, as far as she was concerned, and, oddly enough, that made him hotter.

She got so heavy in his arms, he thought one or both of them was gonna end up on the floor, and he was about to lay her on the bed and join her when he heard Morgan calling him.

"Snap out of it, Storm," Aiden whispered. "It's time to be part of the wedding party again."

"Huh?"

"Drunk on sex. That's my girl." Aiden tried as best he could to set the crotch of her panties back in place. He pulled down her dress and sat her on the edge of his bed. "Are you all right?"

Her face was slick with perspiration, her body so relaxed, he had to hold her up. "You ravished me," she said, and smiled. "I liked it."

He patted her brow, cheeks, neck, and cleavage with his clean handkerchief. "No, darlin', I think it was the other way round, as I'm sure you'll remember in the morning. You started this ravishment before the wedding ceremony, remember? Now, you sneak back up here after the wedding and wait for me, and we'll have wild wicked wildebeest sex all night long."

"No! I mean, we can't," she said. "It doesn't fit in with my—Vickie's plans. She and Rory are using the castle as a getaway for the two weeks Harmony and King are on their honeymoon. They won't want us around."

"Don't worry. We'll sneak out quietly later and take my boat to the mainland. The master suite is in another wing. They'll never know we were here."

Why would she look crestfallen to be getting her way, Aiden wondered, if she didn't have something up her sleeve? Good thing he was getting out of town early, though he guessed he had succeeded in turning the tables, because she looked confused and scared enough to stay away from him for the rest of the night.

He only wished he felt good about that. Why did he feel as if he'd screwed himself as well as her? Well . . . not screwed screwed. *That*, he'd remember.

He kissed her, unexpectedly needing the connection. The thought of distancing himself from her didn't sit well all of a sudden. Damn, but he had to stick to his plans. Too much rested on keeping himself from hurting her worse than leaving would. Besides, life would be better for both of them if he made sure they kept their lives separate.

Heck, he could check a few foundation locations during his two week hiatus. Headquarters was past due a couple of surprise visits, his least favorite sport.

"Aiden," Morgan called from outside the door. "It's time for you to be the best man again."

"I'm coming."

"That's what I'm worried about," Morgan said, and this time, Storm heard him and squeaked in embarrassment.

"You leave first," Aiden told her. "Morgan will escort you downstairs, so you don't fall."

"Escort me? I can't face him, never mind lean on him."

"Morgan, go on down," Aiden called, and they listened to his receding footsteps.

"I'll be down in a minute," Aiden told Storm, kissing

her brow. He stood her up and pointed her toward the door, and with a hand on her fine bottom, he nudged her from the room. Fortunately, albeit like a sleepwalker, she made her way to the stairs.

Aiden needed to get decent before he got to the great hall. Thank God, the castle was about to turn back into a pumpkin. Despite the fact that he now wanted the rebellious goth in his bed more than ever, he was standing firm. Well, his dick was, anyway.

When he got downstairs, Aiden saw that Storm was still so shaken by his unexpected turnabout, she seemed to be standing firm herself, quite the safe distance away from him. His plan had worked. Why didn't he feel victorious?

The orchestra began playing "By the Light of the Silvery Moon" as they got back to the great hall, which meant that Harmony and King were about to leave on their honeymoon.

Thanks to Morgan, he and Storm had returned downstairs just in time.

With the bride on the stairs and mostly unattached females at the bottom, three-year-old Jake caught the bridal bouquet.

At the castle door, Harmony and her sisters embraced, their tears overflowing, while King teased them about seeing each other in two weeks, citing the miracles of cell phones and e-mail.

Aiden read Storm's longing as the castle doors shut behind her sister and her new brother-in-law.

After King and Harmony's honeymoon, he would make sure Storm would be in Salem working at her vintage clothing shop on the days he came here to continue castle restoration.

She looked so forlorn as she stood there watching the closed door that he went to her, despite himself . . . one last time.

"They looked happy, didn't they?" she asked.

"The groom is always happiest between the wedding and the honeymoon," Aiden said.

Storm looked mad enough to knee him. Okay, so he'd pissed her off, but he'd also stopped her from crying . . . and seducing.

"I might be a rebel," she snapped, "but you're one cynical stud muffin, McCloud."

Aiden stepped dangerously close to temptation, close enough to smell sunshine and roses, lazy days of shared laughter, and long nights of hot sex. No other woman had ever had this effect on him. "Cynical?" he repeated. "Yes." *Hot? Hell yes.* "But damn it, I'm jumping-out-of-my-skin prickly with anything that reminds me of a cage without wheels—like wedding dresses and tuxedoes with tails."

"That's why you're the independent wanderer with a no-falling-in-love rule," she quipped, giving his earlobe a hard flick, though he hadn't seen her hand move.

"Ouch. I prefer the term *nomad*. I take my house with me wherever I go. And I go it alone."

"Like a turtle that pulls its head in and hides from life."

"No. Like a sultan. My motor coach is about luxury."

"Take me to never-never land," Storm said facetiously. "Take me with you, Peter."

Aiden frowned. "I do not have a Peter Pan complex. I'm a responsible and sought-after antiques and architectural restoration artist, *not*, as you imply, a slacker who won't grow up."

"Oh, you grew up all right, you just never stopped running."

He turned to put space between them. "I travel. I don't run."

"I scare you," she said with a grin, noting his retreat with a raised brow.

"Get real," he said as Destiny approached her and claimed her attention, an opportunity Aiden grabbed to slip out the castle door.

She aroused him, bothered, bewildered, and definitely bewitched him, he thought, hailing a water taxi. And sure, if he wasn't vigilant, she might have the ability to take him down. But scared?

Oh yeah.

Like a penis in the teeth of a zipper.

Chapter Eight

"WE'RE the last of the wedding guests," Storm said. "Morgan, will you go and hold one of the big water taxis, and tell the other boats they can go, while I find Aiden?"

"Aiden left," Morgan said.

Storm felt light-headed.

She couldn't have heard correctly. "What did you say?"

"Aiden already went back to the mainland."

I'll kill him. "Hurry up, everybody. We have to run."

"What are you gonna do?" Destiny asked her.

"Follow him. Stop him. I don't know. He couldn't have gotten a big head start. We were just talking."

"What's with the cats?" Morgan asked as he followed them out the door.

"We each have our own," Destiny said. "Tigerstar is staying here with Vickie, and Gingertigger is on Harmony's honeymoon. Any questions?"

"Cat family history later!" Storm shouted running toward the water taxis.

"I don't know why we're not sleeping here tonight," Morgan grumbled behind them.

"Because Vickie and Rory are," Destiny explained. "They'll drool over each other at breakfast and make the rest of us lose our oatmeal."

"I've had enough of *that*," Morgan said. "Let's blow this clambake."

"So get in, already!" Storm snapped.

As the water taxi approached Salem, Storm saw Aiden's motor home still parked at the dock, the moon casting an eerie glow on the stylistic dragon along its length, making it look alive . . . and oddly inviting. "Reggie," Storm said before they docked. "Take Jake to the house. The jig is up. I'm on my own. Thanks for covering for me in the shop for the next two weeks."

Reggie picked up Jake. "Happy to help."

Morgan got out first to help everyone from the boat.

Storm snatched the cat carrier from his hand—her bag of clothes stashed inside—and raced for Aiden's motor home, cursing her long gown and spindly spikes. Aiden's driving lights went on, and the engine turned over.

"What do you want me and Morgan to do?" Destiny called after her.

"Wait awhile," Storm said as she watched Reggie disappear down the street.

Storm set Warlock down on the tarmac. "Go to Destiny," she said. "I don't want you to get hit by the big bad motor home, and, Warlock, throw some magick into this spell with me, will you?"

Her black cat yowled and ran toward Destiny.

Storm had only two choices. She had to put *herself*, or Aiden's crying baby, in harm's way. A no-brainer. "I win," she said as she watched her kitten get far enough away.

Storm planted herself in the motor home's path and chanted like she'd never spelled before.

> *"Full moon, blue and bright,*
> *Guide me through this task with might.*
> *Hold me, protect me, now, I pray*
> *Turn Aiden's thoughts rescue's way."*

Joining her fury at Aiden for running, with her dogged determination to save that baby, Storm harnessed the forces roiling inside her and thrust them against the vehicle's forward surge.

Telekinesis had never felt so good.

> *"Earth, fire, water, air,*
> *Stand before me and take care.*
> *Stop the gatekeeper,*
> *His steed beware."*

Storm cast a circle of white light around herself, encompassing the unknown baby, whose suddenly faint cry spoke of hopelessness.

> *"Pure of mind and deed*
> *Insight, not ire, let Aiden heed.*
> *The babe is his;*
> *It's him she needs."*

She turned the circle of white light into a sphere, closing it in on itself, a protective web of magick light surrounding her and the child fate chose her to protect.

> *"The child lost is meant to be*
> *Her father's for eternity.*
> *To find her is my destiny.*
> *If I die trying, so mote it be."*

Storm raised the pet carrier like a beacon. "Engine, stop!"

Chapter Nine

AIDEN drove forward . . . and saw Storm standing in the middle of the road.

Panic shot through him.

He hit the brakes.

Canned goods rolled from a cupboard and hit the floor.

Aiden checked the dock. Fenced in, dead end. Water locked. Low power lines; high motor coach. People everywhere. Nowhere to go.

No choice but to skid forward.

"Damn it Storm, move!"

The engine died, and the coach rolled to a stop.

His heart beating in his ears, Aiden stood and looked for her.

Gone. Nowhere to be seen.

He launched himself from the coach.

Storm appeared in front of him. He jumped and yelled, grabbed her, and kissed her. Fury claimed him anyway. He pulled away and, hands on her shoulders, he squeezed . . . with care or fury or both. "What the hell did you think you were doing?"

She opened her mouth to speak, and he kissed her again. She wasn't dead. She wasn't dead. He couldn't get enough. If he ever did get enough, he'd have to kill her.

"Storm," Destiny called, lowering her hands from her eyes. "You still have it!"

"Have what?" Aiden shouted. "Brass balls? Or sawdust for brains?"

Destiny shrugged as if the answer were debatable. "Telekinesis," Destiny said. "The ability to move objects— or stop an object—without touching it. But she has to be pretty damned fired up to do it."

Aiden looked to Storm for an explanation.

"You heard her," Storm said, squeezing his arms. "You think *you're* mad."

Aiden pulled her against him. "I never wanted to strike a woman more. Why didn't you move?"

"You tricked me."

"You'd be dead if my engine hadn't died."

"Your engine didn't die. I *killed* it."

"*You* could have been killed! Gone! Finito!" Out of his life forever . . . which is what he'd wanted, but he wanted her alive, so she could . . . and he could . . . He felt light-headed.

Hell, he didn't know what he wanted, except *her*, alive . . . and close . . . this close . . . for a long time.

Then he could have himself committed.

"When I looked up, and you were . . ." He kissed her again.

This time she cooperated, wove her fingers through the hair at his nape, which he loved, which she knew.

He pulled back and set her away from him, and when they stood a safe distance apart—safe being relative—he ran a hand through his hair. "You witch! You scared the life out of me!"

"Spell you, I was scared, too."

Aiden rubbed his brow with the fingers of both trembling hands. "Morgan," he shouted. "I can't believe you let her do that."

"Let her? I didn't know what the nut planned."

"Storm, where's Warlock?" Destiny asked.

"Don't you have him? I sent him to you so he wouldn't get hit."

"You'd protect your cat but not yourself?" Aiden snapped.

"To protect *your* baby," Storm answered in the same stinging tone. "Warlock?" she sobbed, and looked beneath the coach.

Aiden unclenched his jaw and looked *in* the coach. "Your kitten's making himself at home, inside."

Storm wilted, and Aiden caught her in his arms so she wouldn't hit the pavement. "That was pure stupid. I take it you wanted me for something?"

"A tour?"

"You risked your life for a tour? I don't think so."

She raised her chin. "You're right. I did it for a belief."

She didn't need to spell it out. She thought she could talk him into driving off with her to follow the sound of the crying baby she said she heard only around him. He didn't know if inspiring the sound made him, or her, crackers. "I'm not taking that trip with you," he repeated. "Besides, dead engine. Not going anywhere. I'll get a mechanic in the morning."

"I'd still like a tour," she said. "I've got a scary feeling deep down that when you leave, I'll never see you again."

"That's quite the sudden burst of sincerity," he said. "I'm glad I don't believe it."

"I gave you reason not to believe me. I understand, but give me a tour? I need to get my cat, anyway."

"You're certifiable, Cartwright."

"Probably, but you thought Harmony was certifiable before she brought the castle ghost out of hiding, didn't you? And look at how that turned out."

"She's right," Destiny said, coming closer, Morgan behind her.

Aiden rubbed his chin. "Guess I'll have to give you that one. I wouldn't have believed it about the Paxton Castle ghost if I hadn't seen it."

"My point exactly," Storm said. "Let me bring you to the crying baby and—"

"*Not* on your life."

"It was worth a shot." Storm shrugged and stood back to examine the coach's exterior. "I love the size of your dragon. At least let me see it."

Morgan fell into a coughing fit.

Storm watched him try to catch his breath. "You okay, Morgan?"

"I must have inhaled a bug," he rasped, and Aiden wished he'd leave, though he should want Morgan to stay and Storm to go.

Storm looked from one of them to the other and shrugged. "Come on, McCloud, give me a tour of your dragon."

"I'm furious with you." Aiden looked hopefully at Morgan for some kind of rescue. "You two want a tour?"

"Sure," Morgan said.

"No," Destiny countered, backhanding Morgan in the gut.

Amazing, Aiden thought, *that might have been Morgan's first experience with foreplay.*

"Honestly, Morgan, I'm beat," Destiny said. "As long as Storm is still alive," she added with a hint of sarcasm, "and Aiden is going to give her a tour, take me home, will you?"

Morgan about stopped breathing when Destiny leaned against him and gave him a simmering look. "Home, please. Bed," she added with a fake squeak, and Aiden honestly hoped his friend was halfway to first base, but he doubted it.

"I don't know," Morgan said.

"Effin' A, Morgan. Just go." Aiden figured Morgan needed to get laid more than he needed protecting from the witch. "Go. You hardly need a tour; you designed the thing."

Aiden shook his head at Storm. "Don't get excited. I'm not taking *you* anywhere, even if I could get the engine repaired in the next two weeks."

Destiny tugged on Morgan's hand and dragged him toward Wharf Street. "Come on, Morgan. Take me home. I'll give you a glass of brandy and let you debunk me."

Morgan swallowed his Adam's apple. "Um, another time, Aiden."

"Wait," Aiden said, picking up Storm's pet carrier and handing it to Morgan. "You might as well take this so Storm doesn't have to carry it herself later. I won't keep her out too late, Destiny."

"Storm's a big girl," Destiny said walking away. "She can stay out as late as she wants."

"She'll be home within the hour," Aiden called, aware that his declaration and his desires hailed from different galaxies.

Chapter Ten

STORM figured it was bad luck losing her clothes and Warlock's carrier, but she'd gotten this far, and she wasn't going to let a little thing like no luggage or a motion-phobic cat keep her from her psychic mandate.

Like Aiden, she watched Destiny and Morgan walk down the street. Destiny leaned on Morgan, who shifted the carrier so he could put an arm around her waist.

Well done, Sis.

Storm turned to Aiden. "May I have that tour now, please?"

"This really is a bad time for a tour," Aiden said. "You blew my engine. I might have to beat you."

Storm pressed her breasts against his tailcoat and breathed in his spicy man scent, a blend that included cloves and cherries. "Beat me, Big Boy."

She raised her chin as Aiden ran a callused finger from her nose, over her practiced can't-deny-me-anything pout, down her neck to the crests of her breasts, the light of the blue moon shining on his silver and topaz ring. Topaz! A boon she hadn't thought to employ. Negativity did not survive around joyful topaz, a quality she intended to harness.

Storm touched the stone of her aquamarine ring to the topaz on Aiden's so the two crystals would work together to enhance and transform their sexual energy into a vibration that could launch her on her psychic journey.

The aquamarine would harmonize them, reduce stress, invoke tolerance, overcome judgment, soothe his fears, sharpen her intuition, and enhance her clairvoyance. The topaz would induce relaxation, trust, and empathy between them, and keep them receptive to love from a new source . . . his child.

Aiden's hand hovered just above her breasts, as if he were unsure of his next move.

Any doubts *she* might have had about her decision to look for his child vanished in the face of their crystals' combined magick, never mind the magick taking place between them.

She took Aiden's hand and led him to caress her more boldly. As she did, moonlight reflected off the topaz and aquamarine together to form crosshatches of light, like a dance of stars, a beacon to light their path, emotional support on their journey, and favor from the spirits.

As their lips touched, Storm added a silent spell to the simmering cauldron:

> *"Blue Moon, cast your light*
> *On our travels in the night.*
> *To find the babe crying,*
> *In spirit, we are flying.*
>
> *"Our path shall you clear*
> *To a child we hold dear.*
> *Love, bind the charm,*
> *Protect all from harm.*
>
> *"This is my will,*
> *Aiden's resistance to still.*

> *And it harm none,*
> *So mote it be done."*

"I should take you home," Aiden said against her lips.

"I think you should take me inside."

"I'm afraid—"

"I know. You were running scared."

"No. I should take you home for *your* sake, because through that door, I see a path of no return."

"The very path I choose."

"Bad idea. C'mon, I'll walk you home."

"I'm too tired to walk. Drive me. You can park in my . . . driveway . . . overnight."

"My engine died. I can't drive it until a mechanic looks it over. Besides, with that heart attack you nearly gave me, you also gave me a good idea that you're willing to play with fire."

She cupped him. "Fire? Is that what you've been hiding in here?"

"Go . . . home . . . now."

"But you promised." Appalled at the moisture filling her eyes, Storm rubbed her cheek against his topaz and prayed for an attainment of goals.

Aiden turned her as if to see her face in the moonlight.

She raised her chin, and he crushed her against him, exactly where she wanted to be. "I never made you any promises," he said, his lips against her ear, his voice rough. "I never made a promise to any woman."

Storm firmed her spine. "You promised me a cure for PMS."

Aiden's shoulders relaxed. "That was three weeks ago. You have PMS again so soon?"

"*That* was a saying on a shirt. *This* is a medical emergency."

Aiden looked toward Wharf Street, back at his coach, and shook his head.

Storm's heartbeat tripled. Had she won? She didn't

dare celebrate too soon, but she did fish in his pocket for his keys, making sure to dig deep and rev his engine.

"What are you doing?"

"I wanna unlock the door. Keys?"

"Keyless entry system . . . and it's open."

"Really? Well, there's a mighty beast of a key in *here*."

Aiden's eyes narrowed as she took her hand from his pocket, pleased to disturb the beast in the process, and then she preceded him into his coach.

"Don't turn on the lights," she said. "This place looks heavenly in moonlight." She watched him take the key from the ignition and deposit it in a cup on the dashboard. She took his arm. "I had no idea how beautiful this would be. I mean, I could tell from the outside that it was big, but it's breathtaking."

Like a cat, she rubbed herself against him, making her intentions clear, making his intentions hugely clear. "Big and breathtaking," she said.

He cupped her in return, and she wondered if he could feel her pulsing womb through her clothes. She yearned for nothing between them—for more of that crazy stunt he'd pulled in his room earlier—as dangerous to her plan now as it had been then.

She pulled from his arms, stepped and rolled on something, and fell against him.

Aiden righted her, collected half a dozen soup cans, and returned them to a cupboard, which he clicked shut. "From hitting the brakes," he said, his annoyance killing the mood.

Just as well. Safer that way.

Storm pretended not to notice his renewed anger as she ran a hand along the leather sofa, her kitten settled in against a silk-fringed throw pillow. "Warlock likes it here," she said.

"He shouldn't get too comfortable. He's not staying long," Aiden said. "I met Warlock before I met you, back when Harmony first came to the castle with his mother and littermates, and Warlock jumped right into my arms. I'm not surprised he likes my place."

"You have all the comforts," Storm said, taking the mock tour, "double-wide fridge, microwave, dishwasher, and a computer station. Oh, a washer and dryer, too. Where do you keep your Harley?"

"In a small attached garage at the back."

"Seriously? This is more beautiful than a house."

"It's my castle. The only house I've got. Built to Morgan's specs."

"One of a kind, hey?"

Aiden placed an arm around her shoulder. "I'm partial to one of a kinds . . . most of the time." He pulled her toward him, hesitated for a beat, and she kissed him.

Storm instigated an onslaught. Staging a seduction in a moonbeam by the sea made it easy to believe she could do anything. It would also be easy to lose her focus within the vortex of a sexual offensive.

She stepped from the kiss to stay in control, but she let her hand ride his tush as he led her forward. They stopped in the doorway of a room with two sets of trundle bunk beds. "For the kids?" she asked.

"Six kids? Are you insane, woman?" His question ended in another kiss, with both his hands on her ass.

"Bathroom," he indicated.

"Shower for two?"

Aiden tilted his head, asking without asking if that had been an invitation into the roomy corner shower.

Let him wonder. Let him want. Let him wait.

Storm subtly moved her hand along the back of his thigh toward the center of his need, as he stepped deeper into his castle on wheels, unaware that he was stepping like a fly into a spiderweb of her witchy making.

She gasped at the sight of his decadent bedroom. "I never expected to find a king-sized four-poster in a camper."

"This is not a camper. Please. You're killing me here. It's a motor coach."

Keeping one hand high on his inner thigh, Storm ran a sensual hand up the tall, elegantly turned post, as if that's what she wanted to do to his dick.

Aiden swallowed hard.

The elegant bedroom had a window across from the bed, but other than that, it was surrounded by built-ins, closets, drawers, an entertainment center, and a luxurious amount of floor space. Not only did Storm want to sink her toes into the plush carpet, she'd like to sink her body into it, too, while Aiden sank himself into her.

Dear Goddess, maybe she wasn't the only seducer in the room.

Chapter Eleven

FOCUS, Storm, she told herself, *get him into bed.*

She boldly fondled ~~his balls and boner and made him~~ gasp as she took in her surroundings. "This is big."

"What is?" he asked, a new light of willingness in his eyes. "The motor coach or . . . what?"

"What," she said, fondling him. "I think *big* is the operative word all around."

She lowered the side zipper on her vintage bridesmaid's gown.

"I like you in blue," he said, "especially your hair." But he seemed to lose his train of thought and his ability to speak when her gown pooled at her feet.

He stepped back, as if he'd just discovered she was contagious. "You're playing dirty, Cartwright." But he came close again, like a magnet unable to resist the pull, his hungry gaze devouring her.

"What do you call that thing?" he asked.

"This?" She stroked the enticing undergarment very near her breasts, her nipples a peek away. "This is called a merry widow."

"I don't know about the widow, but *I'm* feeling pretty effin' merry." He took in every detail of the royal blue merry widow and bikinis. Not removing his gaze from her body, he bent to trace the seam of her silk stockings with a finger, from her garters to her three-inch heels. Then, watching her, he palmed his way back up again, their arousal releasing the musk of their preferred scents, commingling them like an aphrodisiac.

To get herself under control, Storm turned her back on him, hoping the view would heighten and *extend* his desire while hers cooled.

Since Aiden seemed like an ass man, she bent at the waist to pick up a hanger from the closet floor, and his altered breathing pattern told her everything she needed to know on that score.

Returning to him after she hung up her dress, she got the idea he might also be a breast man, he was so focused on watching to see if her nipples would spill from the merry widow. The possibility was good that they would.

She bit her lip on a chuckle as she slid her hands up his tailcoat to his shoulders, pressing against him to the brink of breast spillage and nip revelations, while slipping his tailcoat off his shoulders without a word of protest from him.

After the coat, Storm tackled his silver double-breasted vest, kissing him between buttons, with his undivided cooperation. Yummers.

Except for the kitten circling their ankles, then climbing Aiden's trouser leg, she might be able to concentrate. With a sigh, Storm broke the spell and set Warlock on Aiden's bed before returning her attention to the stud muffin. "It's only fair that I get you down to your boxers so we stand on equal ground."

"Go for it, Snapdragon."

"Snapdragon? Where did that name come from?"

"You'll know soon enough."

"Funny thing about snapdragons: they're said to grow in the colors of actual dragons, which carry a powerful magick protection for the pure of heart. That's me—"

"Hah!"

"I'll ignore that," she said. "Snapdragons ward off the negative intentions of those who are against the pure of heart. So, if I'm a snapdragon, I'm protected from the likes of you."

"I wonder which of us really needs protecting, here."

"I gotta give it to you, McCloud. You're as astute as ever, but off the mark at this juncture."

"Whatever you say. Just don't stop getting me naked."

"Whatever *you* say."

By the time she placed his ascot, topaz shirt studs, and cuff links in the nightstand drawer and removed his silk shirt, Aiden had gotten her knickers in a twist, a damp twist, generated by his hands, yes, but also by his workout pecs and washboard abs, and she needed a different distraction to stay in control. "I love a man with chest hair. It drives me wild when you wear a V-neck shirt."

His green eyes twinkled, his laugh lines deadly seductive.

Storm swallowed at his touch and played in the silken mat of his chest hair with her sensitive fingertips, while his boner danced and thickened against her thigh, demanding her attention. Hard to choose between the sensations he invoked, the look on his handsome face, or the prize in his tux trousers.

Uh-oh, she sounded like she was hooked on the whole package. Scary thought.

With practiced fingers, he distracted her by discovering how ready she was, his light thumb stroke sending shivery sparks through her to land and crystallize in the most amazing places. New places.

Virginal erogenous zones. Who knew she had any left?

Never before had she felt such a deep and primordial need to kiss and to mate, to impale herself and ride her partner . . . hard . . . and long, while eating him up with her gaze, an imperative as cataclysmic as their case of instant lust, but a darn sight more demanding.

Dragon's blood, she wanted to follow through with this seduction, *without* ruining her plan, and she wondered for a minute if she could have her hunk and steal him, too, if she finessed him just right. She stood back and raised a speculative brow.

Aiden placed a hand on his heart. "You're killing me, here, Cartwright. What's going on in that mind of yours?"

She fingered the outline of his arousal pushing against his trousers and practically took him in hand. "I'm thinking . . . the big guy's ready to start without me."

"The big guy had been asleep for ages, but he woke up the day you asked if I was trading King's old chandelier for a jock strap."

"Nah. You were attracted to my sister back then. Admit it. The big guy's been primed since you met Harmony."

"I did think Harmony was hot, but I didn't catch fire until I met you. There's no comparison."

Storm started the slow torture of unzipping his tux trousers while Aiden toed off his shoes, tossing them aside like flip-flops when they probably cost a fortune. She hooked a finger on each side of his pants at the waistband, gave a tug, and they landed at his feet.

He wasted no time in stepping out of them.

Storm about came as his boner tented his silver silk briefs. She opened her purse. "Get on the bed, McCloud. I have plans for you."

"Please," he begged. "No verbal stimulation. I can barely handle the sight of you in that merry make-me-come thing. Talk about killer eye candy. Another word and I'll turn into an active volcano and erupt without you."

She tossed a handful of colored condoms across him and the bed like confetti.

"Storm," Aiden said, "sometime between now and naked, we need to have a talk."

She straightened. "Are you kidding me?"

Chapter Twelve

CAUGHT up in shock, the both of them—her at his words, and him at her actions—Aiden didn't realize she'd cuffed one of his ankles to a bedpost until she cuffed the second one. "Fuzzy purple handcuffs," he said. "I so want to find out why. But listen, Storm, there's something you should know."

She came for a wrist, but he pulled it from her reach and sat up.

"C'mere, Stud Muffin. Snapdragon wants to play."

"Wait," he said. "We need to talk."

"Why for the sake of my sanity would I want to talk now?"

"Because if we talk later, after I'm cuffed, I won't be able to keep you from leaving."

"I'm not the wanderer, here, Scruffleupagus, sweetie. You are. I won't run. Though you'll probably wish I had."

"Storm, listen."

"I'm listening," she said, cuffing one of his wrists, to his surprise.

"Will you cut that—"

His words went the way of his good sense, he realized, when she made a production, or a seduction, out of climbing over him, hands and breasts everywhere, one breast in his mouth, praise be, for one gloriously long minute, while she played with his erection through his boxers, a rod-raising, erotic exploit that could end their sex life before it began.

He tried to remember what he was supposed to tell her. Why he wanted her to stop when he never wanted her to stop.

"Wanna take this big boy out to play?" she suggested. "Does he have a name, by the way?"

"I never named him, but someone else did."

"Oh, yeah? What'd she call him?"

"It's a stupid name."

"Try me."

"Mr. Majestic."

Storm chuckled. "Was she drunk at the time?"

"I resent that."

"I'll call him Mage for short. It's a good nickname. It means wizard or magick."

"Hold that thought," Aiden said, remembering, unfortunately, what they needed to talk about. Effin' A. "Storm, you might wonder why we've never—"

She raised a quieting hand. "I wasn't ready, either. No explanation necessary."

"Damn it, Cartwright, will you listen to me?"

"No." Snap! On went the fourth pair of cuffs. Aiden tested their strength and appreciated the fuzzy fact that they wouldn't scratch his bedposts—small problem compared to the real issue here, but his sanity called for some form of compensation. "Fine, I'm shackled to the bed. I can do kinky," he said. "Boy, can I. Let me tell you about the kinkiest—"

"Save it for when we need it, Ace. Any chance you've changed your mind about us going to look for your crying baby together?"

Her question surprised him. He'd hoped, for the sake of

their sex life, that she had a longer attention span than that. "Stop being a nutcase. I already said no."

"Your call." She took his tailcoat from the closet and slipped it on over her merry insanity maker.

"We can talk later," she said leaving the room, him spread-eagle on the bed, his rod pointed toward heaven . . . awaiting . . . a miracle?

The light went on in the kitchen. Then it went off, and something rumbled. The engine? Nah. She'd killed that.

"Hold on to your shackles," his seductress yelled, and Aiden felt the barely noticeable motion of his motor coach rolling down the road. "I want to get laid," he shouted. "I've got a boner the size of Texas, here!"

"It'll go down," she shouted back.

"It would if I could reach it!"

"Hey! Don't go turning me on. And stop yelling at me!" she yelled. "My PMS didn't get cured, so I'm cranky. *Don't* piss me off!"

"What the hell are you doing? How'd you get my dead engine going?"

"Dragon's blood, you're slow on the uptake when your man brain's doing the thinking. I'm abducting you, McCloud. I didn't kill your engine. I'm not that strong. I only stopped it."

"What the? Holy— I've got a flying cat in here. Wha'd'ya know, it bounces . . . off walls, ceilings. Off me. Hey, your cat just ran over my face! Ouch, my nuts!"

Aiden heard a soft click and looked toward the intercom beside his headboard. "Sorry. I didn't know you had an intercom," Storm said. "He's only a kitten. He can't weigh much. I'll rub your nuts later. Warlock hates to ride; he's motion phobic, according to the vet. He'll settle down."

"Ouch. Son of a— Do something!"

"I did. I brought his cat carrier, but you gave it to Morgan."

Aiden swore beneath his breath. "You planned this!"

"There you go," she said. "Man brain lets real brain take over."

"Have you lost your mind?"

"No," Storm said logically. "You've lost your baby."

"I don't have a baby. I *have* . . . a supersized boner and . . . bruised balls."

"Shrinking, is it?"

"Storm?"

"Yes."

"Your cat bounced up, but it didn't come down." Aiden looked toward the ceiling.

"Where'd he go?" she asked.

"Uh, he's hanging from the rotating ceiling fan, riding around in slow circles. I think he likes it up there. He seems to be calming down."

Aiden heard the intercom go off and realized he was calming, too . . . probably because he'd gotten a reprieve. He wouldn't have to do any explaining until they were ready to do the deed. "Storm?" he yelled, and the intercom clicked on again.

"You called?"

"Oomph." The cat landed on his chest. "What makes you think I won't turn the coach around the minute you un-shackle me?"

"I have my ways."

Had she purred? Oh no, that was her cat getting very close to sitting on his face. "Your cat landed."

"Glad to hear it. Is he relaxing?"

"Imafrddssso."

"Speak up. Your voice is muffled."

"Ctnnmfffface."

Storm chuckled. "I'm beginning to get the picture."

"Humph."

"I know you won't turn us around, because you want to get laid," she said. "And after you do, you'll want to do me again. I promise. Are you tired? I could tell you a bedtime story about a naughty triplet and the man she shackled to the bed."

Please no, he thought. *It'd be so embarrassing coming that way.* He sneezed and dislodged his fuzzy face mask.

The brat in the driver's seat chuckled.

"I'd like to get my hands on you right now," he said.

"That's why I'm staying where I am."

"I'm so damned mad, I could—" *Come my brains out screwing my kidnapper,* he thought. *For about a week. Maybe three.* How sick was he? "When you unshackle me, I'll beat you, then I'll screw you."

"Did you say eat me then screw me?"

"Good idea," Aiden said.

Chapter Thirteen

IT seemed to Aiden that he didn't have a hell of a lot of choices here. The minute she set him free, he would be forced to put the shackles on her and take her back to Salem, though he still didn't trust the engine, and he needed to get it looked at.

Furious as he was at her ploy to abduct him, he was proud of her determination to seek what she believed was her psychic destiny. Frankly, if he ever did have a kid who needed to be found, he'd want Storm on his team.

He was screwed up but not fucked up, and both problems were her fault.

He hated to ignore the obvious promise of wicked wildebeest sex, but he wanted it now, damn it.

Not gonna happen.

"Storm, unshackle me, and I'll ride shotgun."

"I carry the weapons this trip, thanks."

"Come on, I'm all cramped up in here."

"It's called a boner. Besides, I don't trust you. You'll carry me back to the bedroom, have your wicked way with me—which I'll let you do, weak and hot as I am—then you'll drive us home."

Aiden got the message. He did have some leverage. "You want me to have my wicked way with you?"

"Am I still breathing? Hell yes, but that's beside the point, and you know it, which is exactly why you're staying where you are." She clicked off the intercom.

"I have to pee," he yelled.

Storm's laughter, even from a distance, washed over him and made him ready again.

"Try me in an hour," she said over the intercom, "then I'll think about it for another hour after that. You're a regular camel. I've noticed your staying power."

"That wasn't the staying power I wanted you to notice," he muttered. "On the other hand, I noticed that you're a morning person," he said. "What time did you get up this morning?"

"Shuddup!" She yawned.

Oh, the power of suggestion. If only it could get her back here.

"Hey, we're driving in a rather serpentine manner. Do you need a nap? A cup of coffee? Please don't fall asleep at the wheel. Storm, I don't want you to get hurt." Though he'd nearly killed her himself tonight, both during and after her stunt.

"I'm not sleepy."

"Then you need to turn on the GPS system or stop and get a *map*."

"Those things don't help when you don't know where you're going. How's Warlock?"

Aiden listened to the kitty purr near his ear and . . . liked it . . . as if he'd . . . bonded with the beast . . . heaven help him. "He's asleep right here beside me, where you could be."

"Great try."

The motor home climbed a curb and fell off the other end twice, damned near spraining his wrists and ankles each time, while his closet door swung open and barfed half his clothes, because Storm hadn't latched it. Outside, branches—or giant ogre fingernails—scraped the exterior paint job, which would cost a bundle to restore.

"It's okay," Storm called. "Everything's okay." They came to a bouncing stop. "I'm gonna get myself a cup of coffee. Do you want anything?" Her voice now came from just outside the bedroom door, he could tell, though he couldn't see her.

"You *know* what I want," he said, putting as much sex appeal into his voice as he could muster.

Storm groaned. "Hold that thought."

"For how freaking long?"

"Until maybe . . . Connecticut?"

"We're going to Connecticut?"

"I don't know, but we're pointed in that direction, sort of."

"What the hell are you using, a broken Girl Scout compass?"

"I got kicked out of Girl Scouts."

"I gotta ask. For hiding a Boy Scout in your tent?"

"Hey, good guess. For sleeping in the wrong tent during a camperee."

"With a boy."

"No . . . with three boys."

"Effin' A. You're killing me here. Now I'm all hot again. Seriously, what are you using for directions?"

"I'm using the sound of the baby I hear crying. If it's loud, I'm on course. If it fades, I'm off course, and I turn around and go back, until it gets loud again."

"At this rate, it could take two days to *get* to Connecticut."

"We *have* two weeks."

"I will definitely need to pee sooner than that." Aiden stilled. "Storm . . . there's a woman looking in at me. Two women. Three. Storm, I'm a sexual freak show!"

"Get real. You have tinted glass."

"And a surprising sense of modesty. They're grinning like they're starving, and I'm Sunday dinner. Oh for—one is licking her lips. They're pointing, and gathering a crowd. Effin' A, Storm! Someone snapped a picture. Will you come and close the damn shades!"

Storm came into the room looking like . . . a hooker . . . fiddling with his . . . *shades*—his luck.

"How do you close these things? There's no string to pull."

"Power shades. Button's at the—okay. Whew. Thanks."

"You're welcome . . . sideshow freak."

She was trying not to look at him, he could tell. "You can look your fill," he said. "It's not like I can do anything about *you*."

"And aren't you sorry?" She sighed. "No, I can't look. If I do, I'll want to do something about you . . . like jump your bones a couple, three times."

"Do give in to your baser urges and dive right in. I'm begging you."

"No, you're scaring me."

"Why? I'm not mad. I'm not a threat."

"That's what's scary. You should be livid. If that veneer of calm is a ploy, I'm in deep doo-doo. You're a loose cannon stud puppy with a cannon-sized boner, but you could be playing possum, and the first time I turn my back, you could tie *me* to the bed and take me back to Salem."

Aiden appreciated the fact that his grin startled her. He raised a brow. "Honey, if I cuff you to this bed, I will not be thinking about going back to Salem. I shouldn't admit it, because I'm really tired of this position, but the thought of driving this motor coach is not what's driving me." Aiden glanced down at his tented boxers. "Get the picture?" How could he not be turned on with her looking like that? Wearing his tailcoat over that merry boner maker made her look like a pricey streetwalker. "You look naked under there."

She placed her hands on her curvaceous hips with a stance that could only be termed argumentative. "Well, I'm not!"

"If some guy follows you back in here, I will not be responsible for your rescue, because I'll be too tied up to help."

"My knight on a white charger," she said, and he wasn't sure if he should be complimented or insulted.

"Oh, honey, I am so not a knight. I'm the fire-breathing dragon all knights fear, and don't you forget it."

"Another good reason to keep you cuffed."

"What's the name of this place you're going into?" he asked.

"Captain Midnight's, a twenty-four/seven coffee shop and eatery."

"Do yourself a favor and don't eat anything. Stick to the coffee. I'll be waiting."

She bent over him, gave him a glimpse of her luscious caged breasts, and kissed him with plenty of tongue, which made him want to give her plenty of sooo much more than tongue.

When she straightened, she moved to his torso and kissed the tip of his reaching cock through his boxers—the highlight of his night—then she petted her kitten, sleeping against his neck, and she left.

The minute the coach door opened, Aiden heard cheers and applause. Women, it sounded like, lauding Storm for tying a man to a bed. Go figure.

Once the door shut, and he got over the shock of Storm's apparent victory over mankind, Aiden stretched to try to slide the handcuff up an effin' tall bedpost. Cuffed . . . to the rope-twist leather bed he'd fought to have modified and installed, rather than a same ole headboard screwed to the wall.

"Dumb ass perfectionist." *Posts! He'd had to have posts.*

On one hand, he wanted out. On the other, if Storm wanted to have sex with him shackled, she'd have to do all the work, so why spoil her fun—his fun—by freeing himself? Not that he was close to succeeding, but he preferred to believe he held some control over his life, such as it was.

The fact that he stopped trying to escape for the sake of some bitchin' badass sex probably meant that his kidnapper had made him as crazy as she was.

Sex Storm Cartwright. Damn, he wanted to slip it to her.

Chapter Fourteen

IT took Storm longer to get back to the motor home than she expected, because she'd gotten stuck fielding questions from those applauding women and feeding them a pack of lies about why she kept Aiden cuffed to the bed. Of course, she hadn't called him by name. She hadn't needed to. They'd already given him a name in honor of his foxy good looks and silver briefs, the only clothes she'd left him.

She found Aiden sound asleep and drove for another hour, until about three in the morning, when she could barely see straight. Hard to believe, they'd only been on the road for a few hours. No campgrounds in sight, but she spotted a huge open field that called to her with vibes of happy childhoods and parents who cared.

She drove onto the field, well off the road, before she parked, locked up, and closed all the shades, including the power windshield-privacy curtain.

In the bedroom, she tossed her merry widow toward the chair, where Warlock meowed with annoyance and shook it off his head, and she wrapped herself in a blanket.

In the darkness, she noticed Aiden's eyes like pinpricks of fire aimed directly at her, as if he was determined to see into the depths of her soul and extract every mystery she kept hidden there. But she wouldn't let him. "Yes," she said with a knee-jerk defense, "I have years of embedded secrets, but they're buried so deep, even I can't see them."

Aiden gave her a half nod, as if he understood her convoluted thinking. Maybe they were more alike than they let on. "Maybe you refuse to see them," he said. "How many layers are you hiding?"

Storm considered the question. "Pretend I'm an onion. Peeling away my many layers produces tears. If you continue to peel, you allow yourself to be blinded by the tears, so your knife slips, makes a deep cut, and you bleed to death. Take that as a warning, McCloud. I'm not good for you. I'll suck the life right out of you."

"I believe we've already established that." He pulled against his cuffs to demonstrate. "You, Storm Cartwright, have failed Emotion 101. I see what you do. You slip into rebel goth mode to scare away potential emotional intruders."

"Don't go trying to bare my soul," she snapped, spooked by his perception. "It's so dark it casts a shadow like blood on the moon. I think maybe you're so smart because you know a little something about hiding. Let he who carries his protective shell for crawling into bare his soul first."

"You're changing the subject. You don't react well to emotion because you don't know *how*. Has no one ever made you *feel* anything?"

"Screw you, Aiden McCloud."

"I wish the hell you would. I'm way past due."

"I have a headache," she said, telling the truth.

"And I've got a bladder like a water balloon."

She bet he did. "I have to go, too. Wait, I'll be right back."

"Like I have a choice. You're special, you know," he called after her.

She scoffed. What the hell was with him? "Yeah, right," she said.

"I'll just keep telling you until you believe me."

"Cold day in hell, McCloud."

"You can't scare me away."

"The handcuffs and abduction didn't do it for you?" she asked, returning. "I guess if that didn't scare you, you think nothing will, but don't count on it." She held up an empty measuring cup. "Here ya go."

Aiden raised his head. "What the hell is that for?"

"Aim and pee. It's so easy for men."

"I do not pee well in public."

"Don't tell me you're one of *those*. I took you for the kind of guy who could take a whiz on the side of the highway in plain sight."

"Let me rephrase that. I do not pee well while a sexy woman is holding my target."

"And your hose. I'd have to hold that, too, I believe."

"Gee," Aiden said. "I wonder how long a jail term you can get for hijacking and abduction? Thanks to your coffee stop audience, there are now witnesses and photographs."

"Dragon's blood, are you touchy." She unlocked his ankles and one wrist, but she cuffed the other wrist to her own.

"What the hell?" he said getting up. "Oh, it feels good to stretch. You're not coming in there with me."

"I won't watch. We'll stand back to back."

"Fine for now, but it won't work in the morning."

"Yeah, yeah." She'd been hoping that by then, he'd be addicted to having her around and wouldn't bolt when she let him loose . . . which probably meant that she needed some insurance . . . like sex. Fantasmaglorious sex.

In the bathroom, standing back to back, she realized that she'd never found herself in so ludicrous a position, but her giggle seemed to have a direct effect on the sound of running water, as in . . . his stream stopped.

"Now see what you did," Aiden said. "You scared the big guy, and he's not done, so now we have to wait for him to come out of hiding. What's so funny?"

"The women at the coffee stop. One wanted to rent you for an hour. They dubbed you the Silver Fox."

"Wonderful. Why?"

"They saw your silver boxers, and they think you're a fox. Personally, I don't see it. Anyway, they asked questions about you."

"You didn't answer them?"

"Don't worry. I didn't use our names. I told them a pack of lies about paying you to be my traveling sex slave."

"Storm!"

"You're never gonna pee if you don't calm down."

Aiden took a deep breath and told her in boring, step-by-step detail how to go about restoring a great work of art, never mind that she'd already watched him do an everlasting restoration on a wall mural at the castle.

"Great lesson," she said. "But, duh, why?"

"To get my mind off you behind me or to get my mind off your behind. Either way, you're a distraction. I can't keep the big guy on task if we're thinking about you naked back there."

"I'm not naked. I'm wrapped in a blanket, mostly."

"Yeah, and I'm dressed, mostly."

When she got him back to the bedroom, Storm tried to cuff him again. The first arm was easy, because she was cuffed to it. But catching his ankles was like chasing a greased pig, and she didn't appreciate him being so heartily entertained while she tried.

Finally she ended up naked and spread-eagle on her belly on top of him, except that she was facing the footboard and he was facing . . . well . . . enough of a distraction for her to cuff his ankles. His last wrist was a no cuff, but that was okay, because she liked having that arm around her as she snuggled in beside him and pulled the covers over them both.

"Is this it?" he asked. "One arm is all I get?"

"Yes. I need some sleep."

"That sucks. I'd like to hold you with both arms while we sleep."

"It won't stop at holding."

"I have control," he said. "I'm not an animal."

"You have too much control," she said turning to face him. "I'm the animal." She growled like a hungry wildcat. "You're not safe from me. Ergo, you're in protective custody."

Chapter Fifteen

A few hours after falling asleep, Storm woke to the familiar sound of a crying baby. Aiden was already awake and watching her, his morning boner saluting like a good little—no big—soldier, his free hand cupping a breast. She didn't have to think twice. She grabbed the breast-happy hand, jumped up, and cuffed that wrist to the bed.

Aiden sputtered and cursed her witchy ancestors back to Lili in Scotland. "I can't believe you did that," he shouted, but his fury ended abruptly when she grabbed a cherry condom, tore the packet open with her teeth, and straddled him for a morning ride.

Though Aiden groaned at the near skin-to-skin contact, he shouted for her to look him in the eye when she slipped her hand in his briefs, and having him hold her gaze captive was mesmerizing and quite the added turn-on. She grabbed his cock, sheathed it by Braille in its cherry slicker, then she slipped his saluting soldier into her warm, pulsing self.

Aiden raised his hips off the bed with a roar of satisfaction, and as she rode him, he continued roaring and shouting, loud and vocal . . . almost as loud and explicitly vocal as her. Three weeks in the making, with a slow, sweet burn that might freak lesser mortals, this mating was worth every spark of torture.

Nothing had ever felt so good, so long, or so perfectly made to fit snug and deep down inside while stroking impossible-to-reach depths and raising her to impossible-to-reach heights.

Between them, they'd honed abstinence and staying power to a science; only look at the night of sexual torture they'd just survived.

This was Aiden, the man who'd touched an unnamed yearning in her at first sight, the man she'd teased—who'd teased her—for three merciless weeks, who'd suckled her breasts and made her come at every opportunity, despite the clothes between them, the man who came, himself, more often than not, as a result of the same torture.

They had tested each other to that endless most frustrating brink and never consummated their mutual sexual hunger for each other—not even during the ritual midsummer bathing, her naked in the sea and him ready to pop the zipper on his khaki shorts. All that waiting and foreplay had gone into preparing them for this moment, this cataclysmic mating.

Storm felt like a goddess as she rode him, head high, hair thrown back, her wild mount bucking beneath her, taking her to a world unknown, but making her crave the journey the more for his expertise.

She rode him hard and put all of herself into this mutual inferno, as did he, his attention as much on her pleasure as his own.

Panting to increase her staying power when she felt herself rising too high, too fast, too close to the pinnacle of satisfaction, she begged him to stay with her. But she needn't have bothered. He urged her to greater heights with a patience and enthusiasm like no man she'd known.

His warmth and caring touched her in that scary emotional place, but with Aiden, she made the journey anyway, and as her orgasm overtook her, she flew from her body to a trembling zenith, a place of prismatic stars, magick crystals, and brilliant joy.

Wild and soul shattering, body-trembling multiples claimed her, and with Aiden's instigation, she kept rising, one orgasm after another, until she could barely keep from passing out.

She screamed her final release like a banshee as Aiden shouted her name and rose with her, impaling her more times than she would have thought possible—as if he'd experienced a multiple of his own. And when she collapsed atop him, prone, sated, sweaty, sticky, and damned near to passing out, she heard a pounding.

Her heart pumping in her ears most likely.

"The door."

Smoothing the sweat-slick hair from her face, she looked up at Aiden. "Huh?"

"The door," he repeated. "Someone is knocking at the door."

"Breaking it down, you mean. I don't think I can summon the strength to move."

"Uncuff me, then," Aiden said, drawing air into his lungs with a pleased look.

"Good try, but you can't move either, for more than the usual reasons."

"Do you hear me complaining?"

Storm rose and tossed a blanket over him then wrapped herself in another, in case it was the orgasm police, and they'd exceeded their limit for legal multiples in one time zone.

She opened the door . . . and looked up at the skinny seven-foot clown on her doorstep, lost her train of thought, and got a crick in her neck.

Words failed her. Her body nearly failed her.

Passing out seemed an option, not because of the apparition, because of the sex.

The clown squirted her in the face with his lapel carnation.

"Thanks" she said. "I needed that."

Carnival tents and animal cages had sprouted around them, like a hidden fairyland—while they'd slept the sleep of the dead, apparently. Storm tightened her blanket and hid as much as she could of herself behind the door. "Good morning, Bozo."

"We're not all called Bozo, ya know." He raised a bushy blue brow. "How about you don't stereotype, Trixie, and I won't either."

Storm slapped a hand to her mouth and nearly lost her blanket. "Oops. Close call. Let's start again. Hi, I'm Storm, and you are?"

"Winkie."

There ya go. "Good morning, Winkie. May I help you?"

Storm got distracted by an elephant on a leash, led by a purple-haired clown on stilts. She was so diverted, Warlock ran past her and out the door. She saw him leap, as only Warlock could, to the edge of a cage where a full-grown tiger raised its head to eye her three-month-old fur ball.

One tiger hello, and Warlock relinquished the need for a litter box.

Like lightning, her kitten ran and became lost to sight somewhere in the carnival crowd. "My cat!"

Winkie cleared his throat.

Storm apologized and gave him her full attention. "Are we in your way?" she asked. "I promise to leave as soon as I find my cat."

"Uh, no," the embarrassed clown said, removing his blue-striped top hat, banded with black-eyed Susans, to reveal a fuzzy thatch of blue hair. "We don't care where you're parked. It's just that . . . your screams were scaring the children."

Storm focused on the scene, noticed the upbeat carnival music, and smelled the popcorn and cotton candy for the first time. She saw people—midgets, giants, acrobats, and families—everywhere.

Parents, in particular, several sets of them, with children, stood in groups, all of them staring at her, some with wary surprise, a couple with smiles, but most with downright disapproval.

Storm rarely blushed, but the heat in her face could probably start a campfire. She stepped deeper into the confines of the motor home. "Ah . . . toga party," she said, too loud, too fast . . . and too stupid.

The clown nodded and donned his hat, trying to be all business, except that his grin got the better of him. "Sounded like a *great* party."

Her giggle caught him off guard and made him blush.

She cleared her throat. "Will we be able to pull out of here without a problem?"

"Well," Winkie said, removing his hat again and turning it in his hand. "Some people will boo, of course, but a few will probably cheer."

"Not that kind of problem. Is the road clear ahead of us? All our shades are still down, and I can't see what we're facing."

"I'll make sure to clear your way when it's time. Can you be ready to roll in half an hour? I'll bring a few friends to help."

"Not if I don't find my cat. I can't go without Warlock."

"Find me when you're ready to go then. I'm easy to spot."

No foolin'. "Thank you," she said, rethinking her own blue hair.

He tipped his striped blue top hat and honked his bicycle horn several approving times. "No, I thank you," Winkie said. "I haven't started my day with this big a smile in years."

Chapter Sixteen

STORM felt the newly familiar heat wash up her face once more as she shut the door.

"Who was it?" Aiden asked when she went back to the bedroom.

"Some clown says we have to leave." She unlocked his cuffs. "Let's get moving. Warlock escaped out the door when I opened it, and we have to go find him before we go."

Showers were an absolute necessity, but they needed to be quick, so they took turns.

After a futile search for Froot Loops, Storm showered and put on one of Aiden's cotton dress shirts, letting his shirttails hang over a pair of his navy boxers, hoping they looked more like her shorts than his underpants. Worse, she had no choice but to wear her wedding spikes with the outfit.

Winkie would take one look and think *Trixie* all over again.

When she emerged from the bedroom, she found Aiden waiting on the sofa with all the shades up, except for one. "Why didn't you open the windshield curtain?" she asked.

"I keep it closed to keep the sun from fading the interior." He grinned. "There really was a clown at the door, wasn't there? You must have been some sort of tired last night to park in the middle of a carnival. You're lucky you didn't mow down a tent."

"For your information, smart-ass, I parked in an empty lot. The carnival must have rolled in during the night and sprouted up around us. Guess we were both so tired from the wedding—"

"And the abduction—"

"That we slept through the whole thing."

"The clown wants us to move the coach, I take it?"

"No . . . the reason he came to the door is . . . well . . . we were screaming and shouting some pretty outrageous satisfaction, which . . . um . . . scared the children and pissed off their parents." She opened the door. "Let's go find my cat."

Aiden looked pretty cocky as he let her precede him out the door. "I'll take whatever reprieve from the cuffs I can get."

The breeze beneath his big shirt caressed and budded her bare breasts, so Storm crossed her arms. "That wasn't the only reason I let you out," she said, leaning close. "I didn't want the clown to think I was having all that good sex by myself."

"I could go another round," Aiden said. "Yes?"

"Of course, yes. But we have to find Warlock first. I don't want him getting hurt or adopted by a bunch of kids."

"Judging by the trapeze act that cat pulled with the ceiling fan last night, I say we start with the Tilt-A-Whirl or the center ring. Both have Warlock written all over them."

"How about a funnel cake or fried dough for breakfast to keep up our stamina while we search?" she suggested.

"Name your poison. I prefer a corn dog, myself."

Storm called Warlock as they made their way to the concession stands, but as the crowd grew thicker, finding her kitten seemed more and more impossible.

Storm's heart wasn't in her fried dough, so she dropped it in the trash after two sugary bites.

Aiden inhaled his corn dog before she turned around. "Stop worrying," he said. "Where would one fearless cat go in a place like this?"

"He might once have been fearless, but he met his match this morning." She told him about the tiger incident, which seemed to worry Aiden as much as it did her.

"Winkie," she called when she saw her good-morning clown. "Winkie, this is Aiden."

Winkie beeped his bicycle horn and tipped his hat. "Congratulations."

Aiden's spine went ramrod straight. "I'm proud."

Storm ignored their not-so-subtle form of male bonding. "We can't find my cat," she said. "Is there someone here who can make an announcement?"

"Good idea," Aiden said, as Winkie led them toward the nearest concession stand. "I've got another idea that might help."

An hour later, the hundred-dollar reward offer netted eight contenders: five black cats with white boots, one with a white-tipped tail, a stuffed skunk, and the correct pure black Abyssinian. Warlock yowled and leapt into Storm's arms from two feet away.

Aiden handed the hundred-dollar bill to a very happy young lady. "Where did you find him?"

"It was the funniest thing," she said. "He was crawling on his belly in a cage toward a sleeping tiger. I lured him through the bars with cotton candy. He's got a sweet tooth, your cat."

Aiden thanked the girl and scratched Warlock behind his ears. "A sweet tooth," he said as they walked away. "And balls of steel. Wait." Aiden stopped at a shooting game. "Let me win you a prize before we go?"

"You can shoot?"

"After military school?"

"Oh, yeah." Storm took Warlock. "Go for it. I want a big prize."

He didn't miss a target and played until she had the pick of the stuffed-animal litter. She chose a big stuffed purple dragon with wide eyes, a wink, and a grin.

"I can't believe you chose a dragon," Aiden said, putting the gun down.

"I like dragons. I told you that during our Midsummer celebration, remember?"

"Right, at the castle, when Jake wore the dragon costume."

"You got something against dragons?" she asked.

"I guess you could call it a phobia of sorts." He rubbed his hands together in the manner of a personal subject change. "Wanna go on the Ferris wheel?"

"Gee, Aiden. We have supplies to buy and a baby to find."

"I don't know, Snapdragon. I thought you'd be more fun." Aiden waved at Winkie, signaling that they were ready to leave.

"I was a hell of a lot of fun this morning," she said climbing into the coach.

"I have to agree with that." Aiden opened the windshield curtain as half a dozen clowns worked to clear a path for them through . . . an elephant crossing?

Storm chuckled. "Horses, tigers, elephants . . . and what they leave behind."

"I can't drive through that!"

"Why not? It's only elephant poop. You want me to go out and shovel it, throw some sand on it, maybe—"

"Would you?" Aiden looked hopeful.

"Drive, Bozo."

"I am not a clown."

"Of course not. If you were, I'd call you Winkie . . . or Weenie."

"That hurts."

"Hey, you're the one who's too prissy to drive through elephant poop."

"I'd climb that entire mountain of poop if you needed me to rescue you, but don't ask me to spray it on my paint job and undercarriage."

"Nice sentiment, Mighty Mouse, but it doesn't change the circumstances. Drive."

Aiden shuddered, gunned the engine, and drove straight through, splashing elephant poop on the gawkers, like a road puddle.

"I'm proud of you," Storm said, at about the same time Warlock screeched and bounced off the back of Aiden's head.

"We gotta do something about that cat!"

"Judging by your chewed slipper, we should shop for cat food, a cat carrier, and kitty litter, in that order. I saw a mall last night. Turn left out of the parking lot."

"First, we have to find a campground where I can wash the undercarriage, and whatever else needs depooping on this thing."

"I never pegged you for a neat freak. You can't be. You're a . . . a . . . Scruffleupagus. Your hair is scruffy/spiky/wavy, your jeans are torn. You always need a shave."

He gave her a look.

"Aha," she said. "You're fashionably scruffy." She pointed a finger. "*You*, sir, are obsessive."

"Give me a break. I'm an antiques restorer. I make my living being obsessive. And this is where I live, damn it! Would you like living in a house with elephant poop sprayed all over its beautiful Victorian exterior? How'd you like to tell people your house is the color of lavender, sage, eggplant . . . and elephant poop?"

"Okay . . . I see your point."

They were startled by plates falling from a cupboard and shattering on the floor, shards flying everywhere. Warlock swung from the handle of the cabinet door.

"I've had it with catastrocat," Aiden snapped.

"Have you ever heard of melamine?" Storm asked. "Cats can't break melamine."

"Plastic?"

"This is a camper, not a house."

"Effin' A. Enough," Aiden said, and took a *right* turn out of the parking lot.

Storm sat forward to see if he knew of a campground nearby, but he pulled onto the interstate heading north. "Where are we going?" she asked.

"Back to Salem."

Chapter Seventeen

FRUSTRATION and anger filled Storm.

Passionate anger.

They were driving in the right lane, nobody behind them for miles, with a roadside rest looming, so she concentrated her fury on Aiden's hands, and he turned the wheel and exited into the roadside rest.

"What the hell?" He pulled into bus parking and turned off the ignition. "Care to explain what just happened here?"

"It was a physical manifestation of rage," she said. "The same kind of energy that let me stop the coach on the wharf. I guess you get better at harnessing telekinetic energy the more you use it. I didn't even know how powerful it could be until last night. Then again, no one ever makes me as mad, as passionately mad, as you do."

"You mean that you directed my hands to turn that wheel?"

"It's a psychic thing. We were in the right lane, and nobody was behind us."

"Do your sisters have that particular talent?"

"Not that we know of. They rarely get passionately angry."

"I think you were born mad," Aiden said.

Storm thought about that. "If not, then I got mad in the first few hours of my life, and my anger's been compounding like interest since."

"It's about your mother leaving you, isn't it?"

"Dig deeper," Storm said. "It's about me being the unexpected twin, the unwanted twin, the straw that broke the camel's back, the *reason* our mother ran in the first place."

"You don't know that," Aiden said, and Storm appreciated his attempt at comfort, but she didn't like the turn this trip had taken.

"I don't think that Harmony or Destiny have the right psychic abilities to harness telekinetic energy. Focused fury in the present equals focused movement in the present, and my psychic gift is sensing the present. Harmony and Destiny's strengths lie in the past and future."

Aiden got up for a bottle of water. "The fact that you were careful about the traffic doesn't make it any less annoying that you took over the driving from the passenger seat." He got back into the driver's seat with his drink.

"So stop pissing me off, already." She unhooked her seat belt and stood to look down at him. "Get out."

"Of my own house?"

"Of the driver's seat." She was building a new head of steam, but she didn't want to shove him off the seat if she didn't have to. "I'm taking over and turning us back toward my goal."

"I could have you arrested for hijacking."

Storm scoffed. "Wouldn't that make the big, bad biker boy look brave?"

"Give me one reason why we should continue this trip," he said with the kind of challenge in his look that meant nothing—nothing—she could say would sway him, the pain in the—

A full-bodied shudder overtook her as she tried to resist a new surge of anger. She paced the confines of the living area. "I hear babies crying, okay? All the time. And no one believes me. You, this trip; this is my last shot to prove myself. Harmony pulled off her psychic mandate. Why is it so difficult to understand that I'm desperate to succeed with my own? How would you feel . . . if . . . somebody was trying to stop you from doing the work you love?"

Aiden gave her a look that she couldn't read, but she hoped she'd given him something to think about. He rubbed the back of his neck. "If I go with you, I'll only be doing it to prove that you're wrong."

"I appreciate your honesty, and I can live with that, because I'm right. There is a baby out there, and it's yours."

"You should probably stop trying to piss me off now," Aiden said.

"I'm just telling you what I believe. When I'm on course, the sound is loud and vibrant, demanding. The smell of baby powder is strong. When I veer off course, the baby's cry softens to a despondent whimper, and the scent fades, but if I turn back to where the sound raged, it rages once again. That's the honest to Goddess truth. Finding that child is my spiritual mandate. Because of the psychic gifts I've been given, I have a responsibility to the universe to see this through, especially since the crying baby is attached to you."

"Why does the baby being attached to me have any bearing on this crazy stunt of yours? Not, *for the record*, that I believe there *is* a baby."

Storm shrugged, embarrassed. "I don't know why that should matter. Because *I'm* attached to you, I guess . . . maybe . . . in a way."

"I sure in hell wish you were attached . . . like this morning, I mean. Hey, can you use telekinesis during sex?"

Storm raised a brow. "You really want me aiming in that direction . . . when I'm furious?"

Aiden paled.

"Are you gonna let me drive now, or what?" Storm aimed her gaze at his crotch.

He took his hands off the wheel. "After we clean up the

broken dishes, you drive, no question, while I make a list of things we need to buy. Remember, I'm only going with you to prove you wrong."

"Yeah, yeah." Storm tried not to grin in triumph as they swept the broken pieces into a wastebasket.

"I'll be right back," Aiden said and went to empty it at the rest stop.

"We'll have to buy replacement dishes," he said, returning.

"Melamine," Storm muttered as she buckled her seat belt.

"I heard that." He took the passenger seat with Warlock on his lap and buckled up. Grabbing pen and paper from a dashboard drawer, he started his list. "Campground for coach cleanup," he said, dodging Warlock's paws as he wrote. "Cat supplies. What else?"

"A mall. I need underwear, clothes, magick supplies, and you need new dishes."

"Underwear?" Aiden perked up considerably. "Like from Victoria's Secret?"

Storm did a double take, and she liked the twinkle in his eyes. "I'll trade you Victoria's Secret for melamine dishes."

"I pronounce myself a happy man, not that I wasn't plenty happy once already today."

"Twice," she said.

Aiden grinned. "We shop together, right?"

She gave him a look. "Everywhere. Not just in Victoria's Secret."

"Busted," he said.

An hour later, they walked into a gigantic mall. "The cat's fed," Aiden said. "We're fed. The undercarriage, tires, and paint are free of elephant poop."

"Broken dishes are in the Dumpster," Storm added.

"I gotta be honest with you, Storm. When I think about what I'm getting myself into, here, I feel like I'm in the Dumpster."

"Nonsense," Storm said. "You got a kick out of the carnival this morning. You enjoyed yourself. Chill. It's a good day. I have new orange glitter flip-flops, an orange Curses! T-shirt, and a black broomstick skirt that fits. Don't you love yard sales?"

"I love knowing that you're going commando beneath it all."

"Shush. You're weird."

"Starved. I'm sex starved."

"I could tell. How long had it been for you . . . not counting flying solo?"

Aiden swiped a hand down his face, and Storm almost thought he was wiping away a smile. "Let's not go there."

"Give me a time frame, and I'll drop the subject. Months, years, decades?"

"More than a year."

"Dragon's blood. Did you lose a bet?"

"You said you'd drop the subject."

"But you've gone for more than a year without sex!"

"Say it louder," Aiden snapped. "I don't think they heard you in Guam."

Storm stopped in front of a dress shop. "Yummy. A shop for all worlds. I gotta get my goth back."

"I like you in colors."

"I like you handcuffed to the bed."

Aiden eyeballed her, and they both knew it was a draw.

She couldn't believe he'd followed her into a boutique with a bridezilla mannequin in the window.

Two minutes later, he followed her out again. "What's wrong?" he asked.

"I can get what I want in a regular store for half the price. Besides, I took one look at the dressing room and remembered that I needed to buy underwear first."

"Wait!" Storm stopped walking and put a hand on his arm. "I hear a baby crying, and it's here!" She looked around the mall and focused far into the distance. "Stop!" she yelled, then she shot across the mall in a marathon sprint.

Chapter Eighteen

AS Aiden took off after Storm, he figured she thought she was following the sound of a child, and he wondered if maybe this witch could be a few twigs short of a broom. She'd stood in front of a moving vehicle, cuffed him to the bed, and abducted him. Except . . . wha'd'ya know, he came across a hysterical woman calling for help.

Aiden hesitated a minute beside the woman and lost sight of Storm, but when he turned a corner, he saw her jump a thug and ride his back. The guy started to twitch as if he were dodging invisible bullets . . . or experiencing a random series of stabbing pains.

Though Storm's bucking bronco ride added a burden of weight to his botched escape, and he shouted and cursed with each invisible . . . jab . . . the thug never let go of the screaming toddler hanging like a sack of grain from beneath his arm.

Aiden's heart sped as his instincts took over, and he snatched the little girl from the man's grasp then brought her to the woman running over. Accompanied by a mall guard, she grabbed the toddler and clasped her so tight, the little girl wriggled to get loose while she cried, "Mommy, Mommy. My scared, Mommy."

The guard and the woman mistook him for the rescuer, and when they tried to thank him, Aiden pointed. "Your hero's over there," he said, button-busting proud. Then he went to save the kidnapper from Storm. Hell, she had the guy on the floor in the fetal position screaming and twitching in pain every other minute while she stared down at him.

May *he* never make her that mad, Aiden thought, lifting her away from the scum by her middle, despite her instinct to fight him. And while he held the wildcat to one side, Aiden shoved a foot against the kidnapper's belly to hold him for the police team running their way.

As it turned out, Storm had bagged a menace to society.

By the time thanks had been said, the kidnapper ID'd, and the police finished questioning them, Aiden was exhausted, and only the thought of accompanying Storm to Victoria's Secret kept him going.

The fact that she had foiled a kidnapping—and saved a crying baby that *he* had not heard—wasn't lost on him. She really had heard a baby crying.

"Has anything like this ever happened to you before?" he asked as they window-shopped their way toward the opposite end of the mall.

"What? Hearing kids cry in my head? Too often to count." She caught her reflection in a window and finger-combed her hair. "But saving a baby that nobody else heard? Never." She grinned, looking exhilarated and good enough to take to bed. "I wonder who's shaking more right now, me or you," she said.

Aiden figured it was him. "At least we can go back to Salem now."

Storm stopped walking. "What makes you think so?"

"You found the crying baby."

"I found *a* crying baby. Not *your* crying baby. Yours is still in my head with her baby powder scent. And apricots. I often smell apricots when she cries, and I get a craving for Froot Loops."

Aiden grinned. "I love Froot Loops."

"See? We can't go home. While I was giving that piece of garbage what he deserved, the scents, tastes, and sounds I associate with your baby became stronger as you came closer."

Aiden felt a little queasy about the possibilities, but what he'd just witnessed didn't necessarily mean that *he* had a child somewhere. Only that Storm might really hear babies crying . . . like that wasn't a shocker in itself. Either way, Aiden's resignation was laced with apprehension. What if he did have a kid somewhere?

Walking into Victoria's Secret took the edge off his anxiety, and everything but the thought of Storm's underwear went out of his head.

Since she normally wore black—unless she was a bridesmaid—Aiden expected her to choose black underwear, so his day got brighter when she chose camis, panties, V-strings, and any number of sexy little man-hardening teasers in turquoise, raspberry, peach, ruby, and cinnamon—all those spinning colors making him dizzy . . . happy dizzy . . . as did the sight of them in sheer, opaque, lace, and spandex.

"This is like a dream come true," she said.

"You mean that you dreamed you could make me come just walking me through a lingerie store?"

She elbowed him. "I dreamed I could buy all new underwear."

"Can I help? Can I? Please?"

He'd amused her, as he intended, and she let him choose a couple of one-piece beauties, a bustier and a teddy, which she needed to identify for him, and which he loved.

She took every dreamy choice to the register, and when the salesgirl said "Cash or credit?" Aiden handed her his credit card.

Storm gave him a questioning look.

He pulled her aside for a minute. "There are dreams," he said, "and there are dreams come true."

After she bought the underwear, she asked if she could

go into the dressing room to change into one of her new purchases.

When she came out, Aiden got up close and personal. "Which ones are you wearing?" he asked, but she chuckled and refused to answer.

In the department store, she chose all black items to bring into the fitting room, but when she sent him back to the racks for different choices, he picked clothes in bright, outrageous colors and patterns. He handed them to the sales-clerk to bring to Storm and was rewarded by her "Curses, McCloud," but she sounded more entertained than angry. He was really surprised when she came out wearing a sailor-type playsuit with short shorts in red, white, and blue. She postured and posed as if she was a leggy, over-paid runway model, and he was her million-dollar client.

"This is pure retro," she said. "Wha'd'ya think? Too *Debbie Does the Coast Guard*?"

Aiden winked and relaxed in the comfortable chair he'd found outside the dressing room. "I like the outfit, but I'm not sharing you with a branch of the armed forces."

In a patchwork jacket, she looked like a mod sixties refugee, and he gave her a thumbs-down. "Looks like you've been Dumpster diving."

"Eeyeew." She turned and marched back into the dressing room.

She modeled every outrageous outfit he sent in. "Flower child does a garage sale," she said about a high-waisted print minidress.

She called the sleeveless red dress with a black T design, "Middle-aged substitute teacher."

"Thigh-high boots with this skirt," she said, modeling it, "and I've got a 'bad slut/good slut' look going."

While she poked fun at his choices, she did try them on, and she had a good time doing it. This Storm—the one he was seeing for the first time—was like a kid playing dress-up, which made him wonder if her goth trappings weren't a form of camouflage all their own, as if she *meant* to hide the real Storm. Watching her explained why he'd found her so charming and enchanting from the moment he met her.

Did her goth alter ego try to make a bad impression, so the world would think she *didn't* care what they thought? If goth *was* simply a role she played, why? To protect herself from the world? Or to protect the world from her?

Will the real Storm Cartwright please stand up?

She'd caught his attention with this unexpected peek, and he was honored she revealed herself to him. He'd gotten a glimpse at the wedding, but not like this.

Yet another side of her had come out when she caught the kidnapper, which made him wonder just how many sides there were to the puzzle called Storm.

He'd been up-front with her by telling her why he was going on this trip, but because he'd like to see Storm the woman as happy as Storm the hidden child, he almost—almost—wished she wasn't wrong.

If she was right, he had a kid to deal with, but he'd cross that drawbridge if it ever lowered itself into his path.

More than likely, she'd make a fool of herself, but he'd be there to pick up the pieces, if he could, and protect her from the worst of it.

Funny, he'd never thought of himself as someone who rescued damsels in distress. But if Storm were the damsel, he could pretend to be a knight.

The saleswoman came from the dressing room with her arms full and gave him the mound of clothes Storm had chosen. All black. Not a color among them. He was disappointed in a way, because he liked Storm the child, though Storm the woman was one sexy handful, one he could really fall for.

Where did that thought come from? He was probably light-headed and disoriented from hyperventilating in Victoria's Secret. That was it.

"Your wife asked me to give you these to hold. She said they'd survived the first cut."

"What? Who?"

"The lady with the blue hair?"

"She's not my wife."

"I apologize," the saleswoman said. "I based my assumption on the fact that you're sitting in the husband chair."

Aiden stood so fast he got a head rush.

He looked in every direction, tossed the black clothes on the chair, and headed for the closest exit sign.

No way could he be a knight. Not even for a goth in colored underwear.

She'd have to find another schmuck.

Chapter Nineteen

STORM was disappointed to find Aiden gone when she left the fitting room, but when she checked out, the salesclerk told her how he'd reacted to "the husband chair." Hell, he was a man who carried his house around like a turtle. Talk about not wanting to be tied down. No wonder sitting in a cushy commitment chair scared the stuffing out of him.

She found him on a hard man bench in the mall watching a bunch of sugar-shot toddlers in a gated childcare facility.

Since she still couldn't believe that he'd trusted her instincts enough to assault a stranger in a mall on her behalf, she let his defection slide.

Look at him. He might be afraid of the words *husband* and *father*, but if the way he was smiling at those kids' antics was any indication, he'd make a great dad—a good thing, because he was about to become one.

He didn't notice her until she cut off his view of the kids.

"Get everything you wanted?" he asked.

Not quite, because she was beginning to want him, perish the thought. Sure they'd been playing sexual games for three weeks, and the body chemistry was off the charts, the sex mind-blowing, but what was with this *want* thing? "Almost," she said. "The salesgirl said the mall's got a store called Dragon Pearls where I should be able to find the magick supplies I need."

"Dragon Pearls?" Aiden stood, shook his head, and took her bags. "I'm not sure I'm up to a magick shop."

"If you don't like it, you can leave. You're aces at leaving, Turtle."

"Lead the way, Cruella."

To give him his due, he didn't so much as wince at the display of athames and chalices in the window.

In the store, the petite blonde salesgirl in a wispy pink ritual robe, with a rose quartz heart between her breasts, looked like she must be hiding pointy ears and fairy wings.

"Righteous," the sales fairy said, as Storm perused the crystals beneath the glass counter. "You have a spirit attached to you."

Storm looked up. "My baby? Is it my baby?"

"What baby?" Aiden asked.

Storm came back to her surroundings with a jolt, turning to the clerk for an explanation.

"Not you," the girl clarified. "You," she said, pointing at Aiden, who stopped breathing and stood dumb as a toadstool.

"Is the spirit attached to him a baby?" Storm asked.

"No," the fairy said. "It's a woman. Red hair, blue eyes, a paisley scarf. Jingle jewelry. She's gorgeous, and the way she looks at you. Love struck. Oh, she's fading, but she's still with you. She has been for a while. Haven't you sensed her?"

Aiden tried to speak, but no words emerged.

Storm saw the determination it took for him not to turn and run.

"I'd like a witch ball, please," Storm said, changing the subject. "Black corner candles and white tapers—"

"Eye of newt?" Aiden suggested.

"Right," Storm said. "That, and some mugwort, hemlock, and belladonna for his breakfast cereal."

Aiden was not amused.

Storm perused the shop from where she stood. "You know what else I need? An angelite crystal."

"I have one, but it's expensive. What did you want it for? Maybe I can suggest something more reasonable?"

"I'll take the angelite," Storm said. "I need it to enhance telepathic communication and psychic channeling."

"Righteous. You know what you're doing, then. Angelite it is."

Storm raised a brow Aiden's way before she turned back to the girl. "Do you have anything like a travel magick kit? We left in a hurry."

"Yes, I have a kit with all the basics."

"Good. I'll take that and this essential oils energy spell bath and body basket."

That perked Aiden up, Storm noticed. While her purchases were being wrapped and rung up, Aiden pointed out the magickal supplies he recognized. He'd taken part in Harmony's midsummer castle cleansing ritual, so he wasn't new to this, but Storm was glad he was curious enough to ask questions.

After the magick shop, she bought some Doc Martens chukka boots and two pairs of spikes, then they headed across the parking lot toward Aiden's motor home, stopping when they saw the crowd gathered around it.

They continued to the periphery. "What's going on?" Aiden asked a bystander.

"Oh," the guy said, "that's the tail wagon, or should I say the dragon tail wagon?"

"Never heard of it," Storm said.

The guy pulled a folded newspaper from his back pocket, the kind famous for fractured stories about movie stars giving birth to alien babies. The owner unfolded the paper and flicked the front page.

Storm read the headline: "Woman Keeps Sex Slave Handcuffed to Bed."

Chapter Twenty

AIDEN whipped the newspaper out of her hand.

"Oh, look, dear," Storm said, trying not to grin. "There's a picture of the sex slave, spread-eagle, all right, but it's too dark to tell what he looks like or if he's wearing clothes. Too bad." She took the paper from him to look at his picture more closely.

"Let's see what it says, *dear*," Aiden replied, taking the paper back. "'Observers testified to seeing a man they called the Silver Fox, and to speaking with his keeper, Snapdragon McGee, a *nymphomaniac* who says she keeps her slave well-paid, well-fed, and very happy.' A nymphomaniac, hey?" Aiden raised a brow.

"Is that all?" Storm asked the bystander.

"No, turn to page five for more pictures."

Storm swallowed. "Oh, goody."

Aiden found page five. "Yep, here's a picture of that Snapdragon dame. Oh they think that's an alias because of her dragon motor home. She looks good, but she's covering her face. Too bad. Still, bare legs that go on forever and a tailcoat over nothing but a . . . well, whatever you call it."

Aiden swatted Storm's arm with the paper. "Why don't you ever wear anything like that?"

Storm put her hands on her hips. "Why can't you be satisfied with me the way I am? Men!"

"Quit whining," Aiden said while their informer looked on with an understanding smile. Aiden shrugged at the guy. "I can't imagine why people think this could be the same motor coach."

"Turn the page," the guy said. "There's a great picture. The coach was parked under a streetlight."

Aiden took a deep breath, and Storm's heart picked up its beat. "You're right," Aiden said. "Great picture."

Storm started walking away, and Aiden followed her, and by the time the guy yelled for his paper, they'd ducked behind a van and were threading their way between cars.

Aiden took Storm's arm, and they hunkered down behind a Honda Element. "I should probably beat you now as a matter of principle."

"But that was fun," she lied.

"McGee, your nose is growing."

Aiden's cell phone rang. "Crap," he said. "It's King. You think they get that newspaper on the islands?"

"Answer it. I wanna talk to Harmony."

Aiden answered and put it on speakerphone. All they could hear was the sound of King laughing. "Hey, Silver Fox," Harmony broke in. "Let me talk to my sister."

"I'm here, Harm."

"That's how you got him to go with you? You cuffed him to his bed and hijacked his motor home? I thought you were going to seduce him into it."

"I did . . . in a way. Are you having a good time?"

"Hell, it's my honeymoon, but I don't think I'm having as much fun as you are."

"I resent that," King said, no longer laughing.

"Well then, let's go buy some handcuffs, Paxton."

"Good idea," King said, and the line went dead.

Aiden folded his phone and put it back in his pocket. "I'm never gonna hear the end of this."

"You think those gawkers will ever leave?" Storm asked.

"Eventually, they'll get tired and go home."

"I'm glad we left the air on for Warlock."

"I'm glad I bought the optional generator so we could."

The Honda owner caught them crouching and looked like she might call for help.

"We're hiding from my abusive ex," Storm said. "Is he still there, honey?" she asked Aiden.

Aiden stood, looked around, and shook his head. "No, I think we're safe. Thanks for the use of your shield. Nice car, by the way."

The woman nodded as she watched them go.

Inside the mall, Aiden stopped and stared her down. "I've got an idea."

Storm cringed. "But I'm too young to die."

"Then shut up and follow me." They cut through the mall and went out a side door at the opposite end, circling back to the exit nearest the coach. "You wait here at the door," Aiden said. "I'll be right back. Be ready. We might have to make a quick getaway."

Storm watched him sneak up behind the coach, which was backed up to the building and sandwiched between a couple of buses. She was glad the crowd had gathered by the front of the coach, near the door, because Aiden was able to open his garage, unnoticed, and slide his Harley down a ramp. He left their purchases in the garage, locked it, and walked his hog to where she was waiting.

He handed her a motorcycle helmet, put on his own, and when she got on behind him, they took off.

She was surprised when he parked near the carnival where they'd awakened that morning.

"You offered me a ride on your Harley the first day, remember?" she said, getting off.

"A motorcycle ride isn't really the kind I was offering."

"I knew that. What now?" she asked. "Gonna feed me to the tiger?"

"No, but dumping you in a mountain of elephant poop sounds pretty amusing."

"The poop or the tiger? Didn't we have to read that story in grammar school?"

Aiden caught her in an affectionate shoulder hug. "Lets take a walk on the midway and grab some carnie junk food for supper. Amusements like this always attracted me, but—"

"But?"

He shrugged. "No fun going to a carnival alone."

That was all Storm needed to hear. Aiden didn't know it, but that was the closest he'd come to saying he was glad they were together. "Good enough," she said. "What are we gonna do about the crowd around the camper?"

"They'll get tired of trying to see through the shades. When it gets dark and no lights go on, they'll give up and leave. Even gawkers get hungry."

A few minutes later, sausage rolls and pizza in hand, they sat in the swinging seat of a gigundous Ferris wheel and started their slow climb as each seat emptied and re-filled.

At the top, Storm stole a bite of his pizza and made a sound of ecstasy at the decadent taste. "The world looks beautiful from up here," she said. "Look, I see the merry-go-round. I love carousel music, and I can smell . . ." She sniffed. "Belgian waffles with strawberries . . . and baby powder."

"It sure does look beautiful," Aiden said, but he hadn't taken his eyes off her. He hadn't caught the baby powder reference, either.

"I haven't been on one of these since my eighth grade date with Melvin Pickles."

"Neither have I."

He was watching her with such intensity, he hadn't heard anything she said. "So you dated Melvin Pickles, too?"

"What?"

"Do I have pizza sauce on my nose?"

"No," he said. "You have a lot of layers, and discovering them is fascinating and disconcerting. You thought the spirit of your baby was attached to you. And you were filled with joy when you did. Wanna tell me about that baby of yours?" He looked so concerned, so caring, that Storm had to work not to tear up.

She looked out over the midway at the lights and balloons, couples hand in hand, couples pushing strollers. Happy families. That's what she'd sensed when she pulled into the empty lot last night. Carnivals must set up here regularly.

She looked at Aiden, watching, waiting.

She usually didn't talk about it, but she sensed his willingness to hear it, and more surprising, she wanted to share it with him.

She sighed. "I was a junior in high school, and I got pregnant. I knew that I'd be on my own. My father would be no help." She fought her emotion, but Aiden got fuzzy.

He handed her a clean napkin, but she refused to use it. "I wished I wasn't pregnant, wished the baby would just go away, you know." She shrugged. "And it did. I miscarried."

She rolled her aquamarine ring around her finger. "I was afraid that I'd inadvertently gotten rid of my baby with wishful magick, which would make me worse than my mother."

"Oh, Storm." Aiden gathered her close.

"I can't believe I told you," she said. "I didn't know that I already loved that baby until I lost it. I miss him every day. Not that I'm sure it was a him, but I sensed . . . him . . . almost the minute I started to bleed, like he was saying good-bye."

Aiden nodded his understanding. "That's why your sisters don't take your talk of crying babies seriously."

Storm crumpled the napkin. "They think it's grief."

"Maybe it is."

"I never heard my baby cry. I only sensed his presence. Your baby, I hear."

"And other babies, you hear, too, judging by your stunt at the mall."

"That's right," she said, pleased all over again. "As long as we're sharing," she said as the Ferris wheel began picking up speed, "do you have any idea who the woman attached to you is?"

"Not my mother. She wasn't attached to me in life. Claudette, I guess, Claudette Langley, an old girlfriend."

"You must have had other girlfriends."

"I did, but none of them are dead, that I know of, and Claudette was . . . my most recent . . . companion."

Dragon's blood, he couldn't even say *relationship*. "Did Claudette pass away while you were together?"

"No, she dumped me, or I assumed she did, because one day, half my closet was empty. No good-bye. No explanation, though we'd had a disagreement earlier."

He shook his head with regret. "A few months after we split, a mutual friend told me that Claudette had died in a car accident."

"She lived with you in your motor home when you were together?"

"On and off for a couple of years. I had a smaller coach then. It was nice, but she wanted a house."

"Attached to the ground. In one place, you mean."

"Roots, that's what she said. She wanted roots."

"Which you can't grow."

"I think I must be root challenged." For half a beat, his expression changed. He blamed himself for Claudette's death. Storm knew it as well as she knew his child was out there.

"I'm no better for you, Storm, than I was for Claudette."

"I'll be the judge of that. I take it she couldn't have been pregnant when she left?"

Aiden put an arm around her. "You're amusing company, Snapdragon McGee."

Change of subject. She got the message.

"Where to after this?" he asked.

"Merry-go-round, Tilt-A-Whirl," she suggested. "I get

the feeling that we can't go back to the coach until well after dark."

"I mean, where to when we get on the road again?"

"Who knows? We're on the right track. The sound of the baby is strong. I say we try to get in a few hours' driving before we stop to sleep."

"We'll need to find a campground tonight. Time to hook up."

"Star showers later tonight," she said. "Want to watch them with me?"

"Will you be waving a wand?"

"No. Will you?"

Chapter Twenty-one

AIDEN sat in the passenger seat several hours later knowing that by failing to drive them back to Salem he'd agreed to go looking for a baby he didn't believe existed, which probably made him as crazy as Storm, except that she was a good kind of crazy, and funny, and smart, and he liked the lunatic a whole lot more than he should.

Plus he had a two-week vacation, which he hated, because, well, being alone got old, and working helped fill the void.

"I'm glad you've made up your mind to come along," she said. "Even if it is to prove me wrong. Do you realize how often you've tried to run, figuratively, and literally, in the past twenty-four hours?"

"You're reading me again."

"You don't seem to mind as much."

He felt pretty good not being in hiding. "I can live with it, especially with you anticipating my every sexual need, you nymphomaniac, you."

"They did not get that word from me."

"No." He grinned. "They got that impression from you,

and I gotta say, I think they're close enough to the mark to make this an interesting journey. Makes me glad I decided to come . . . along. Gives me an incentive for sticking around."

"We all have our reasons for running and for sticking. I'll bet the reasons behind my determination to follow through on my psychic mandate would surprise you."

"Care to elaborate?"

"Not all at once, okay? I'm private by nature. Surprises you, doesn't it? And I'd get the bends if I laid all my secrets bare in one sitting."

"I might suspect some of them, but never mind that. Let's not dig too deep for a start. What's the first reason that pops into your head for almost letting me run you down? Hell, I need a tranquilizer just remembering."

"First reason that pops into my head? That's easy. My sisters and I are illegitimate. We hate it. So, I hate the thought that you might have an illegitimate child somewhere. I hate that the child might *need* you."

"What makes you think this supposed child needs me?"

"If life was good and everything okay, she wouldn't be crying loud enough to reach me."

For a minute, Aiden had taken her statement as if it were a birth announcement. Could he have a *daughter*? Naming the sex of the crying child made it feel so damned real. Heaven help him, was he buying into this? "She?"

"I don't know. I'm new at this. I never followed one of the crying kids in my head before today in the mall, and look how that worked out."

"It worked out great."

Storm grinned at him from the driver's seat. "It did, didn't it? Be honest with me. If you did have a child, wouldn't you want to know?"

"I reiterate: It's not possible, but, yes, if . . . and that's a big if . . . I had a daughter . . . who needed me . . . I'd want to know, by damn." The thought of claiming an unknown figment of Storm's gothic imagination was as crazy as this search. "You're a nutcase, you know."

"I know you think I am."

"A cute nutcase."

"Cute is pretty bland."

"You, Snapdragon, are not bland. You're hot and smokin', and workin' it even when you don't know you're doing it. You're . . . irreverent, rude, sassy, prickly, passionate, impulsive, seductive . . ." She was, in fact, everything he wanted in a woman . . . oxygen, please . . . if he wanted a woman.

"Here!" Storm hooked a left, almost too late, into a campground on freaking campground row.

"Effin' A!" he snapped when all four wheels were finally back on the ground. "There are campgrounds for fifty miles in both directions, and you lay rubber to bring us into this one? What the hell is wrong with you?"

Storm considered the question. "This is the right campground?"

Aiden tried not to go for her throat, because killing her would put a distinct crimp in the sexcathlon he planned for tonight, which should scare him, because he really liked Storm . . . the first crack in the structural collapse of a . . . great friendship . . . if ever he heard one.

Midnight had come and gone by the time they pulled into their spot and he got the coach hooked up to the amenities. Then he needed a shower, and when he came out of the bathroom, the coach was empty.

He pulled on a pair of jeans and found Storm outside, sitting on a quilt Claudette made, wearing her new watermelon sports bra—be still, his heart—and a matching pair of watermelon lady boxers, which could easily be taken for sportswear. She also wore Claudette's old copper sea horse pendant, which she found in a kitchen drawer. Yes, he'd said she could have it, but now the hair on the back of his neck stood and saluted.

What did Storm like to say about paying attention to the signs? If he believed in signs, he'd think that Claudette was trying to tell him something.

Aiden rubbed the back of his neck and dismissed the possibility as ludicrous.

"C'mere, Big Boy." Storm patted the spot beside her. "Let's watch the star showers and let the heavens sprinkle us with tranquility while the crickets lull us to sleep."

He'd expected to find her in bed wearing something like that powder blue babydoll cami and matching G-string, and maybe her new leather boots, though if he'd found the nympho waiting for sex, it would have been time for him to fess up, so he guessed this was better. He lay beside her, put his head on her pillow, and she slipped her hand in his. For half an hour, she pointed out the clusters of shooting stars—the view *was* spectacular—and she talked about anything and everything except sinsational wildebeest sex.

"You're really ticking me off," he said.

She rolled his way and winked. "Hey, McGrumpy, I can *off* you in a lot of ways. Is that your problem?"

"I don't have a problem."

She chuckled, unzipped him, and slipped her hand in his jeans to find him primed and ready.

"You sure do have a problem," she said, and as his blood turned south and his man brain—as she liked to call it—took over his thinking, he was glad he wasn't going to have to reveal his problem tonight after all.

Determined to give as good as he got—and he was getting him somethin' grand—he found her wet and ready, and it didn't take long before a star shower lit the earth as well as the sky.

A short time later, Aiden woke and saw that the stars had continued showering without them. Storm lay curled around him, her hand in his jeans, him rising to fill her palm, one leg over his, her face in his neck, a different sort of heaven than he'd expected tonight, but one he could get used to.

He moved close and made her more comfortable by slipping his arm beneath her head. She mumbled something about crying babies and went back to sleep.

What a witch, and he meant that in a good way. He shouldn't be in lust or serious attraction. In the last day and a half, the sexiest triplet witch east of the Mississippi—one who could assault him without touching him, if he wasn't careful—had seduced, undressed, handcuffed, and kidnapped him. Yet—he should face the facts—he'd stupidly agreed to this no-destination road trip . . . just to be with her.

Her ability to psychically assault people was some witchy power, and he sure hoped that raging passion didn't take hold of her often, unless, of course, she could use it in the sack. He wasn't sure she'd been honest about that earlier when she was fighting to get her way. If she could turn his wheel . . . maybe she could, actually . . . turn his wheel.

But he was being selfish. The parts of her past that she'd shared made him suspect the depth of her pain. Storm the cryptic cynic was bruised, deep down, but he wouldn't change her; wouldn't want to. He could only try to make her happy with the means at his disposal. He'd show her that he cared, because someone should—besides her sisters. The trick would be to keep an emotional distance at the same time.

Storm wrenched from his arms, nearly ripping his dick off at the root, and she shot to her feet. "She's lost!"

Aiden shook her to make sure she was awake, and when she focused on him, she sucked in a breath and ran to the coach. She nearly knocked him over running out the door in jeans, T-shirt, and Doc Martens, then she started banging on the camper door one site over.

Aiden slipped into his shoes and shirt and followed her.

When their neighbors opened their camper door—in their sleep—she asked if they had a child missing, even though they were about ninety-nine years old.

When the answer was, of course, no, Storm ran to the next campsite to wake a family of tenters. By the sixth invasion, a few vocal souls were talking about a lynching.

Eventually, the campground lights came on, and a police car pulled up.

This time, she was gonna get them both arrested.

Chapter Twenty-two

AIDEN tried to stop her. "What are you doing?"

"A lost child . . . crying." Storm said running toward the next campsite.

Conundrum. She'd already saved a lost child. Could he afford to ignore this? Would the police put him in a strait-jacket when he tried to explain? Because Storm wasn't about to stop long enough to tell them anything.

When they couldn't talk her out of knocking on doors, two police officers physically detained her. Storm took a deep breath and screamed, "One of your children is miss-ing!" loud enough to alert the campers.

A few minutes later, a woman came running their way. "Leslie! My daughter's not in her bed. It's my daughter," the woman told a police officer. "Have you found her?" she asked Storm. "Is that why you've been shouting?"

The officers let Storm go.

She gave them a dirty look and adjusted her shirt. "I needed to know *who* was missing. Do you have a picture of her?" Storm asked the woman.

With the officers, she followed the woman to her camper.

Storm studied the snapshot and handed it to an officer. "Call for a search party and an ambulance! Chop-chop!"

The campers formed their own search party and headed toward a nearby quarry, but Storm asked the campground owner to point her toward water, a lake or a pond, maybe, and he sent them in a different direction.

At the edge of the lake, Storm shook her head. "This isn't right." She looked toward the stars and closed her eyes. "She's hurt, and her cry has a gurgle in it, like water is filling her nose and mouth."

Aiden thought of Storm's experience at the mall, and it worried him that, this time, she wasn't running headlong toward a rescue.

Without a word, Storm bolted in another direction, down a hill and into some woods, Aiden right behind her.

When they got to a rope bridge high over a rocky stream, Storm stopped so fast, Aiden passed her and was halfway across the bridge before he realized she wasn't behind him. He'd lost her. Where had she gone?

"Storm?" he called. "Storm? Where the hell did you go?"

Below the rope bridge, miles below, it seemed, he saw her climbing over a sharp outcropping of rocks. Adrenaline shot through him as he backtracked and took the hill at a run.

He heard Storm scream, got distracted, tripped, rolled, and came to a stop at the same outcropping, but Storm was gone.

Aiden climbed over the rocks, but he still couldn't see her.

She wasn't nuts. *He* was nuts for letting her get hurt. If something happened to her . . .

On the opposite side of the rocks, he found that the steep hill continued, and he followed it down. Then he saw something shimmering in the moonlight, the sea horse, hanging down Storm's back. Far above him, she clung to the edge of a bigger rock cliff than the first, trying to get a toehold.

Something moved at the edge of the water. The girl.

His heart tripped. Helplessness grabbed him by the throat.

"Hold on, Storm," he called, going for the girl.

"Hurry," Storm said, glancing back. "She'll drown."

The child lay at the edge of the stream, her body nearly submerged. Thank God for the stream's irregular flow; water covered her face erratically, so she could take air every now and then. As Aiden got closer, the child's gurgling finally reached *his* ears.

"I'm gonna take you out of the water," he told the kid, glancing up at Storm, praying she wasn't heading for disaster.

"My arm," the girl said. "It hurts."

Aiden got in the water and placed an arm behind her back and another beneath her knees. She screamed anyway until he set her down in the dirt.

Then he stood directly beneath Storm. "Jump, Storm," he called. "I'm going to catch you."

That fast, she let go . . . and landed on him.

The girl's giggle told him she was going to be fine, though his sprained cock was another matter.

"Did I squish you?" Storm asked, getting up and going to the girl.

"I think her arm's broken," Aiden said. "Let's splint it before we take her back to camp."

A half hour later, Aiden carried Leslie the long way around the rocks and up the steep incline, with Storm at his back, trying to keep him from falling with Leslie in his arms, though Storm stumbled a few times herself.

When they emerged from the woods, people came running. Leslie's parents repeated their thanks. The police and a news crew were waiting, as was the ambulance that whisked Leslie off to the hospital.

Aiden asked the news crew to turn off their cameras. All they needed was for the dragon tail wagon to be filmed and recognized.

The police took his statement.

Everyone in the campground must be there, Aiden thought as he got slapped on the back, though the girls' parents had known who really saved her.

He found Storm standing as if in a daze, watching the road the ambulance had taken.

"Can I take your picture?" a camper asked her.

"No, please," Aiden said, placing his arm around Storm's shoulder to walk her back to his coach.

Aiden took her inside, turned on the shower, stripped her, and got in with her. He shampooed her hair, washed her face, and scrubbed the dirt from beneath her broken nails. Afterward, he wrapped her in a towel and put antiseptic ointment on her scratches while he stood there still dressed and dripping on the rug, then he pointed her toward the bedroom. "Go roll up in a blanket. I'll be with you in a minute." He stripped and showered.

When he got to the bedroom, a towel wrapped around his waist, he found her wide awake. It was seven in the morning by then, and if they'd gotten more than an hour's sleep, he'd be surprised.

He lay down beside her and took her in his arms, gazed into her wide, wide eyes. "Why are you looking so lost? She's safe."

Storm rolled tight into him. "While I was looking for her, I . . . *felt* her parents' anxiety, which was making it hard for me to hear Leslie. I guess—I know—that when you found me staring after the ambulance, I was sharing their joy at her safe return. I never felt the love of a family before. The feelings were so foreign and so utterly amazing. I think I was . . . wallowing . . . in love."

"You looked like you'd been shot and didn't know enough to fall."

She buried her nose in his chest hair. "I felt like I'd been shot."

"Why?"

She looked up at him. "Because I didn't know until then what family love felt like. Didn't know what I'd missed."

"You have a family. Your sisters."

"Our love started in the womb. It's unconditional. Maybe I take it for granted, but it's sibling love. Until that moment, I didn't know how different that was from mother love or father love."

"I wish I'd felt it," Aiden said. It would have been new to him, too.

She cupped his cheek. "It was the most beautiful feeling in the world."

"You deserved it for finding her."

"I didn't do anything but use the gift I've been given . . . twice this trip." She smiled, the light coming back into her blue green eyes. "Wait till I tell my sisters that I have a gift for finding lost children. They thought I was crazy, but they're wrong! I could dance, I'm so happy. You wanna dance?"

God she was beautiful. Breathtaking.

"Cat got your tongue?" she asked.

"No, *he's* got my slippers."

"I'm sorry Warlock fell in love with your slippers."

"Very expensive Italian leather," Aiden said, "but you could make it up to me."

"How?" she asked, looking rather kittenlike, herself, in the way she moved her body into a naturally seductive, feline pose. He wanted to know more about the child hidden inside the seductress, as much as he wanted to know the sex storm goth with attitude, in the biblical sense. Except that he needed to get both of them past the stupidest mistake he'd ever made.

Though he'd be forced to confess, he got hard thinking about what he wanted to do to her, which must have set off some kind of witchy hot button, because she began rotating her hips, kissing his neck, working her hand beneath his towel, and generally arousing the hell out of him.

Maybe if he got her good and ready, she was already halfway there, she'd be too hot to let anything stop them—please God—and maybe he'd confess, and she'd accept the results with equilibrium, and they'd have an amazing sex storm conflagration.

Still, she *could* turn from him in disgust . . . If his towel fell before she was primed, D-day would arrive precipitously, and he might never . . . arrive.

Better he should initiate the unveiling, rather than run from it.

The fact was, he couldn't stand the suspense.

No more games, no more running.

Aiden stood, turned on the light, and whipped off his towel.

Storm focused, gasped, and reared back.

The object of her shock shriveled in embarrassment.

Chapter Twenty-three

A surge of disbelief shivered through Storm.

She stood on her knees and inched forward for a closer look. *Weird* was the first word that came to mind, *joke*, the second.

Except that it was real. The mortified look on Aiden's face said it all, and her heart went out to him. "You have a penis tattooed on your dragon. I mean, a dragon tattooed on your penis."

"I figured you'd notice."

"It's kinda . . . pink, hot pink."

"Pale violet red," Aiden said. "With maroon trim."

"Yeah, that . . . with its tail curled down your thigh and wings halfway to your waist. I guess I would notice. No wonder you wear boxers."

Storm reached for his dragon but pulled back and looked up at him. "I'm not the only one who acts before they think." She indicated the dragon. "I submit exhibit A . . . which is raising its head and looking up at me as if it could devour me for breakfast."

"It could."

"That's the longest dragon neck I've ever seen."

"Why, thank you, Storm."

"Did you ever notice that when he raises his head, his wings seem to get wider, as if for flight?"

"I'm looking at it from the wrong angle."

"What possessed you in the first place?"

"Liquor and plenty of it, a need to prove my independence, and a bet I wanted to win."

"How rational of you."

"Hey, the tattoo artist was a Tahitian beauty, as were her topless multitalented assistants, who held my balls and my dick, and did wicked things to keep me entertained. I had a bet to win. I love women. I'd been dumped. We had our moments."

"Topless assistants. No wonder you didn't notice it was pink."

Aiden opened his mouth and closed it again.

It was both the weirdest and most arousing thing she'd ever seen. "How did you stay long that long?"

"The tattoo artist's assistants handled . . . everything, but to be truthful, it isn't all that arousing getting needled, and it's less bloody if you're not hard."

"Did it hurt?"

"Not as bad as I expected. There's skin anesthesia and new methods. It barely scabbed. It's a tame version of what I've seen out there."

"It doesn't look tame now. Did you win the bet?"

"Yeah, for what that's worth, but I lost my sex life . . . until you . . . maybe. That's the part I didn't think through. How I would feel about revealing my . . . lapse in judgment . . . to a woman."

"How have other women reacted?"

"You're the first who's seen it, and you're shocked out of your mind."

"Well, not out of my mind. You must have expected some surprise, or you wouldn't have gone celibate."

"It's hideous," he said.

"No, it's . . . kind of a turn on, the way it's looking up at me, all expectant-like. And it's my favorite color. But why did you do it?" She patted the bed beside her.

He hesitated, then he accepted her invitation to join her on the bed. "I'd been dumped . . . again. That can only happen so many times in a man's life before he does something . . . brainless."

"Claudette dumped you."

Aiden nodded. "King and Morgan wanted to cheer me up, so they took me sailing to the islands, and over a week that I now remember as humiliating, I let this happen."

"It's like those dragon tattoos on the Internet, but different."

"That's where I got the idea."

"Why didn't Morgan and King stop you?"

"They were getting their own tattoos."

"Not—"

"No . . . mine's the most outrageous. King's is almost sane."

"Harmony will tell me about King's, but what's Morgan's like?"

"We swore never to tell, and I knew by the look on your face when you saw it that King kept his vow and didn't tell Harmony."

Storm got closer, slipped her hand up his thigh, felt him shudder, and watched his dragon come to life. "So . . . you got drunk because your ex broke up with you, and you got a tattoo?"

"No, I got drunk because I got dumped, and while I was drunk, I made a stupid bet. I had to get sober to get the tattoo—something to do with liquor thinning the blood and the consequences."

Storm tried not to roll her eyes. "You loved Claudette that much?"

"No. I was mad at her. She wanted commitment, and I didn't, so she dumped me. I did this to assert my independence."

"Nearly a year and a half without a woman, because Mr. Majestic got a makeover? I don't think so. What aren't you telling me?"

When Aiden didn't answer, Storm shook her head. So he wasn't ready to face the real reason. She could respect that.

She touched the wrinkled beast and discovered that when in full flight, it was actually . . . beautiful. Either that, or she liked this man a whole hell of a lot more than was safe or sane for her. "So, I'm the first woman, other than the tattoo artists, who's ever seen it?"

Aiden nodded, holding his breath as if waiting for a verdict, as if it might actually go his way, as if he didn't deserve it to.

But he did deserve it. This was Aiden. And Storm wanted to see his dragon fly.

She stroked its neck. "I'm the first woman you're aroused by who's ever touched it?"

"Easy," Aiden said. "This is his first time out in female company, and he's feeling . . . cocky. Since you haven't decked me or run away, he's primed, and I'm afraid he'll breathe fire before either of us is ready."

"I'll take that into consideration," Storm said, petting the reaching beast and tracing the curled wings raised above its neck.

"Oh," Storm said rising to her knees. "I almost forgot. He has a friend." She turned her back to Aiden and lowered her blanket to show him the Celtic dragon tattoo at the base of her spine. "Meet Elektra, my dragon totem, a powerful guardian and guide, a sea goddess who gives me the courage and wonder to tap into my psychic power. Elektra protects me, helps me grow, and adds power to my magick."

"A scarlet lady dragon," Aiden said. "I always thought of dragons as male, probably because of my own, but I suppose dragons once needed to make little dragons, didn't they?"

Storm faced him. "Your dragon is getting bigger as I

watch." She tilted her head. "He's every bit as beautiful but not quite as detailed as some I've seen on the Net."

Aiden shuddered. "I didn't have the details in me." He turned her so he could see her dragon again.

Storm felt the nerve endings at the base of her spine rising to meet Aiden's fingertips as he caressed every scarlet scale. "Elektra," he said with a reverential awe. "It's a fine name for a lady dragon."

"The goddess Elektra was the mother of storms and rainbows," she explained.

"Elektra's beautiful, just like her namesake. What would you name an *ugly* dragon?"

Hearing the insecurity in Aiden's voice, Storm turned to worship and befriend his dragon with her fingertips. Gentle touches, soft, sweet, slow, taming him, and bringing him to life. "I was shocked when I first saw him," she admitted. "But he becomes less frightening as he . . . grows . . . on you." In full flight, he was rather beautiful. "I believe he's a water dragon," she said. "Many of them have only one head—"

"Praise be," Aiden said.

Chapter Twenty-four

"HOW about if we call him Triton, after the god of the sea who calms the waves. Triton can be Elektra's mate . . . for now. No commitments there, either, so don't go shrinking into your shell."

"Witch," Aiden said. "*You* become less frightening by the minute." He cupped her face in both hands and stroked her lips with his thumbs. "I wonder if you heard my dragon crying. I think it wept in silence when it couldn't reach you, even though it trembled in utter delight when you were near."

Storm liked Aiden's attention so frightfully much; she suddenly wished *she* had a shell to retreat into. "As a water dragon, Triton brings hidden memories to the surface," she explained. "He helps us face our painful pasts and gives us courage and balance to face our futures."

"Triton. I like his name," Aiden said. "And revealing him sure as hell made me face a painful past."

Storm petted the beast. "Let's raise his purpose to a giver of courage, then. Triton is a powerful god, but Elektra is almost more powerful, because she's his seducer."

"Is she now? Let's see how that works."

Aiden's voice had become so sexy, his dragon so gorgeous in flight, that over the next few hours, Storm learned Triton the dragon's many fine qualities and talents. He could make her scream, and cry out in rapture, make her beg for rest and beg for flight.

The longer Triton and Elektra performed their mating dance, the more beautiful Triton became, until he lifted the stormy Elektra and carried her to the heavens, star by star, climbing higher and higher, the most beautiful dragon in the galaxy, surpassing even Draco the constellation on his own home turf, so to speak.

Storm fell asleep on her stomach with Aiden petting Elektra, and woke as Triton began to . . . mate . . . with her again, but this time Aiden also wanted to kiss Elektra, so he raised her hips and entered her from behind, slipping his dragon so deep, it kissed her pulsing womb.

No man in Storm's experience had ever had the length to enter her in this way, though two had tried. But with Aiden's dragon stroking her, hard and determined, against slick and willing, her milking him with involuntary bursts of greed, she experienced a primordial tempest of sensation that no human or vibrator had ever matched.

Later, Aiden let Storm bring his dragon to life with her lips and her hands and the ring on her pierced tongue. She gave him kisses on his wings, along his neck, on his head and eye. And then she took him in her mouth and suckled him, until Aiden shouted, rolled her beneath him, and rose over her to ride the waves he could tame, if only he would, until he commanded her to rise with him, and she did. They flew to the depths of the sea, then rose on mighty crests, more than once, until that final almighty crest lowered them to float and rest.

"I think my dragon is dead," Aiden said, hours later.

Storm could barely raise her head to check. "It died happy."

The next morning, she woke starving, and got up craving Froot Loops.

Aiden walked proudly naked into the kitchen and opened the refrigerator.

"Aw, look, Triton is sleeping," Storm said.

Aiden raised a skeptical brow. "He's dead, I tell you. Nearly a year and a half's worth of happy in one day was too much for his celibate heart, though I think we set a new world record for dragon fire dancing."

Storm dropped the blanket from around her.

Aiden dropped the milk carton.

Triton lifted his head in true dragon fashion to see what he could get into.

Her, Storm thought; he could get into her. "I think he might be well on his way to a miraculous recovery. He looks like he's about to straighten his spine and sing the national anthem."

"Well, he should," Aiden said. "Tomorrow's Independence Day, after all, and isn't independence what you and I are all about?"

"Totally," Storm said, yet there was something that had changed inside her last night. She recognized it when Aiden took care of her in the shower. She'd never had anyone take care of her like that—other than her sisters.

Between his empathy and concern and her taste of family love, she now heard several babies crying, but she didn't think that Aiden was ready to hear that. "I never told another soul the things I've told you about myself on this trip," Storm said.

"No other soul has seen my dragon."

"King and Morgan?"

"Hell no. They saw the drawing and the bill."

"Not even your doctor has seen it?"

"I hate doctors."

"Well that has to change. You need to take care of yourself. You're a father, now."

"I am not. We found a crying child. Hell, we found two. Damn it. That can't be right, can it?"

"Yours is still crying. But I have a confession to make."

"Give it to me, baby. Oh, I'd better stop talking like that," Aiden said. "I'm turning myself on."

"Triton the insatiable." She led Aiden to the shower. "Dragons love water, especially Triton. I'll get your clothes while you shower."

"Wait," Aiden said. "Aren't we going back to bed?"

Storm turned on the shower. "We're getting on the road. We have a quest to fulfill."

"There are quests," Aiden said. "And there are dragon quests. Which one would you prefer to follow?"

"Both. Now take your shower."

When he left the shower, Aiden heard Celtic music and found Storm standing beside the freshly made bed—wearing a pair of clear spikes, red thigh-high fishnet stockings, his tool belt, and a lacy red bra. From a bear-shaped honey jar in the tool belt hung the bikinis that matched the bra.

"What have we here?" Aiden dropped his towel, while his dragon prepared for flight.

Storm gave him a Cheshire cat grin. "I figured that after so long, you and your dragon might need a tune-up."

"Where did you find the tools?"

"Here and there." She lifted the contents from each pouch on the tool belt, one by one. "Honeysuckle candles for mood and scent." She put them in the holders, lit them, and turned off the light. "Makeup brushes—very erotic." She whisked one up beneath his dragon's neck, and he shivered with arousal.

"Bath powder and puff." She powdered his navel. "Edible raspberry massage oil from my magick bath kit . . . in honor of Triton the raspberry titan. Handcuffs—your old friends—but I thought you might like to use them on me for a change, along with anything in the tool belt that strikes your fancy. Your assignment, should you accept it, is to find my third tattoo."

Triton jumped at the opportunity. Aiden grinned. "What's the honey for?"

Storm raised a brow. "I plan to use it on you. I found it in your cupboard." From the tool belt, she took a small plastic tube that she shook like a rattle. "Honey first, then chocolate sprinkles." Storm looked down and cleared her throat. "I can see that Triton's agreeable. What about you?"

Aiden or Triton—it was hard to tell which—roared and took up the challenge in a very big way.

It was a full three hours before Aiden drove the coach away from the campground, because after all, dragons who'd been deprived of tune-ups for so long deserved a lube job once in a while.

"You don't think that Elektra's jealous because Triton fell in love with your sea horse, do you?" Aiden asked.

"Nah, Elektra and Ceres have different purposes. Ceres is a goddess of fertility, which doesn't apply to us. She knows that Triton belongs to Elektra. She was just warming him up a bit."

"Triton thinks he's gone to heaven," Aiden said. "But he's probably gonna get hard every time I see a tool belt from now on."

Storm raised a skeptical brow. "I can't imagine what King's construction crew is going to think about that."

"I'll have to stay out of range, and Elektra will have to visit Triton regularly until the castle is finished."

"That could be arranged. Do you feel mellow enough to hear my confession?"

"Uh-oh," Aiden said. "Was that tune-up a ploy so I wouldn't want to beat you again?"

"No, the tune-up was pure fun, which doesn't change the fact that I have something to confess." Storm took a breath, but the crying in her head was confusing her. "Wait. Take a left. Now a right. Left again. No, turn around."

Aiden pulled into a restaurant parking lot. "Would you like to drive?"

"Yes, please, since our mapping system is in *my* head." Before they set off, they got takeout and ate at a picnic table behind the motor coach. The way she parked, Storm had blocked a corner table closed in by bramble bushes on two sides. And for dessert, their dragons got naughty on the picnic table in broad daylight.

Back in the motor coach, Storm got into the driver's seat. "Confession time. I now hear several babies crying."

Chapter Twenty-five

"HOW many, in your book, is several?" Aiden asked a little too loudly. "Sorry, I'm overreacting." Hell, he didn't want to hurt the love of his dragon's life. She was . . . *Elektra* was . . . something . . . special.

He took a calming breath. "How many babies?"

"I don't know," Storm said, biting her lip, as she took random lefts and rights.

"Two, three, four?" he asked. "Don't try to tell me that you think I have triplets?"

"No, but you sound like you believe you might have at least one baby." Storm looked hopeful, which ticked Aiden off, probably because he was afraid she could be right, and that a baby of his—one baby—might exist somewhere.

She'd already pulled two child rescues out of her magick hat, and he didn't know what else she had in store. "Where the hell are you going?"

"Beats me." That was when they heard the siren. Aiden looked into the rearview mirror. "Storm, the officers in the police car behind us want us to pull over."

"I wasn't speeding!" She pulled into the first mall parking

lot she came to. "Oh, do you think somebody saw us on that picnic table?"

By the time the officer got to the driver's side window, the rag-reading dragon tail brigade was starting to circle like buzzards.

"Tell the officer to come inside," Aiden told her.

Great, Storm thought, and then she turned to the officer and invited him in.

He brought his partner. They stood in the doorway and took off their hats.

"Was I doing something wrong?" Storm asked.

"No," the macho officer said. "We saw the dragon camper, and after that sex slave story the other day, we called it in, because we wanted to be sure nobody was being held against their will."

Storm raised her chin, her breasts rising with it, and crossed her arms to give herself some mighty fine boobage—on purpose, Aiden thought. "Do I look like somebody who could abduct a man?" she asked them. "Seriously?"

"If you hire paid sex slaves, miss," the rookie officer said, "can I have an application?"

Macho gave Rookie a look with *Shut the ef up* written all over it.

Rookie elbowed Macho. "You're just jealous that you didn't ask first."

Macho turned to Storm. "Mind if we take a look around?"

Storm looked surprised, and Aiden worried about what she'd do or say next.

"Don't you need a search warrant for that?" she asked.

"Storm, stop making matters worse," Aiden said. "We have nothing to hide. Take a look." When the rookie flirted with Storm, Aiden indicated that the officers should precede them, and he took Storm by the hand.

"Jealous?" she mouthed.

He showed the officers every room, watching them open closets and cupboards, and in the bedroom, Rookie found

Storm's cuffs in the nightstand with an array of confetti colored condoms. "It *was* you, then," Rookie said, all smiles.

Aiden thought the macho officer was going to deck his partner.

"We're consenting adults," Aiden said. "Snapdragon thought she'd get funny and leave me stewing while she went in for coffee, but she attracted the wrong kind of attention."

"May the Goddess forgive me," Storm said, and Aiden squeezed her hand to shut her up.

"Snapdragon's not your real name, is it?" the rookie said.

"She didn't commit a moving violation, but you know who I am because you ran my license plate. You know this is my coach and that I'm squeaky clean."

"Hell," the rookie said. "We even know how much you donate to the police retirement fund."

"Stan, will you shut the hell up!" the macho officer said.

Storm went back into the living area and opened the fridge. "Can I offer you a glass of lemonade before you leave?"

While Rookie nodded, Macho said an emphatic, "No thanks." With an apology, they left, and did some crowd control so Storm could drive the camper from the parking lot.

"The things you get me into," Aiden said. "Now I'm a sex-slave icon."

"Don't blame me. Why did you have dragons painted on the sides of the motor coach, given the fact that you were keeping such a . . . ginormous . . . secret?"

"It made sense at the time." Aiden sighed. "Sort of. I knew when I had the coach painted that my motives and emotions were bumping up against each other. Part of it was getting the dragon out in the open . . . so to speak . . . an honest statement about who I really am, even though no one would understand but me."

"That makes a weird sort of sense." Storm took a quick left.

"Will you slow down? I can't believe they didn't ticket you."

Storm raised her chin, a sign she was ignoring him on purpose. "So having a dragon camper was a bid for self-respect, despite Triton," she said, giving him something else to think about.

Aiden nodded tentatively. "Or a warning . . ."

"Or all of the above," she said.

"Probably. Dragons are highly respected, so maybe driving around in a dragon coach had to do with making peace with myself. Kind of like telling myself to get over it already, though if I'd known I'd have you and your sarcasm to look forward to, I never would have produced any of my own."

Storm glanced his way. "Glad to be of service. Has it helped?"

"No, but the way you accepted Triton did."

"I understand your motive for wanting the tattoo, if not the fact that you actually stayed until the dragon was done."

"Thanks, but I could have stayed days longer if I wanted it detailed. The spikes were supposed to be detailed in scarlet and black."

"See, you're smarter than we both thought."

He gave her a dirty look. "Do you still hear several babies crying?"

" 'Fraid so."

Aiden sighed. "Mind if I just sleep through the next nightmare?"

"Suit yourself," she said, taking a right. "Dragon Boy has had a *hard* day."

Aiden looked over at her, absurdly glad that she'd cuffed him into taking this trip to wonderland, and he fell asleep.

Sometime later, he woke up to an ocean view out one window and Atlantic City's famed boardwalk out another. Here? She was going to find babies here? Aiden went looking and found Storm asleep in his bed. He crawled in beside her and took her in his arms to coax her awake with kisses. "Rough day?" he asked.

"Um-hmm," she said, pressing her breasts against him while slipping her arms around his neck. "First, I gave my favorite dragon a tune-up, and then he got a splinter in his paw and growled at me."

"Triton was a jerk," Aiden said.

"Yes, he was."

"He apologizes profusely."

"And I got stopped by the cops." She curled a finger in the hair at his nape. "Thank you for protecting my identity, though yours was blown to bits."

"Yeah, I'm a regular dragon in tarnished armor."

Storm sat up. "Does that mean you'll take orders from me? Throw your coat over the elephant poop in my path?"

"My coat, but not my coach."

Storm patted his sleepy dragon. "How do you feel about taking a walk toward the casinos?" she asked.

Ten minutes later, she led the way down the boardwalk.

"How many babies do you hear?" Aiden asked.

"A nursery full."

Aiden missed a step. "Are you sure we're not going to rescue a set of triplets?"

She took as random a turn into a casino as she took into the campground. Random like the mall they'd chosen, and the roads they'd taken, except that his random was her real. Two lost children back with their families proved that.

They wandered inside the casino for a while, lefts and rights, and straight ahead, among blackjack tables and slot machines of every conceivable type, where eager hopefuls hit buttons or pulled cranks and rubbed screens for luck, while the machines themselves devoured their money with cunning avarice.

Aiden almost lost her, but he caught up. "Are you still listening to the babies in your head? Though I don't know how you can hear anything with this racket." Upbeat music and gripping tunes battled with coins hitting metal trays, flashing lights, and spinning drums with attention-grabbing graphics. "Storm?" Damn, she was concentrating, and not on the chaos around her, but on the chaos in her head.

Storm, with her hard outer shell and large, hidden heart, had a huge psychic ability that was either a gift or a curse.

She stopped, and when Aiden saw why, he stopped, too. Talk about surreal.

Facing them stood a casino hostess in the establishment's signature red halter top, miniskirt, black stockings, and spikes. Balancing a raised tray of drinks on the palm of one hand, the hostess could be Storm's double, except that Storm was already part of a triple.

Chapter Twenty-six

BOTH women stepped forward. Both with colored hair, dark lips and nails, and heavy eye makeup.

"Do I know you?" they asked at the same time.

"No," they answered together.

A bouncer-type thug came around the corner, and the hostess winced. "Gotta get back to work. I have a supper break in fifteen minutes," she told Storm. "Meet me in the Malachite Lounge upstairs." The woman left without waiting for an answer and began to distribute drinks to high-roller slot machine players as if Aiden and Storm didn't exist.

"That was weird," Storm said. "She looked a little like me."

A little? Aiden thought.

"Did you read her name tag by any chance?" Storm asked.

"Sorry," he said. "We'll take a look at it when we meet her in the lounge."

Fifteen minutes later, the hostess no longer wore a name tag, though Aiden saw signs of the missing pin. Why would she remove it, unless her name proved as spooky as her resemblance to Storm?

"This is my supper break," she said. "You don't mind if I order?"

"I'm hungry, too." Storm picked up her menu. "Mind if we join you? I'm Storm, by the way." She reached across the table and offered her hand.

The woman hesitated but shook it, barely. "Marvelanne."

"Marvelanne," Aiden said. "That's an unusual name."

"It is," Marvelanne said, blowing a gum bubble and sucking it in with her pierced tongue. "My mama was into the Marvelettes, and she was playin' 'Please Mr. Postman' on the record player when she and my daddy did the deed and conceived me."

Aiden firmed his mouth so his jaw wouldn't drop. "Aiden McCloud," he said, introducing himself with his last name, hoping that Marvelanne—the Southern casino hostess, or so her accent indicated—would add her last name, but she didn't.

Her first name wasn't even one you could shorten. No one would call the nicotine-stained, smoke-scented woman a marvel.

The waitress came to take their orders, and Marvelanne shut her menu. "I'll have a bacon cheeseburger, blue cheese instead of cheddar, sweet potato fries, and a side of mayo."

Storm slowly lowered her menu, revealing a look both amazed and wary. "I'll have the same."

Aiden ordered a scotch.

"Are you a goth, like Storm?" Aiden asked Marvelanne. "You're wearing the casino's uniform, I know, but your hair and makeup are similar, though your hair's purple and hers is blue, then there's the tattoo . . ."

Storm focused on the woman's wrist. "The symbol of three in a heart, a Celtic triquetra," Storm said, pulling her top aside a bit to reveal the edge of the triquetra on her breast. "Mine's blue, and yours is red."

Aiden's scotch appeared before him. "Do you have triplets, too?" the waitress asked. "That's why Marvelanne has a triquetra."

Marvelanne slapped the table.

"Too much information, I guess, huh?" The waitress looked from Storm to Marvelanne, and back. "Cripes, you two could be sisters."

"Sylvia!"

"Sorry. Food'll be out in a minute." Sylvia popped her gum and left.

Storm looked uneasy. She shook her head and crossed her arms in a protective gesture. "How old are your triplets?" she asked. "I'll bet they're teenagers. Must be a handful. Boys? Girls? Or a mix?"

Marvelanne shrugged. "I didn't keep 'em."

"But the tattoo?"

"A form of birth control."

"Has it worked?" Storm asked, and Aiden choked on his scotch.

"Are you all right?" Storm leaned over to slap his back.

Aiden nodded and took a sip of Storm's water. "You'd think there wouldn't be anything else you could do or say that would shock me."

"You should talk," Storm said, turning back to Marvelanne. "How old were you when they were born?"

Marvelanne took the gum out of her mouth and stuck it to her wrist triquetra. "Anybody ever tell you that you're nosy?"

"I mean, did your parents force you to give them up for adoption?"

"Nah, my old man never knew. I ran the minute the brats were born. Daddy would have killed me."

"Did the number of babies you had matter?" Storm asked, sitting forward.

"What the hell does that mean?"

"Would you have kept one baby? Or two, maybe? But three were just too many? I mean, was the third baby the straw that broke the camel's back?"

Marvelanne mocked her with a laugh. "I wouldn't have kept *any*, honey. One baby would have been every bit as much trouble as three."

The waitress brought their food, and when she left, Aiden was still comparing the two women with his gaze, still shocked by the resemblance. "I'm sorry," he said to Marvelanne, "but aren't you the least bit curious about what happened to your children?"

Marvelanne raised a brow. "You want to know if I feel guilty, don't you?" She took a bite of her hamburger, chewed thoughtfully, took a drink, and then another bite, before she set her burger down. She checked her watch. "On the clock," she told him. "Gotta get back to my shift on time."

"Of course," Aiden replied.

"I never look back," Marvelanne said. "Guilt is a wasted effort." She emptied the container of sugar packets into her purse and added a honking big wad of napkins.

Aiden wondered if she'd take the catsup bottle, too.

"I did the right thing," Marvelanne said, closing her purse. "You don't miss what you never had."

"That's not true," Storm said. "Don't you even want to know who adopted them, where they are?"

Marvelanne examined Storm with dead eyes. "I left my babies in their daddy's care."

Storm sat forward, the light in her eyes fading. "Maybe their daddy *didn't* care."

"His mother would have. She was a pushover."

"Maybe his mother would have killed him, like your parents would have killed you, so he didn't tell her until the triplets were too old to need her."

"He wasn't afraid of his mother. He was older than me. He'd been married before."

Storm pushed her plate aside, but when Aiden coaxed her lips open with one of her fries, she ate it and gave him a wan smile.

"What about later, when you left your parents' house, Marvelanne?" Aiden asked. "Did you try to look for your triplets, then?"

Marvelanne shrugged. "I had enough trouble support-ing myself. Kids drag you down no matter how old you are." She raised a hand to wave at their waitress. "Sylvia, bring me a piece of strawberry cheesecake. Do you two want any dessert?"

Aiden put a fifty on the table, certain that Marvelanne would make a tidy profit.

"Dessert?" she asked them again.

"No thanks," Storm said, standing. "I don't feel very well."

Chapter Twenty-seven

AIDEN took Storm's arm. "Come on, I'll get us a room for the night."

At the last minute, he turned to Marvelanne. "Nice meeting you," he told the cocktail hostess with no heart.

"I sure hope you were lying," Storm said as they walked away.

"About the room?"

"No, about it being nice to meet her. It was awful." Storm's fingers and legs tingled, while a suffocating heat closed around her and threatened to smother her. She was that scared she might have met her mother, the woman who gave her away without a second thought.

In sensing the present, she'd been almost sure, except that she'd spent her life wanting to find her mother so badly, she was afraid that her need was playing tricks on her psychic good sense. But who wanted a mother like that?

Talk about a dream crashing and burning.

Aiden sat her on a cushy sofa in the lobby as if she was made of spun sugar, and went to register.

When he came back for her, Storm tried to smile for him. "Nice to know I'm not the straw that broke the camel's back."

He held up a credit-card-size passkey. "Nice to see you got your equilibrium back."

"I'm not in denial, if that's what you mean. There are some pretty strong arguments for that . . . loser . . . being my mother, though I can't believe Marvelanne has enough generosity and sensitivity to have allowed anyone the use of her uterus for nine months."

"Why didn't you just ask her the name of her triplets' father?"

"I didn't wanna know. This way, I'll always have hope. Can we go play hide-and-seek with the dragon?"

"Is this *you* running away now?"

They stepped into the elevator, and the doors closed them inside, alone.

"Share your turtle shell for a while?"

"Ouch."

"Kiss me, Dragon Boy."

They kissed, and kissed, and Aiden had her up against the wall kissing her senseless when a cough interrupted them. When they broke the lip-lock, the elevator door stood open, and an impatient, mature, and expensively dressed couple stood waiting to get on.

"Oops," Storm said. "Did we forget to choose a floor?"

"Oh, right," Aiden said. "Penthouse. Gotta use the passkey in the elevator to get up that far." Which he promptly did.

"Are you coming?" Storm asked, biting her lip at the couple's appalled expressions.

The two disapproving up-tights got on the elevator, and though they pressed the third floor, Aiden had used his passkey first, so the two couples rode up twenty floors together in silence.

Storm and Aiden got off at the penthouse floor, and the minute the elevator doors shut behind them, they laughed, but somewhere between amusement and hilarity, Storm's crumbling defenses collapsed, and she found herself sobbing in Aiden's comforting arms.

He lifted her off her feet, carried her like a bride to their door, and, after only two tries, he aced using the passkey with his arms full.

Entering the penthouse was a little like entering her sister's castle, though the furniture, art, and chandeliers were newer and more traditional, though no less pricey or elegant.

Poor Aiden had to carry her through a foyer, living room, dining room, and past a small bedroom before finding the master suite.

Entranced by the lush and brilliant palette of earth tones accented by brick red, Storm was surprised to feel the most amazing mattress at her back and then nothing but the warm comfort of Aiden's weight protecting and encircling her.

His arms became her haven, his words soothed her like a balm, washing over her with gentle care. "Storm Cartwright, don't you dare let what you came from get you down. You've risen above your beginnings in so many wondrous ways. You're beautiful, generous, determined, hardheaded, tenacious, stubborn, a little bit crazy, and very, very addictive."

As he brought out her smile, he raised her self-esteem, and that made her fall a little bit in love with him.

She didn't know how long she wallowed in tears, so rare her sisters wouldn't believe they existed. She knew only that the sun went down and the room went dark, then Aiden's lips were on her everywhere, her hands on him, as a slow and sensuous pressure built inside her, a need to be taken to the gratifying world of mating dragons where neither reality nor broken dreams could intrude.

They kissed forever, ravenous and magnificent, tender and satisfying, kisses made of healing, not sex, of caring, too—on her part, though maybe not on his. But that was okay. She cared enough for both of them.

Aiden had foreplay down to a science. His glorious preliminaries created an enticing promise of sexual fulfillment and oblivion. He looked her straight in the eye, focused, and she could see that he was determined to raise her up, make her his, and tame her in the process, a plan she embraced.

"You're aptly named," he said during their slow, sensual foreplay, "and I mean that in the best of ways. Storms energize," he explained. "They force new life from barren lands. They're exciting and turbulent. You're the storm who captured me, clearly the most beautiful tempest I've ever made dragon love with—okay so you're the *only* woman I've ever made dragon love with—and I can't believe you're also the woman I swore a few days ago to stay away from."

Dragon love, he'd said. Did he even realize he'd used the word *love*? Probably not, or he'd be on his way to cardiac care.

"I never thought you'd admit trying to stay away from me. Uh-oh, looks like you're sorry you admitted it," she said, reading the sudden surprised look on his face, and not because she was slipping her hands beneath his shirt. "Or do you think I'll misunderstand your intentions? Don't worry. Let me explain mine. This is sex, McCloud, not commitment. I'm a rogue storm, and you're a rogue dragon, and we each wreak our own brand of havoc, alone. I'm as independent as you."

Aiden's relief made Storm happy because she'd pleased him, but a bit sad, too, deep down, because she wished he liked her as much as he liked storms. She wished he could come to appreciate her value, however turbulent, that he could . . . love . . . *her*.

"I thought I was supposed to be comforting you," he said.

"Oh, you were, make no mistake, but now we're both comforted, aren't we?"

"You have no idea."

Storm lay the back of her hand on her brow. "I don't expect you to fix a lifetime of hope gone up in flames, Aiden. Just help me forget, for a while, that my most cherished dream might've become my worst nightmare."

"I know something about living with nightmares," Aiden said as he cupped her face, a touch she cherished, and he pulled her so close, his dragon wings caressed her. When had she lost her panties?

He opened his talented mouth over hers, as his dragon soothed her deep down and lifted her, body and mind, with pleasure.

It was still difficult to tell who consoled who. She didn't think Aiden knew, either, maybe because he sensed the change in her and understood her no-commitment ploy—her lie. Or he realized that he cared more than he wanted to, which spooked him.

Either way, he took to ravaging her lips in a bid for mindlessness, caressing every inch of her that he could reach, nearly tearing the rest of her clothes from her body with an enthusiasm she welcomed and returned.

A kiss like magick, he gave her. Like a first kiss in a parked car, enthusiastic and unreserved, but this was the kiss of a man who gave pleasure, not a boy who took it. A man with experience, unafraid of breaking her, body or spirit, despite her fragile emotions.

Storm pulled back, pushed him down against the pillows, and pulled his shirt over his head—he must have lost his boxers around the same time she lost her panties—then she made love to his dragon, took it in her mouth to torment him, while he thrashed and begged for mercy, and then she took his dragon deep into her womb, where she made Triton sing, and roar, and breathe fire.

This from a man likely as broken as her, though stronger and more doggedly resilient. This man, this dragon god . . . she could very well come to love.

Chapter Twenty-eight

SHE caught fire, too, so much so that she rose above her thoughts and touched that magick place where pleasure obliterates pain. There, amazingly—because she was riding him, not the other way round—Aiden took her to a place where sadness disappeared, and ecstasy held sway.

"You taste of sweet life, and I'm a man starving for every bite." He gasped as she took to riding him harder.

She shouted with the burst of her orgasm and with her power to take him with her to the brink of the abyss, where he cursed her and blessed her and begged her never to stop. "You're like . . . the wind off the sea," she told him, "a run through the woods in the black of night, like an earth king who believes in . . . me . . . despite the odds."

"I am that," Aiden said, changing their positions and taking charge with a jaunty play of kisses dancing their way down her torso.

Storm raised her hips so his lips and licks wouldn't miss her hoped-for target, but Aiden missed it anyway, and she pouted for all of a second before he began again at her toes and nibbled his way upward.

"I haven't trusted a woman for nearly a year and a half," he said, "hadn't slipped inside one for as long, until yesterday with you, a prickly witch who speaks to a part of me hidden so deep, I don't know what it's called."

"Let's call it trust," she suggested.

"That's safe," he said, his instincts of self-preservation still sharp amid so much pleasure.

He skipped her slick and aching center for a second time, which made her scream.

He chuckled. "I want your mouth again, first," he said. "Your lips are like overripe plums. I can't get enough of your nectar." He kissed and nibbled those plums, and who was she to complain?

With a practiced hand, he found her center slick from when she'd impaled herself on his dragon, and when he replaced his hand with his mouth, he all but consumed her, petal by petal, matching his rhythm to a magick mating dance among the stars.

"I've never—" Storm's orgasms hit her like swells pummeling the shore in a gale, each greater than the previous, the tempest ending in a tidal wave of pleasure that wiped away all the sadness in its path.

Breathing deep, gasping for air, Aiden took a moment to rest, and Storm chuckled. "You've just ruined my best vibrator's track record for staying power. Now I'll have to go sex toy shopping again."

"Can I come?"

"Sex toy shopping?"

"Okay. Sure. That, too." Aiden got right back down to business, but despite his slick pulsing dragon arousal, he raised his head from his oral ministrations. "Did you just admit to using a vibrator?"

"How else do you think I survived the three weeks before you finally came out of your cave, Dragon Boy? What's a girl to do?" Storm rose on her elbows. "For that matter, what's a boy to do? What did you do, during your lengthy . . . dry spell?"

Aiden rose up to kiss her, so she tasted herself on his

lips, and then he collapsed on the bed beside her. "Sorry I asked."

Amused at his reticence, considering his exhibitionistic dragon, Storm chuckled. "Dragon's blood, how else could you survive if you didn't let your dragon fly across the night skies? How often did it take wing in the last three weeks? What kind of an effect did I have on you? Seriously. Details, please."

Aiden groaned. "You're something, you know that?"

"I'm a lot of things, so my sisters keep telling me. Brat and pain in the ass come up most often, but an unambiguous replacement for the word *something*, from you, could give my poor negative ego a positive boost."

Aiden looked down at his dragon preparing for renewed flight and winked at her. "Does this give you any indication?"

"Which would make me . . . dragon bait?"

"A dragon dream."

"His wet dream, you mean?" Storm put his dragon exactly where they both wanted it. "I can live with that."

STORM woke around ten that night to find a note on the bedside table. "Be right back."

What had she done, passed out from exhaustion?

Wondering when he'd left, she ordered room service. For some reason, she'd gotten her appetite back in spades.

She had time to take a quick shower and was thrilled to find complimentary lavender shower products in the luxurious bathroom. Lavender would be great for cleansing away the negative energy she'd likely absorbed during her encounter with the cocktail hostess from hell.

Storm hung the sachet she'd found on her pillow on the showerhead so the water would run through the lavender. She visualized herself beneath a waterfall and asked to be cleansed in the name of healing. With three deep breaths, the lavender water and body silk washed away her negative tension and stress—body, mind, and spirit. Even her aura felt cleansed. As she toweled dry, the lavender-scented air empowered her positive healing as well.

Wearing the hotel's lush terry robe and slippers, she signed for a midnight snack of no small proportions.

When Aiden got back, he handed her a plastic-draped hanger, a tiny Naughty Nightie bag, and a shoe box. He put the men's store bags to one side and let her tear into her goodies while he uncovered the food and went to town. "Guess you worked up an appetite, too."

Storm loved the short black strapless sundress he bought with its tiny, scattered, red-stenciled sea horses, but she squealed over the black, fringed Prada slingback spikes.

Aiden smiled and picked up one of the shoes to hold in his palm. "As soon as the salesgirl said these were a bold and risky choice, I knew they were perfect for you. Inside the Naughty Nightie bag, you'll find everything you need to wear beneath the dress."

Storm emptied the bag and hooked a finger through its only contents, a pair of black lace V-string bikinis. "You can be my personal shopper any day."

"You can be my dragon rider any day."

Storm joined him at the formal dining table, an elaborate amber Victorian chandelier above them, and a brick-colored Oriental carpet beneath them, for strawberries and champagne, melon with prosciutto, cracked crab, and raspberries in chocolate baskets.

"Quite the feast," he said.

"I'm an eclectic witch," she said, cracking a crab leg. "What's in the big brown paper bag? Groceries?"

"Supplies to get us through the rest of the night."

"That's one whopping big bag of condoms. What are you? Super Dragon?"

After they finished eating, Aiden emptied the bag on the bed.

Storm whooped. "Every kind of vibrator I've ever wanted to try, butterflies and rabbits, gnomes and hummingbirds, oh my. Hah! You even found a dragon vibrator!

Let's see how it stands up to the real thing." She wiggled her brows.

She held up one of the toys. "Aiden, this is an extender. You sooooo don't need an extender."

"Which reminds me, I bought larger condoms. More room to fly."

Storm sighed and placed a hand on her heart. "Triton the majestic dragon."

Aiden bowed, his killer grin dangerous.

Falling-in-love-with dangerous.

Chapter Twenty-nine

"WE could play for days with all this stuff," Storm said, aroused by the possibility, as she picked up armfuls of sex toys, like they were hundred-dollar bills, and dropped them back on the bed. "Flavored condoms, stimulating jellies, slick lotions, and a few plug-in thingies I don't know how to use."

"Don't worry," Aiden said. "They all come with instructions, and I have huge expectations."

"*You* have a huge . . . dragon . . . and a truckload of sex drive. You're insatiable."

"Horny, nearly a year and a half's worth of horny, and you're the best cure ever."

"We so know each other's secrets," Storm purred. Approaching him like a cat on the prowl, she licked his lips.

Obviously appreciating the act, he petted her from her spine to her bottom. "Probably not every secret, but outing more will be half the fun."

After they'd peeled off every item of his clothing and made a meal of each other, he carried her into a spa room.

"Dragon's blood!" she said. "I never saw such a gorgeous

room." The underwater theme carried to the scallop-shell tub. On the counter stood a footed teal opalescent shell-shaped bowl filled with a gorgeous assortment of starfish, sea urchins, and seashells. Small soaps were shaped like shells, and accessories like towel racks, sconces, and picture frames were decorated with shells. "This looks like a mermaid cave, and it's bigger than your motor home."

"Coach. It's a coach."

"You won't use the word *home* for anything, will you?"

"Stop trying to analyze me. It really is called a motor coach, which I prefer."

"Ah, like Cinderella's coach, except in this case the driver is a dragon, and you did buy me a new pair of slippers. Where to, my prince?"

Aiden sat her on the edge of the spa and turned on the nautilus-shell spigots to fill the bottom-lit, multijet spa, a sea-green, pearlescent scallop shell, deep and wide enough for a ménage. "I have a request," Aiden said, his smile sexy enough to curl her toes.

"Sure, anything."

He crossed her lips with a finger. "Be still, my erotic imagination. Never agree to *anything*, unless you mean it, Snapdragon."

She ran her beringed tongue down his chest. "Dragon's blood," she purred. "Anything."

"Hold that thought. Before I take you up on *anything*, could you find another expletive besides dragon's blood? It makes me think of my poor dragon, wounded, and, well, bleeding."

"Oh." She petted the poor thing. "We don't wanna think of our sleepy little dragon coming to harm."

Said dragon raised its curious head, as if it understood it was the object of interest, the subject of discussion, and it resented being called little, so it grew to new lengths.

Aiden shook his head and emptied every scented bottle from the basket on the tub's edge into the water.

"You're mixing scents," Storm cautioned him.

"I'm mixing a specially scented water spell," he said, surprising her.

Storm stroked his bare backside as he bent over the tub. "I'm the spell maker here. Let me do the honors." She took one of the cinnamon sticks from the basket's sea green bow and waved it like a wand.

> *"Sex for two*
> *In rainforest blue.*
> *Ease sad woes*
> *With orchid and rose.*
> *Bring orgasmic joy*
> *To Dragon Boy.*
> *With harm to none,*
> *So mote it be done."*

Aiden straightened, frowning. "That's not the right spell."

Storm rose in indignation. "Not good enough? I mean, I wasn't going for the gold, just sinsational sex in the spa."

"No," Aiden said. "I didn't want you to cast a spell for *me*. I wanted to cast a spell for you." He held her shoulders. "You're the one who's had a hard day."

Storm's heart filled, she was so taken aback and humbled by his concern. Not wanting him to see how close her emotions sat to the surface, she focused on the sweet-scented soap bubbles floating in their bath. "Say out loud what you want for me," she whispered, her voice rough with overflowing emotion. "Just say the words."

"Damn it, Storm, I can't rhyme."

She looked up at Aiden then, at the caring and concern in his eyes, and her wounded heart began to heal. "You don't need to rhyme. Magick lies in the fact that you wish good for someone. Saying what you wish sends it into the universe. Go ahead."

Aiden hesitated and charmed her with his uncertainty, the big, bad, shy biker.

"Here goes." He pulled her into his arms, tucked her head against his heart, as if he didn't want her to watch, and cleared his throat.

> *"I want to bring you peace,*
> *A healed heart.*
> *I'm glad you were born,*
> *As are the children you saved.*
> *Their parents are glad.*
> *Your sisters are, too.*
> *You're not the last straw,*
> *You're the star of the triad,*
> *The center diamond,*
> *Outshining your beginnings*
> *With a flawless heart*
> *And clarity of mind.*
> *This is my spell.*
> *These things you should know."*

"Damn," Storm said and burst into tears.

Aiden stepped away from her and ran a hand through his hair. "You said I didn't have to rhyme!"

"These are tears of happiness, Aiden. Your spell was beautiful, heartfelt, and brilliant. I'm healing just from hearing it."

Tears of happiness, Storm thought, wiping her eyes, like Vickie's tears had been over the honor of spelling the unknown baby's safety. She'd try to be more patient with her sisters' emotions in the future. This love stuff— Oops. Careful there, Cartwright.

Aiden had been watching her, and now he shook his head as if he couldn't win for trying. "Get in the spa. Must be the PMS. I'll give you my cure and heal you some more."

Storm took his hand, climbed into their scalloped sealike playground, and lowered herself into the luxuriously soft and scented water. "Purr. This is like sitting in champagne," she said, swept away by the pleasure of a gazillion bubbles, stroking her like hordes of minivibrators . . .

Aiden turned on the jets and left the room.

"Hey?" she called. "What the—"

A minute later, he returned with every waterproof sex toy he'd bought. He sat on the edge of the tub and attacked a hard plastic package with a letter opener, like a maniac.

"Aiden, get my purse."

"You carry sex toys in your purse?"

"One-track man brain. No, Sherlock. I brought scissors."

The packages were opened in minutes, while playing with the contents could take hours, days, months, years? Oh, what a tempting thought.

She was in over her head here and drowning . . . happily . . . so happily she could be tricked into thinking that here, in this suite, they'd been making love. Oddly enough, she liked the idea and guessed this was the place to play out the fantasy. What harm could a short trip to never-never land do?

Aiden got in and came for her, pulled her over him, down on him, so she took him to the hilt, her head on his shoulder, his hands in her hair, stroking her as if from the inside out, bringing her a peace and sense of worth she'd never known.

Drifting, she was so relaxed, she noticed through the open-shuttered Gothic window, the moon peeking in, blessing them with light and bathing them in an aura of sensuality.

"Let's try this," Aiden whispered against her ear, turning on the vibrator billed as the naughty gnome. "Turn around," he said. "I'll use this on you from the back so I can watch Electra dance while you run this hummingbird along Triton, for an orgasmic good time."

As convoluted as his plan sounded, the result was magnificent on every level. Foreplay took on new meaning. Time stood still.

After Storm experienced several multiples, Triton couldn't seem to stay away, which she approved, so Aiden faced her and moved her along his body, impaling her with his ponderous and happy dragon, playing inside her so slowly—since he'd come before they got to the spa—that Storm rose languidly to pleasure.

Aiden dragoned her until she reached an outrageous release and shouted with triumph. At that moment, outside the window, the night sky blossomed with a wash of wild, sparkling color. Fireworks. Midnight. Independence Day— a sobering thought—but she refused to let the reminder intrude. Instead, she wallowed in dragon-driven ecstasy.

Aiden provided her with a series of climactic fireworks of her own to go with every burst of red, white, and blue, then with purple, yellow, green. Kaleidoscopic bursts. Multibursts, in color and scope—every time.

No man had ever given such full attention to *her* pleasure. Time he had a multiple of his own. Storm worked her womanly magick, milking him, urging him to come, raising him to the edge but stopping and holding him there. She watched his eyes darken, his lids lower, caught the set of his jaw, and knew how hard he worked to hold back, to give her more pleasure, until she cupped his balls and rotated her hips to unman him.

Voice rough, he begged her to stop, as if the ultimate ecstasy depended on him not coming, when for her, it actually depended on him coming his brains out. And after he did, she didn't let him go but held him inside her, squeezing and pumping that dragon back to life and making them both come their brains out one more time.

Hard to tell where one fireworks display began and the other ended—which display was made of air, which of water, which of earth . . . and which of them was a true fire of the heart.

Chapter Thirty

AIDEN couldn't get enough. He and Storm had had more sex in these last few days than he'd had with Claudette in the two years of their relationship—his longest ever—and he hadn't gotten enough of Storm yet. Wasn't sure there was a yet.

Fireworks marching beside climax, he ravaged Storm's mouth and celebrated her lack of willpower. At this moment, prolonging the inevitable end of this inconceivable attraction made more and more sense.

For nearly a year and a half, he'd feared he'd never be intimate with a woman again, certain he'd never find one who could bear the foolish sight of him. He certainly didn't expect to find one who was turned on by his self-inflicted proof of independence.

Yes, rather than receiving his just desserts for his wretched mistakes, he'd found Storm, instead.

Now he'd reached a new and more confusing crossroad. He couldn't bear the thought of letting any other woman but Storm near his dragon. How dangerous and enervating a concept.

He didn't want to touch another woman, but he didn't want commitment, either. Yet separating himself from Storm didn't bear thinking about. He should put a stop to this zany romp down fireworks lane, this false sense of happiness, but having her was like a glimpse of paradise that he couldn't let go.

In the midst of their erotic dance, which had gone on for so long, her tongue ring doing wild things to his dragon, Aiden feared this was an out-of-body view of life as he wished it could be, without secrets, with a partner who understood and accepted him—red violet flaws and all—and liked him anyway. Liked him, lusted after him, the way he . . . liked . . . and lusted after her.

If only he'd shared his every secret while he had the chance.

Storm raised her head, tilted it. "It's not your fault that Claudette died in that car accident. You shouldn't feel guilty. And while we're on the subject, I don't believe it *was* the dragon that kept you celibate, but your guilt over Claudette."

Ah, and there it was, his last secret, laid ugly bare, except that Storm was the one who'd bared it. "You spook me when you read me like that," Aiden said as he stood and got out of the spa in a snit.

"I didn't mean to send you running for your shell," she said, rising like a water goddess with moonbeams for a gown.

"That turtle talk is getting old," he snapped, annoyed she was still turning him on when he was . . . well . . . annoyed. "What am I, a dragon or a turtle? Pick one or the other. Which is it?"

"Turtles and dragons have a lot in common," she explained. "You may be inclined toward both. You can have two totems, you know?"

"And that's another thing. What the hell is a totem?" His anger came from all the foreign emotions he couldn't name, he thought. And rather than wallow in and enjoy this sexually stimulating nonrelationship of theirs, he feared it would disappear, pink-dicked idiot that he was.

Storm took his hand, and her touch was enough to soothe him. He brought her fingers to his lips, he was so grateful.

"An animal totem," Storm explained, unaware of his rioting emotions, "represents elements of your deepest self, including some of the qualities you might someday need that are hidden inside you. Don't feel that the turtle is weak because it's small. It's a powerful totem said to have brought the earth up from the sea on its back to give people a place to live. For my own totems, I chose the sea horse in addition to the dragon, and a sea horse, as you've discovered, is much smaller than a turtle."

Aiden lowered himself to sit on the side of the spa, his dragon clearly passed out on the edge, his gaze focused on a blue-haired goth with a huge heart.

She gave his dragon a pointed look and raised a determined brow.

Aiden shook his head. "You wake him, you have to pay the price, though I think he's in a coma. What do the dragon and turtle have in common?"

"Okay. Ahem." Storm cleared her throat and tried to direct her gaze away from Triton, but when she couldn't seem to resist, she turned her back on him. "The dragon and the turtle are both water creatures," she said, facing a wall depicting a shimmering, underwater, silk seascape.

Aiden slipped back into the spa to see her beautiful face. "Continue, please."

"Both are one with the environment. They have amazing survival skills and strategies, and they can sense vibrations on land and in water that warn of danger. I'm not putting you down when I call you a turtle, except for the hiding part, which you've aced. But I love that the turtle awakens the senses on both the physical and spiritual levels by stimulating psychic awareness, especially clairaudience."

Aiden perked up at that. "Do you mean that by my very nature, I stimulate your ability to hear those babies crying when you're near me? Snapdragon, you have a truly skewed way of thinking."

"One baby cries when I'm near you. Yours. Don't go taking credit for my gifts, now." Storm ran both her hands up his chest and along his shoulders and arms. "Both the turtle and the dragon have nearly impenetrable shells."

"Hey, I'm penetrable."

She scoffed. "Please, if the hard shell fits, wear it. The turtle teaches us not to gather more possessions than we need and to choose our responsibilities wisely."

"That, I can get behind." He slid around her and pulled her against him, her back against his front, and he rubbed her silk-soft belly to heighten her arousal, as he felt Elektra practically calling to Triton . . . again.

"One more thing," Storm said. "The link between water and land has significance for both dragon and turtle—as it does for the sea horse—in terms of where they raise their family. That's why I think you like the island."

"I'm not raising a family."

"Not yet."

"Okay smart-ass. How about I tell you something about yourself? I don't know from totems, but this is what I've discovered about the Storm witch. Inside, you're hiding a child playing dress-up, a child filled with wonder, lovable, charming, and enchanting."

"Don't be an idiot. I'm none of those things."

"Outside, you're the cryptic cynic, a brilliant goth, world-weary, who works overtime to keep your child inside. But when you're not looking, and the child escapes into the woman, you're a stunner."

"Shuddup!" She pushed him away and went to pout on the opposite side of the huge scallop.

That girl did not like being understood, Aiden thought, any more than he did, he supposed. "Too bad you don't let your inner child stick around," he said. "You cover the slip with a rant or a stinging insult, anything to turn the attention away from your true self."

Storm continued sulking, her arms crossed in a protective gesture, her blue hair doing the natural in the moist heat— curling in every direction, and turning him on like crazy.

"You are so full of turtle poop," she said. "Go hide in your shell."

"There she is, the rebel goth who can't deal. You don't react well to emotion, mainly because you don't know how, I suspect. You slip into rebel mode whenever anyone reveals your character, because revealing your true self scares you half to death."

Aiden knew that the only way to get Storm out of rebel mode was to give her an easy out, so he changed the subject. "Will you give me an A for reading you right, if I admit that you read *me* right? My guilt over Claudette eats away at me. If only I hadn't done . . . what I did . . . that made Claudette dump me, she would have stayed, and not been in that car accident. If not for me, she'd be alive today . . . somewhere."

"Enough." Storm got out of the tub, and Aiden followed.

She handed him a hotel robe from the closet and wrapped one around herself, another form of self-protection.

"Do you know how insane you sound?" she asked.

"As insane as a woman who can hear a phantom baby crying, a woman who stands in front of a moving motor coach . . . and stops it! A woman who fights a stranger in a mall for a kid that might well have been his?"

"Yeah, that's how stupid you sound. Let's get some sleep. I'm beat."

"I can't imagine why." Aiden dropped his robe and threw back the covers, spreading sex toys like glitter on the Oriental carpet.

Storm nodded. "That's what I'm saying."

She fell asleep quickly, but something, or everything, she said was combating his guilt and fear and wreaking havoc in his mind, and he couldn't make it stop. As a matter of fact, his thoughts were becoming more focused and more brilliant by the minute.

Aiden got up, put on his robe, and took his cell phone into the bathroom, where he speed-dialed King's cell. "King," Aiden said softly. "I hope I'm not interrupting the honeymoon, but do you have plans for the windmill on the island? I wanna buy it. I'm thinking of turning it into a house, actually." Aiden rolled his eyes. "I *know* I can't drive a windmill."

After King agreed, Aiden made another call. "Morgan. Hi, am I interrupting your sex life? Same to you. *You* have a sex slave? Hah. You should be so lucky. Hey, remember the plans you drew up for Windmill Cottage? Well, dig them out and start turning the place into a house. I just bought the windmill from King. No, I am *not* done to a turn and ready to be served with garlic potatoes!" Not quite.

When Aiden got back into bed, he closed his eyes, and sleep came with satisfaction.

A few hours later, the phone on the nightstand rang.

"Spell them," Storm grumbled from the depths of her pillow.

Aiden answered, listened to the surprising voice at the opposite end of the line, agreed, hung up, and rolled into Storm's waiting arms.

"Well, are you gonna tell me?" she asked.

"We have a breakfast date."

"With who? Nobody knows we're here."

"Think again."

"I can't imagi—not . . . Marvelanne?"

Chapter Thirty-one

STORM got out of bed and went to the deck to look out over the ocean. "Marvelanne's up to something," she said.

Aiden brought Storm's robe and wrapped it around her from behind, holding her as they stood together, showing her without words that he was there for her. "Yes, she's up to something. Shower for two?" he asked.

She turned in his arms, the wicked tilt to her brow meant to entice. "I'm too tense."

She was playing hard to get. "I can fix that."

"I doubt it."

Triton was up for the challenge.

As they stepped out of the shower an hour later, Aiden felt like crowing, because he *had* fixed her tension . . . until they got off the elevator.

At the appointed spot, around the corner from the casino, they waited for Marvelanne, but by the time their coffee arrived, she still wasn't there.

The diner's red and gray plastic and Formica was not re-production retro but the real thing. Duct tape played a big role in the seating decor. A dive, maybe, but their coffee tasted better than at any big-name corner coffee shop.

Aiden tested the sixties tabletop music selector, put in a quarter, pressed a couple of buttons, and the jukebox clicked and whirred. "Angel Baby" wafted from gigundous fifty-year-old speakers.

Storm leaned against him, and Aiden kissed her temple. "I can't take away the case of nerves you're cultivating, but I'm here for you."

"You don't know how much that means to me."

Marvelanne arrived twenty minutes late.

Aiden frowned. "I thought you were bringing someone for us to meet."

Storm rounded on him. "You didn't tell me that!"

"Don't grind your teeth," he cautioned. "It's not good for the jaw."

"You should know."

A waitress removed the condiments and sugar packets with an evil eye toward Marvelanne, and Storm's eyes twinkled, though she gave none of her amusement away. Aiden cleared his throat to keep from chuckling.

"My guest will be along in a minute," Marvelanne said before she ordered the lumberjack breakfast with a side of grits. Once the waitress left, Marvelanne fished a paper from her uniform pocket and looked up at them. The eight-and-a-half-by-eleven colored picture looked like it had been printed from a computer. Marvelanne handed it to Storm. "I wanted you to know," Marvelanne said, "that I don't invite every good-looking goth at the casino to have dinner with me. That won a photography prize on the Internet, by the way. You're pretty, you and your sisters."

Aiden chuckled. "They look just like—"

"Don't say it!" Storm snapped.

"Sorry." But they did look like Marvelanne.

Storm examined the picture the wedding photographer had taken of "just the triplets," when he'd insulted her for her blue hair.

"Hmm," she speculated. "Guess I *didn't* keep him from

winning his prize, un-freaking-fortunately." She set it on the table between them. "So?"

"So, where are Harmony and Destiny?"

Storm took the picture and checked it, front and back. "There are no names on this."

Marvelanne forked a piece of ham. "I looked you up on the Internet."

"How could you do that without knowing—" Storm stopped and shivered.

Aiden put an arm around her. She had no choice but to face the truth. Marvelanne knew their names for a reason.

Marvelanne nodded, acknowledging their unspoken perception. "I found Harmony's wedding pictures in a story on the society pages. She married well, didn't she? A castle and her own helicopter. My stars."

Storm rose from her seat like an avenging angel. "If you think—"

"I'm just saying . . . Sit down and lose the attitude," Marvelanne said, actually sounding like a mother. "If you hadn't already told me which one you were, I'd know now. I named my triplets the only time I ever held them. The first gave me a sense of peace, so I named her Harmony. The second gave me a sense that the future would be doomed if I kept her, so I named her Destiny. And the last scared the hell out of me—not because I didn't expect a third, which I didn't. Some twins you three turned out to be. No, I named the last one Storm, because I knew that tempestuous little being would fight just for the fun of it. *You* would give anybody a run for their money."

Marvelanne looked at Aiden. "Am I right? You know I am."

Aiden grinned. "Destiny would say that there are runs, and there are . . . runs."

Marvelanne waved his answer aside. "Men! Always thinking with their dicks. I invited you to supper last night because I needed to know which triplet you were."

"You're heartless," Aiden said. "You *knew* she was your daughter at first sight, after twenty-seven years, and you showed no joy at meeting her, felt no regret for abandoning her?"

Marvelanne poured a quart of maple syrup on her pancakes and dug into them with gusto. "I did what was best for her and her sisters."

"You did what was best for *you*," Aiden countered.

"Call their needs a perk I embraced," Marvelanne said.

A little girl came to their table, ten, eleven years old at most, a Catholic school–uniformed version of a goth—at least in the makeup department—sporting a thick head of long, paprika screw curls and a wash of freckles across her nose. She smacked her backpack on the table so hard, coffee sloshed over the rims of their cups.

Ignoring their scramble for napkins, the minirebel turned an insolent gaze on Marvelanne. "I told you," the kid said. "I didn't want to come to this dump."

Aiden wondered who she was and why Marvelanne put up with her sass.

"That's why I didn't give you your lunch money before I left."

Aiden put his coffee down. Good grief, what did that mean? Marvelanne and a rebellious kid with attitude? Déjà vu all over again.

Storm looked a little green.

Marvelanne dangled a fan of one-dollar bills like a flag in front of Little Red Juvie Hood, and when the kid reached for the bills, Marvelanne snatched them back. "Say hello to my guests."

Red glanced their way. "Bite me," she said, turning back to her tormentor. "What gives? You don't know from guests."

Okay, Aiden thought, Red knew Marvelanne pretty well, and she was a good judge of character, too.

"I told you I had triplets," Marvelanne said, pointing her fork Storm's way. "She's one of them."

The kid grabbed the bills and dragged the backpack off the table. "Lucky you." She looked at Storm for the first time. "*You* got away." The smart-mouthed kid tried to get away, too, but Marvelanne hooked a finger in the waist-band of her plaid skirt.

"Does she have a name?" Storm asked.

Marvelanne rolled her eyes. "Oh, yeah, Pepper's not a pleasant sort, but I thought you might like to meet her. She's my *other* kid."

Chapter Thirty-two

"DUH," Pepper said. "I'm here, ya know. I can hear you."

Helpless, Aiden watched Storm go still, stop breathing almost, her expression changing so fast from shock to joy to hurt, he'd have missed it if he blinked. She ate Pepper up with her gaze. "We have *another* half sister?"

"Another one?" Marvelanne asked. "Oh, you mean the legit brat your old man had before we met?"

"That brat kept *your* triplets from living in a van on the streets not so long ago."

Marvelanne shrugged. "We all have our bad days."

"Don't let her kid you," Pepper said as she made true eye contact with Storm, her smile wicked. "Marvelanne's having a bad life."

"Sure looks that way," Storm said.

Pepper elbowed her mother. "I think it started the day they gave her that dorky name: Marvelanne."

Marvelanne's eyes narrowed. "And look what I got for a consolation prize: a potty mouth with attitude and a temper to match her hair." Marvelanne shook the kid by her waistband like a rag doll, and Aiden saw fury build in Storm, in her narrowing eyes and tight fists, and in the stiffness of her body, until Marvelanne yelped, pulled her hand back, and let Pepper go.

Marvelanne made a fist and rubbed her forearm. "What the hell? I feel like I just got electrocuted."

"Divine retribution," Aiden muttered.

Storm looked at him beneath her sunglasses. "Why, thank you, dahling."

He caught Storm's wink and couldn't believe it. She'd stun-gunned Marvelanne with that telekinetic fury of hers. Be still, his heart . . . his dragon could get zapped, too.

"Another sister," Storm said, pulling Pepper by the hand toward their side of the booth, helping her escape a repeat of Marvelanne's Raggedy Ann treatment. "Where do you go to school, Pepper?"

"Around the corner. Crappy private school." Pepper pointed behind her with a rude thumb. "*She'd* never put a dime out for it, but my old man insists on the best."

"You're married?" Storm asked Marvelanne.

"Hell no."

"No offense, Pepper, honestly," Storm said. "But, Marvelanne, why did you keep Pepper and not me and my sisters?"

"Your father was a loser. Pepper's father is as rich as God. He pays big bucks for child support and all the . . . extras."

"Told'ja," Pepper said. "She's all heart, and she has an 'extra' every other day. I've had my tonsils out twice, and wha'd'ya know, I still have tonsils. If the old man was giving her my tuition money instead of paying the school, I'd be in public school, and she'd have a better wardrobe— another of her 'extras.'"

"That's what I get for introducing you to your sister, you damned brat?"

"Didn't cost you to introduce us, did it?" Pepper pointed out.

Aiden hated the way Storm flinched, as if she'd been slapped, when the woman called Pepper a brat. He wanted like hell to comfort her, because she knew what it felt like to be talked to that way. Hadn't she said she'd mostly been called a brat or a pain in the ass growing up?

"There's the school bell," Pepper said. "I gotta go."

Storm hooked an arm around Pepper's waist to keep her there, took a napkin, wrote her cell phone number on it, and stuffed it in Pepper's blazer pocket. Storm tried for a hug but let go when the kid stiffened her spine. "Call me if you ever need anything, or if you just wanna talk."

"Yeah, right," Pepper said, but for less than a blink, she leaned into Storm without being coaxed, except that it happened so fast, Aiden wasn't sure it did, before Pepper pulled forcefully away and ran . . . and he did mean, she ran. She *escaped* out that door as if all of hell's demons were chasing her.

It seemed to Aiden that her mother's browbeating hadn't fazed or frightened Pepper anywhere near as much as Storm's kindness had.

Storm slid from the ratty booth. "Marvelanne, thanks for the loan of your uterus. I guess that's something."

"Damn straight it is," Marvelanne said.

Aiden took Storm's hand as they walked down the street, heading away from the coffee shop, but something made him look back, and when he did, he thought he saw a head of bright red curls peek out from between two buildings not far behind them.

A few minutes later, he looked again, and once more those paprika curls disappeared. Pepper, covertly following them.

Aiden stopped walking, but Storm pulled him forward without looking back. She should know, and yet he couldn't bring himself to scramble her rioting emotions any further by telling her. What good would it do?

After they cleared the boardwalk, he looked back, again, and Pepper stood in plain sight little more than an arm's length away. When they made eye contact, she mouthed the words, "Take me with you."

Aiden hooked an arm around Storm's waist and turned her around, but Pepper had disappeared.

Chapter Thirty-three

STORM climbed into the coach first, only to get hit in the chest with Warlock. "Oh, baby, did you miss us?" She'd never felt more comforted by her kitten, as if Warlock shared her sadness. "Oh, his food bowl is empty, poor baby, though I did mound it before we left yesterday, in case."

"Well he didn't starve. I came by last night and filled it, again, before I went shopping."

"Then you could have taken clothes for us from here. Why did you shop?"

Aiden shrugged. "I wanted to cheer you up. Besides, there weren't any sex toys here."

Storm hugged Warlock to her neck and wilted. "I think I need to go shopping again."

"You're really down, aren't you?" Aiden nudged her to the sofa and sat beside her. "Because you have a mother who sheds her skin regularly?"

"Because I have a sister who's miserable. Wait until I tell Harmony and Destiny, though I wish I didn't have to. We dreamed about finding our mother. Such stories the three of us made up over the years about a wronged princess, sad, lonely, pining for her children. Chumps. But I have to tell them, because Pepper deserves a family."

Aiden took the passenger seat. "Where to, next?"

"You don't have to be cheerful for me. I'm fine. You can drive."

Aiden switched seats. "Me driving. That's a sure sign you're not fine. You want I should follow the sounds in your head?"

"The sounds are gone. I wish I could still hear your baby crying, but all I can think about is Pepper, and all I can hear is . . . silence. A heavy silence."

"Maybe I don't have a baby?" Aiden scoffed. "Listen to me, talking like I'm sorry we're not chasing my phantom baby." He took her hand and squeezed, which Storm appreciated. "Not that I believed you about my baby," Aiden said. "Well, I did *start* to believe after you saved those two kids. But you did hear several crying babies before we got here, and now . . . none?"

"I think some of them must have been echoes of me and my sisters as babies."

"One of them might have been your own baby," he added. "Don't you think that psychologically, you could have been looking for the baby you lost?"

"I can't believe I found . . . *Pepper's* mother," Storm said, ignoring Aiden's impromptu bit of psychoanalysis.

"One crying baby might have been Pepper," he suggested.

"*One* might have been," she said, "but Pepper doesn't need rescuing. That girl can hold her own, and she's got a rich father to boot."

"You'd have to be able to hold your own with Marvelanne. Pepper probably learned her survival skills in the cradle. I don't think she ever sees her father, though, do you? What kind of father pays for two tonsillectomies without asking questions?"

"The kind who gets his secretary to write the checks is my guess." Storm looked over her sunglasses at Aiden, a puzzling question hovering, and then she lost it and shook her head. "Nah, I would have sensed it, if Pepper was in trouble. This is me, remember? I sense the present."

"Do psychics get blocked?" Aiden asked.

"I suppose."

"Could a psychic get blocked by, say, a trauma like meeting 'the bride of the damned,' and learning she's her mother?"

Storm shrugged.

Aiden started the engine. "Want me to drive toward the campground where you started hearing multiple babies crying?"

"Sure. Where are you going?" she asked, because he zigged when he should have zagged.

"I'm taking a circuitous route through town to see if Pepper pops up on your radar screen and maybe you can get a reading. Let me know if the spirit of a child in trouble moves you," he said.

"What are you getting at?"

"I'm thinking that maybe Pepper is too hardened to cry, in which case, you wouldn't hear a cry for help."

"*If* she needed help," Storm said.

"Absolutely," Aiden agreed. "Children in trouble is your territory, not mine."

"Look! There she is, the stinker," Storm said, sitting as far forward as her seat belt would allow. "She bunked school! Oh no, look, she spotted us, and she's running up the school steps." They watched her disappear into the building. "That one's a survivor, mark my words. She's fine. At least here, her father knows where to find her."

"Sure," Aiden said. "If he cares to."

Storm swiveled her seat his way. "You going soft, Mc-Cloud?"

"Lock your seat facing forward," he said. "Hey, if I see kids in need around every corner, it's your fault. You invited me on this ludicrous journey."

"I didn't invite you. I abducted you on this *prudent* journey. Give credit where credit's due."

"Hear any babies crying yet?" Aiden asked, finally taking

the highway out of town. What was with him anyway? First he hates that she hears babies crying, now he's trying to shove them down her throat.

"No more babies," she said, as disappointed as him, which meant that he must have come to believe in her at some point. That was cool. A compliment, really. "Maybe I only heard a baby around you, because you were supposed to be with me when I found my mother. I'm honestly glad you were."

"And when you met Pepper."

"Yeah. Thanks for that." Storm smiled. "How old do you think she is?"

"Eight or nine?"

"With that mouth?"

"Look who raised her."

"For money, no less." Storm fisted a hand and sighed. "I'm not sure which of us was luckier."

"Storm?" Aiden asked. "Do you think that Marvelanne is hard like you because she's hiding her pain, like you?"

"Don't go there. I do not want to feel sorry for that woman. What do you mean, *hard* like me?"

"Vickie told me about the rebel goth with attitude who first invaded her house, and I caught glimpses of you on the wild side from time to time when you were fighting the castle ghost. You *can* be hard, Cartwright. Sharp, prickly, brash, bold, abrasive—"

"I get the freaking picture. I am *not* like Pepper's mother. End of discussion. Do you want to go home?"

"You mean, to Salem?"

"That's right," Storm said, snapping her fingers. "You can't call anyplace home, can you?"

"Not if I can help it."

"You even call your motor home a motor *coach*," she pointed out.

"Because that's what it was called in the brochure. It's a coach. See the length, the styling. It's a luxury coach, and Morgan's unique design made it even more luxurious."

Storm knew Aiden was doing some hiding of his own,

but maybe not the running away from responsibility kind, as she originally suspected. What he was hiding was the little boy inside him—to borrow his phraseology—nose pressed to the window, watching the happy family inside, with no chance of getting in, so he shuns home, pretending he doesn't want it.

"You know what I think," Storm said. "I think you want a home so badly that while you wander, 'home' is your unacknowledged destination. You never know where you're headed, but you're certain, deep, deep down, that eventually, if you search long enough, you'll find a place that will claim you."

"This, from somebody with a savior complex."

"What complex?"

"You go around saving children because you were lost, and your child was lost, and you need to make it all up to the universe or something."

"I never saved a single child until we took this trip. So there."

"Well you're searching for *something*," Aiden said. "Are you trying to find yourself?" he asked. "Or are you trying to find acceptance?"

"None of the above, thank you very much."

"In that case, you're either searching for the reason you were born or the reason you were tossed away."

Chapter Thirty-four

"I know who I am, though *you* confused me into thinking that I needed more than myself for a while . . . a little while."

"You heard kids crying long before you met me, Cartwright, but you chose to pin your hopes on a baby you claim is mine. That was low and self-serving."

"Talk about self-centered. You carry your house on your back, so you can escape into it, like you did the night of the wedding."

"I was running from a nutcase who—"

"Saved two kids guided by the voices in her head."

Storm knew that in military school, Aiden must have been taught to be regimented and not want frivolous things, so in rebellion, he had a frivolously luxurious motor coach and was as far from regimented as a man could get. "I shouldn't admit this," Storm said, "but we're fighting for nothing. I think your Harley-riding nomadic lifestyle and erratic work schedule match my goth trappings."

His smile nearly dissipated her ire. "Your goth *costume*."

"What's your point, Scruffleupagus?"

"You are so off the mark with me."

"I doubt it. You grew up in military school with King, right? So where were *your* parents?"

"Making money, giving it away, defending the down-trodden, feeding the hungry, sheltering the homeless. Flying their high-profile jet around the world, collecting camera crews and grateful spectators. They were famous do-gooders, hugging kids for publicity while I watched them on TV from military school."

"Dragon's—"

Aiden whipped his gaze her way.

"Fire? Can I say dragon fire?"

"Let's leave the dragon out of this."

"How come you can call me Snapdragon?"

Aiden gave her a cocky grin. "Me man. You woman. Man like his dragon snapped by woman. The visual pumps me, ego and dragon. Makes me proud."

Storm shook her head. "You're so shallow that being re-minded of your libidinous excellence gives you a euphoric high, like getting shot with endorphins, minus the choco-late."

"Only better. Wait, you think my libido is excellent? Want to pull over for a quickie?"

"I am so *not* turned on right now. Besides, I've gotta find a new expletive. I understand your problem with the gruesome bloody dragon picture—now that I know what you keep in your shorts—but I'm getting the bends with you pissin' me off and no comeback.

"Wait! I'll steal Harmony's favorite expletive. Wither-ing witch balls! Are you telling me that your parents are the McClouds of the McCloud Foundation? You're filthy rich, Scruffleupagus. Good cover, working for a living. Who'd a thunk it? But I haven't heard about any of your parents' stunts in a while. Wait. You *inherited* your nomadic lifestyle. It's in your genes. Who'd a thunk that?"

"My parents were the opposites of turtles, believe me. If my mother worked in a casino, she'd have been a showgirl, not a cocktail waitress. But nomads, oh yeah. Hey, did I distract you enough? Any babies crying in that head of yours, yet?"

Storm shoved his arm for the ploy. "Where are your parents now?"

"I have no idea, but we're pretty sure they're dead. One minute their jet was a blip on the radar screen over the Peruvian jungle, and the next, nothing. Search parties looked for months before they gave up."

"What happened to the foundation?"

"I've still got it. I carry on their work."

"Without the fanfare?"

Aiden nodded. "I like it better that way."

"Do you have a desk in a big office building that's attached to the ground somewhere?"

"Lots of them, but I haven't sat behind one in years."

"Do you miss your parents?"

He gave her a double take, and she really wondered what he was thinking. "Marvelanne believes that you don't miss what you never had," Aiden said. "You say that you do. I'm split down the middle on the subject."

"Fair enough." Storm sat straighter. "Hah! I hear a baby crying."

"Just one?"

"Yep. Yours. Pull over at the nearest rest stop, so I can take the wheel."

"If I do have a baby out there, I won't know what to do with her. I don't know how to love."

"That's okay. Babies have a way of teaching us how to love." Storm drove from then on, listening to the baby in her head and getting clearer snapshots in her mind. Racks of jewelry. Trinket boxes, rings, bracelets, necklaces. Sea animals, seashells, turtles. *Lots* of turtles in gold, silver, and copper. Somebody who knew Aiden.

"I think you're as flawed as me," she said. "That's why we get along so well."

"From the minute we met," he said. "You think our attraction had *anything* to do with flaws?"

"No, that was lust and pheromones. You've got some hot and hopping pheromones, there, Scruffleupagus. We're on the right track," she added. "The crying is really loud now, and I can see—"

Aiden's heart was about to be tested, and the need for a silent spell became strong in Storm:

> *Mother Goddess, Father God,*
> *For she who pines,*
> *I seek love's signs.*
> *A father, if my wits speak true.*
> *None can save her but you.*
>
> *A man good of heart and deed,*
> *Soul lost and love in need,*
> *He seeks a home*
> *No more to roam*
> *With she who shares his genes.*

"Please," Aiden said. "Tell me."

"What?"

"What you see. Are you all right?"

"The snapshots are clear. Now, instead of gold, silver, and copper discs, I see jewelry from the sea, like this." She lifted the sea horse pendant she'd found in his coach, made the connection, and dropped it as if it singed her fingers.

"Dear God in heaven," Aiden said.

Chapter Thirty-five

AIDEN'S heart pumped as if he'd run the Boston Marathon.

"What's wrong?" Storm asked.

"We're heading into Cape May, where Claudette lived and worked. She designed the jewelry she sold in her shop, Jewels of the Sea."

"Now I'm beginning to scare myself," Storm said. "You're not kidding, are you?"

"I wish the hell I was. She made that sea horse." He was about to tell Storm to park as close to the row of Victorian cottage shops coming up as she could get, when she pulled into a parking lot across the street and stopped, facing Claudette's shop.

"There," she said pointing.

No kidding, he thought. Aiden nodded, got out, and crossed the street to the shop, but he couldn't speak. Claudette had shown it to him once, and then she drove him by her mother's house, though she'd refused to take him inside to meet the woman. She said her mother only understood men who put down roots, so she wouldn't understand about their relationship.

He'd respected that then. Now he just felt like a shit.

The Victorian sign, Jewels of the Sea by Claudette Langley, still hung over the door, but Claudette's store was empty. That shouldn't jar him, but it did. Until now, he'd never seen proof of the news about Claudette's death, and now he was being forced to face and accept it. She was really gone.

He hadn't loved her. She wasn't the lovable sort, not like . . . Storm. Strange thought. But Claudette had been a good companion when she wasn't trying to change him.

Frightened for some nonspecific reason, Aiden looked across the street at Storm sitting in the driver's seat of his coach, watching him, probably giving him time to come to terms with losing his ex, except that all he could think about was Storm herself.

Storm, the bad-girl seductress with a nurturer crying to be set free, who'd wheedled her way into the heart he didn't know he owned. A storm cloud who could be charming when she wasn't being sarcastic. A Snapdragon, tenacious, a natural energizer, the most insecure of the triplets, and, oh, how he liked her.

He *liked* her . . . a whole hell of a lot more than was good for his sanity.

When she'd seen his dragon for the first time, her eyes had taken on a stormy sea-green shade; shock, definitely. Then when she fell in love with Triton, or so she said, her mischievous smile brought a bright aquamarine glint to her eyes. Then a muted gray blue rolled in like a fog when true arousal had hit her—had hit them both.

Storm stood in the coach and crossed her arms—a telling gesture. Was she afraid of losing him to a ghost? How could she lose something she'd never had? But she wasn't the one asking the question, now, was she? Maybe she did have him. Maybe he was up the proverbial creek with nothing to do but sink . . . or grab a handy Storm cloud.

She left the coach, stuck her hands in the pockets of that sea horse sundress he'd bought her, and ambled over to him on the sexy three-inch heels he'd also chosen, her blue hair still rather tame, hardly a spike in sight.

She stopped in front of him. "You okay?"

"I'm a little shaken," he said. "I won't kid you."

"I think you loved her. You'll feel better if you admit it and allow yourself to grieve."

"I liked her. We . . . got along. The companionship was good. The sex was . . . okay. Not to be disrespectful to the dead, but sex with you is better than anything I could *never* have imagined."

"That's because you can be your real self with me. I'm another misfit, an independently flawed creature who won't fall in love. You can identify with me, and you feel safe with me. That's all."

He placed his hands on her shoulders, gazed into her gorgeous eyes, and pulled her toward him. "Is that all?" *He* wasn't so sure.

She nodded, and he kissed her.

When he came up for air, he combed the rebel-blue hair from her eyes. "I'm overwhelmed by guilt, not grief."

"I told you. It's not your fault Claudette took off and had an accident—"

"The guilt is because I care more about you than I ever did about her."

"That can't be right."

"Why can't it?"

"Because I'm barely tolerable, never mind likable."

"You keep thinking that," he said, "and I'll keep thinking different. We'll agree to disagree on this one, shall we?" He hooked an arm around her shoulder and walked her back to his coach. "By the way, Claudette didn't die the day she left me; it was months later."

"Then you're really stupid for feeling guilty."

"You still hear that baby crying?"

"Louder than ever."

"That makes my heart race, and not in a good way. Let's get going. You drive."

Storm's street choices made Aiden begin to clench. First

his gut and his chest. Then, as they got closer to the water-front, his neck and shoulders. He ground his teeth, set his jaw, and the more familiar the roads became, the more Victorian the houses, the tighter his fists. When Storm stopped the motor coach in front of Claudette's mother's house, Aiden nearly jumped from his skin. "I'll never doubt your psychic instincts again," he said. "The crying baby is in *my* head now, too."

"No, Aiden. That's called hearing." Storm stepped out of the coach. "Come on."

They followed the sound around the white Victorian cottage trimmed in sage and lilac to a spectacular seascape view out back. From the side, a white porch said welcome with potted trees and a lush pot of hydrangeas. Baskets of yellow, pink, and purple flowers hung from the eaves, the calico cushions on the weather-worn rattan furniture echoing every color.

But when they rounded the porch corner, a different sight stole his breath. An old woman sat in a wheelchair beside a play yard, in which a toddler in pink ruffled coveralls accepted a piece of apricot from a bowl on a weathered side table.

The toddler's big crocodile tears stopped when she saw them.

Aiden's heartbeat went into overdrive.

He could barely breathe.

His lungs had clenched as well.

The old woman's surprise turned to shock, then her expression crumpled. She pulled her apron over her eyes and rocked her body back and forth as she sobbed. Aiden had never seen anything like it.

"Cots," the toddler said, showing him her treat.

"Yum," Aiden said, and the dark-haired child nodded and popped it into her mouth. Did she look like him, or was that his imagination?

"Are you all right?" Storm asked, kneeling in front of the woman.

The old lady nodded, but she kept crying.

Aiden stooped down as well, purposely covering the little girl's soft fingers as she clutched the edge of the play yard, her hand so tiny, so perfect; then he gave his attention to the woman. "We're strangers. Are we frightening you? Do you want us to leave?"

The old woman shook her head. "You're not a stranger," she said into her apron.

The toddler kissed Aiden's hand, surprising him, melting him. When he looked at her, the little one smiled, and he was sure that his heart turned over in his chest, and it would never be the same again.

"Can I get you something?" he asked, turning back to the old lady, his insides all atumble. "A glass of water? Anything?"

She lowered her apron to wipe her eyes with a corner of it, and then she clutched it to her heart. "Yes, you *can* get me something. Go into the house and get the picture on the mantel in the living room. You'll know the one I mean when you see it."

"I don't think—"

"Please."

Aiden went into the house where Claudette grew up, and an overwhelming grief rushed him. Crystal remnants of her rock-hounding addiction sat on tables and windowsills. He remembered every squeal of delight when she struck crystals. He remembered her laugh, the smell of her hair, the snuffle of her breathing beside him in bed at night.

When he got to the mantel, Aiden did know which picture. Beautifully framed, it was one of him and Claudette standing in front of his old motor coach, the last picture before their last frustrating discussion about him *not* settling down. A camping neighbor had taken it fifteen minutes before his snarky, "Go hound a rock," from the seat of his revved Harley, a moment in time he hadn't realized would haunt him. "Jack-effin'-ass," he called himself as he grasped the picture. Those were the last words he'd ever spoken to her.

He should be shot.

He didn't take his gaze from Claudette's likeness all the way to the porch. She was the anti-Storm: attractive but pale with a boyish figure, so soft-spoken, she couldn't say *sex*, a chore she valiantly bore to please him. Now that he thought about it, she was so prim, she probably thought of it as love, or she couldn't have borne it.

His dragon would have given her a heart attack. But she was kind and generous. Talented. Fun. She liked to dance. He wasn't any more worthy of her than of Storm, and both of them damned well deserved better than him.

Claudette should have cut him out of the picture and thrown his half away. He sure didn't deserve a spot in the old lady's home, he thought as he handed her the picture.

From the porch, he saw Storm, barefoot, ambling along the sandy beach with a bounce in her step and a toddler in her arms, a small head of dark curls on her shoulder. Beneath Storm's rebellious goth demeanor hid a nurturer in disguise, determined to rescue every crying baby in her head.

Claudette's mother tugged on his shirt, and Aiden turned his attention her way. He lowered himself to her level again and for a moment covered her hand, her skin paper-thin and cool to the touch. Claudette had been lucky to have a mother who cared so much she was raising her granddaughter, or so he assumed. Glancing back toward Storm and the baby, he caught Mrs. Langley's movement and gave her his full attention. She had taken the picture from its frame and was trying to hand it to him. "Read the back," she said.

On it, Claudette had written the date, her name, and . . . "four months pregnant" . . . then his name and . . . "the father of my child."

Gut-punched by an invisible hand, Aiden rose and read it again.

He looked across the sand at Storm holding . . . his daughter . . . and his pathetic life passed before his eyes. "I . . . didn't know."

Mrs. Langley nodded. "Claudette told me you didn't."

He'd thought Claudette had left because their life goals differed too greatly. She was a homebody who wanted roots and, *eventually*—or so she'd said that last day—a family. But he was a wanderer; happy driving his motor coach wherever his work took him.

She'd wanted him to stop roaming and put down roots.

Too frank and too loud, he'd told her in no uncertain terms that he didn't want to be tied down.

When he got back, she was gone.

Now their parting would haunt him forever.

She'd left because she'd carried the means to tie him down, and she'd refused to use it.

Chapter Thirty-six

MRS. Langley nodded as if she could read his every regretful thought. "Claudette's friends brought me that picture after they cleaned out her shop."

"I'm sorry about Claudette," Aiden said, his voice cracking.

Her mother teared up. "So are we, though Becky never met her, and Claudette never saw her baby."

Aiden pulled a rattan chair to the wheelchair and sat down. "I didn't know about Becky. I would have come sooner if I had."

"Why did you come now, then?" she asked.

"My friend." He looked toward Storm, heading their way, kissing the baby's crown of dark curls. "She's psychic and has a pretty outstanding gift for finding lost children."

"Storm," Mrs. Langley said. "We introduced ourselves when you went for the picture. And please call me Ginny, both of you. Thank you, Storm, for leading Aiden to us, and not a day too soon."

"I welcomed the opportunity to use my psychic gifts for

such a good cause." Storm gave him a look, not quite an I-told-you-so, but close.

Aiden regarded the baby's small fingers in Storm's hair.

She must have read him, so she put the baby in his arms. "Here you go"—she glanced down at the picture and saw the inscription—"Dad."

"Da Da," the toddler said, patting his cheeks then clapping her hands. "Da Da!"

Despite being poleaxed, a wash of protectiveness made Aiden pull his daughter close. He looked at Claudette's mother for an explanation. "Da Da?" he asked.

"We practice with your picture," Ginny explained. "Becky's been able to identify you for a while now."

"For a minute, I thought she was psychic like Storm," Aiden said, "but she can't be more than, what, a year old? She's smart for her age, isn't she?"

"Spoken like a true father," Storm said, and Ginny looked pleased.

"What did you mean about it not being a day too soon?" Storm asked her.

"Social Services doesn't consider me fit to raise Becky, because I'm confined to the chair, of course, but losing her will hurt so much. They're coming to take her tomorrow and put her in foster care."

"No!" Storm and Aiden shouted.

Aiden checked his watch. "A little after noon," he said. "Good." He handed his daughter—his daughter, shock of shocks—back to Storm and took out his cell. "I'm calling the foundation lawyers to get them started on putting a monkey wrench in the plan. When you feed the poor and shelter the homeless, you work with Social Services. If anybody knows how the system operates, the foundation lawyers will." He walked away to make the call but turned to Ginny during the conversation. "Is my name on Becky's birth certificate?"

"No, Claudette was in a coma when they took Becky by C-section. I hadn't seen that picture yet, and I didn't know.

I was tempted to put you down. But I didn't want to make a mistake that couldn't be rectified."

Aiden shook off her apology. "Can you give me the names of the social workers involved, telephone numbers?" he asked, his hand over the mouthpiece.

Ginny sent Storm for her records.

The older woman sorted through the papers and handed Aiden what he needed. He read the info to his lawyer at the other end of the line. "Get a cease and desist or something," Aiden said and hung up.

After two hours of playing with his daughter and holding her while she napped in his arms, Aiden discovered that he'd fallen head over heels in less than a day. And he hadn't thought he knew how to love. Hah.

With Becky asleep on his shoulder, he looked up, surprised, when warmth spread across his chest and down his lap. "Storm, Ginny, I think my lap is wet."

"Oh," Ginny said. "I should have changed her before she fell asleep, but you both looked so content."

"No," Storm said. "Stay where you are, Ginny. I think it's time Aiden learned how to change his daughter's diaper. Let's go, Papa Bear," Storm said.

Aiden got up carefully so as not to wake Becky, and followed Storm into the nursery.

"Becky's room is really lovely," Storm said.

"Becky's daddy is really wet," Aiden said, "though I hate to wake her, but . . . oh, hello there, Sweet Stuff." Becky pulled away to look at him. "Did I jostle you awake?" Aiden asked her.

But she looked like she was going to cry, as if she didn't know who he was, which about broke him. He jiggled her and said, "Da Da!" with a big grin, and watched her features change to recognition, until she smiled shyly. Oh, brother was he hooked.

"This is the dressing table," Storm said. "And here are the wipes and powder."

"So?"

"So lay her on her back on the dressing table, and stay in front of her, so she doesn't roll off."

"Done. Next?"

"Take off her dirty diaper."

"How dirty?"

"That's part of the surprise. You won't know until you take it off, though there is a distinct odor."

Aiden gave her a double take. "You're getting your jollies out of this."

"Who me? Miss 'You-have-a-child' enjoying some overdue payback for 'you're-nuts'?"

"Point taken. How do I get her out of this to find the diaper?"

"You know," Storm said, "I watched you take an antique chandelier apart and put it back together again. This is a pink ruffled playsuit."

"On a moving target."

Storm bit her lip. Every time Aiden got Becky on her back again, she squirmed around and was up on all fours. "Talk to her," Storm said. "Tell her a story to keep her attention on your face and voice."

"Once upon a time, my darling Becky, there was a turtle—" Aiden started to unbutton her shoulder straps, but Storm pointed to the snap crotch. He rolled his eyes and pulled the snaps apart while Becky tried to get up again. Gently, he got her on her back again. "That silly turtle didn't think he had room enough in his shell, or his heart, for a family—"

"Good grief, don't pull the diaper down, pull the side tabs off. Better containment that way."

"But one day that silly turtle fell in love with a beautiful little fairy princess—holy crap—who stank to high heaven! Stinky, stinky, stinky!"

Becky giggled and raised her legs as if waiting for him to clean her off.

"Figures," Storm said. "You get a daughter who cooperates when it's important."

Aiden grabbed a huge handful of wipes, and Storm

nearly laughed, but he did get Becky cleaned up, and hardly gagged at all.

"If I didn't need you to tell me how to put another diaper on her," Aiden said, "I'd throw you out of the room right now. My weak gag reflex stays between us, Cartwright."

Storm crossed her heart and handed him a new disposable diaper.

"It's flat," he said. "And she's not."

"Open it like an accordion. Pictures go in the front. When they fade, she needs to be changed again."

"How do you know so much?" Aiden asked. "There are no babies in your family yet."

"Vickie's friend Melody Seabright has two kids. I've changed her daughter's diaper more than a few times."

"Melody Seabright of cooking show fame, the one who runs the Keep Me Foundation?" Aiden asked. "I've done business with her. I knew she came from Salem, but I never made the connection."

"How do you two do business?"

"The McCloud Foundation donates heavily to the Keep Me Foundation's causes."

"And here you are, about to keep a baby of your own."

"This playsuit is too wet to put back on her," he said.

"Oh goody, I get to go through her outfits."

"It's fashion all the way with you, isn't it?"

"Since I became part owner of the Immortal Classic, it is. Before that, you don't wanna know."

"Maybe the McCloud Foundation should invest in some kind of child find organization, possibly in conjunction with Melody's Keep Me Foundation." He cupped his daughter's face and bent to kiss her brow, her nose, and then the fingers she placed against his mouth.

The way Storm looked at him made his heart turn over. "What?" he asked.

"Nothing," she said. "I like *this* outfit."

When his cell phone rang, Aiden could see that it was the foundation. Becky clapped, and he and Storm changed places at the dressing table so she could dress Becky while he took the call.

His hands were shaking when he answered and more so as he listened. "Try!" he said, hanging up a minute later.

Ginny had wheeled her chair to the doorway of Becky's room when she heard his phone. She was waiting for a verdict. Aiden wished he had a better one. "Everything is a mess," he said, "but they're working on clearing it up. We have every reason to hope for the right outcome."

Aiden took Becky from Storm, all clean and fresh, and kissed her tiny baby fingers. "I can't believe I've only known you existed for a few hours, and the thought of someone taking you away from me is making me crazy."

Back in the living room, Storm made Ginny a cup of chamomile tea while Aiden went out to the camper for a dry shirt. "Mrs. Langley—I mean Ginny—I couldn't help but notice your curio cabinet. The crystal and coral are amazing, as are the spectacular jewelry pieces displayed with it. Is the jewelry Claudette's work?"

"Yes, I put some of my favorite pieces of hers in there, but I have boxes more in the garage. Aiden," Ginny said as he returned, "see the sea horse cuff links and studs on the bottom shelf? They were for you. Why don't you take them?"

"I can't take your memories, Ginny."

"You don't understand. Claudette made them especially for you. She told me several times that they were yours when she was working on them."

Storm put a hand on his arm, a connection Aiden needed more than air just then. "Aiden, take the cuff links," she said, "and wear them to Becky's every birthday party, school play, and graduation, from nursery school to grad school. That way you'll have a bit of Claudette with you when you celebrate your daughter's milestones."

Ginny grabbed Storm's free hand and squeezed. "Claudette would have liked you."

"I know I would have liked her, especially if she was anything like her mother. You said you have boxes of her work in the garage? Would you like me to take them home and sell them in my shop? It's called the Immortal Classic, it's a vintage clothing and curio shop, and I know the Salem tourists would love Claudette's work. The profits could supplement your income."

"I hated to think about what would happen to her work if/when I was forced into assisted living. Getting Claudette's work to people who would cherish it would make me very happy."

"It's settled then. I'm taking Claudette's stock back to Salem with me. Now, how about letting me make dinner?"

Storm cooked while Ginny caught Aiden up on Becky's life, antics, and quirks.

After dinner, Aiden sat back, sated and happy. "I didn't know you were such a good cook, Storm. That was delicious."

"I told you, my sisters and I raised each other. The three of us have been cooking for ourselves since we were five, maybe."

"That's terrible," Ginny said.

"That's survival," Storm said. "You know a little something about that, Ginny."

"Well," Aiden said, "between Storm's beef Stroganoff, Becky for entertainment, and you for company, Ginny, it was an especially wonderful dinner. Thank you for inviting us, but Storm, you and I should go find a campground for the night."

"Nonsense," Claudette's mother said. "Pull into the driveway. You can tap into my water and electricity so you'll be comfortable. I've only got two small bedrooms, and one's a nursery, or I'd invite you to stay here."

Storm cleared her throat. "Um, can we take Becky to spend the night in the motor coach with us? Unless you think you need to get to know us better. I would understand if you did."

"I know Aiden from all the talking Claudette did about him. My daughter was dreadfully in love with you, Aiden." Claudette's mother turned away at Aiden's discomfort.

"Storm," she said, "not only did you figure out a way to include Claudette in Becky's life by having Aiden wear her jewelry to Becky's special events, I heard Becky call you Mama a while ago."

"I'm sorry about that," Storm said.

"Don't be. That was instinct. She's a pretty good judge of character, our Becky. I'll pack her an overnight bag with everything you'll need, and she can sleep in her play yard, which converts to a travel bed. Come in for breakfast in the morning. The door will be open."

"What time?" Aiden asked.

"Becky time." The woman chuckled. "She runs the show. She'll let you know when she's awake and ready for breakfast." The woman dabbed at her eyes. "Forgive an old lady her emotion, but I can't tell you how happy I am not to be losing Becky tomorrow."

Aiden felt a deep sense of guilt for not telling Claudette's mother how dire the circumstances were at this late date, and how slim the chances of keeping Becky with her. But he guessed that one out of the three of them worrying was anguish enough, and it was time he took some of the torment off Ginny's shoulders.

Chapter Thirty-seven

BEFORE they went to the coach for the night, Ginny gave them so many instructions, Aiden had to write them down, which amused the daylights out of Storm.

In the coach, after Aiden put Becky in her play yard/travel bed, she watched him check the list for like the fifth time. "For a man who swore he couldn't possibly have a child . . . anywhere . . . and didn't want one, you're quite the fanatic."

"Never mind. This is a tiny person here." He shook Becky's bare foot, and she giggled. He let go in surprise. "She laughs."

"Usually if they cry, they laugh. If they eat, they poop. With a kid, it's pretty much a set of unexpected twofers."

Aiden ignored her, but Storm didn't mind as he grabbed Becky's foot again for more jiggling and lots more Becky belly laughs. After a while, her laughter became contagious, and it was hard to tell which of them laughed hardest.

"She's glad you're here," Storm said. "I think you're glad, too. I told you when I kidnapped you that you would be."

Aiden pulled her into his arms and kissed her. "Thank you for my baby."

The highly charged words reverberated between them: intimacy meets terror, times two.

When Becky yawned, Storm stepped away from him. "You change her and get her into her jammies, Dad, and I'll warm her bottle."

Storm took a few snapshots of Aiden feeding Becky her precious bedtime bottle, their gazes locked as they held the bottle together, her tiny hands over his huge, capable ones, revealing that Da Da was hers to command.

Love she saw in their eyes. Unconditional, forever love. Adoration. Baby-I'll-never-let-anyone-hurt-you love. Daddy-you're-my-world love.

After Aiden finished feeding and burping her, Storm sang Becky to sleep as she walked the length of the coach, bouncing her. Sweet summer savory, this little one felt perfect in her arms. If she wasn't careful, she'd be going home with a broken heart, times two.

She and Aiden stood beside the play yard watching Becky sleep for a long while.

"After the last couple of nights," Aiden whispered, pulling his shirt from his pants as he moved away from the play yard at the foot of his bed, "I think sleeping through the night will do us both some good."

Storm smiled as he lay beside her and wove their fingers together.

A few hours later, she woke from a nightmare about Pepper, with a look of abject misery on her face, leaving school to search for her. Storm opened her eyes, glad it wasn't real, to find Aiden sitting at the foot of the bed watching Becky sleep. She crossed the mattress and put her hands on his shoulders. "What are you doing?" she whispered in his ear.

He turned to kiss her. "I'm thinking."

"About?"

"Where to raise her, how to do my job, getting day care, or a babysitter, or a nanny, maybe."

It was all Storm could do not to volunteer. "Houses and fences and roots . . . babies and nannies and diapers, oh my, oh my."

Aiden caught her to bring her around and onto his lap. He kissed her then held her head against his shoulder, tucking a stray curl behind her ear. "I will not let Social Services take Becky away."

Storm grazed his cheek with the back of a hand. "I never expected for a minute that you would."

Aiden kissed her hand. "Will you help me get it all sorted out? And before you agree, you should know that the sorting will be a good deal scarier than I let on. Social Services does *not* want to let me have her, and they won't let Ginny keep her. My lawyers have a lot of red tape to unwind. It would have helped if I was listed on Becky's birth certificate, but the last time Claudette and I talked, I practically told her that I didn't want the burden of children."

"Oh, Aiden," Storm said. "I'm here for you, however long it takes for Becky to become legally yours."

"Thank you for abducting me."

Becky whimpered, "Da Da," in her sleep, and Aiden leaned over to knuckle her cheek and tell her he was there. "Daddy will take care of you, Becky," he promised, and Becky sighed, rolled to her stomach, and went back to sleep.

"She was dreaming about me," Aiden said, his look filled with wonder.

Storm pushed him back on the bed. "She's probably always dreamed about you."

They crawled to their pillows and fell asleep like two spoons in a kitchen drawer, with a tiny snore coming from the foot of the bed.

To Storm, nothing had ever felt so right.

Becky time turned out to be four in the morning.

Chapter Thirty-eight

"GOOD God," Aiden said, waking up to find his daughter, with Warlock in her arms, watching him, a pouty look on her face.

He picked Becky up, and Warlock leapt to the bed, where he went to curl up between Storm's legs. Aiden loved the feel of his soft, warm morning Becky, but he did spare a moment of jealousy for Warlock's prime piece of property.

"You want to snuggle?" he asked Becky as he put her in the bed between him and Storm, who'd barely cracked an eyelid.

"Loops," Becky said, sitting up.

Aiden laid her back down. "Loops?" he asked.

"Breakfast," Storm said, sitting up and rubbing her face. "Froot Loops."

Becky sat up again and nodded. "Loops."

Storm tickled Becky. "So you're the reason I've been craving Froot Loops, and loving the scent of baby powder and apricots. Do you like chocolate milk with your Froot Loops?"

Becky let go of her own foot and nodded.

When Storm stopped tickling her, Becky tickled her in return, then she tickled Aiden, which really made them laugh—not the tickles as much as her attempt at mimicking their play.

After another leaky diaper incident, Aiden washed, changed, and dressed Becky while Storm packed her bag to go back to the house.

"I learned the hard way," Aiden said, "that I change her diaper before naps, after meals, before bed, and especially upon rising."

"And in between," Storm said.

"Right."

"Aiden, you should ask Ginny where Claudette is buried so we can pay our respects and bring her some flowers, unless you'd rather do that alone."

"No, I'd like your company, if you don't mind. Claudette should know who led me to Becky."

He got to carry the play yard into Ginny's house, with enough clothes, toys, and equipment for a day at the beach, while Storm carried Becky, dry and dressed, and Becky carried Warlock.

In the old-fashioned kitchen, waiting on Becky's high chair tray sat a bowl of dry Froot Loops and a sippy cup of chocolate milk. With her tiny baby hand, Becky lifted a red loop and showed it to him.

"Loops," Aiden said. "I see."

"Red," Becky said and offered it to him.

"For me?" he asked, and when she nodded, he was so touched, he bent down and let her force it between his lips, which made her laugh. He couldn't believe he'd not only accepted a limp Froot Loop, but he was eating it with joy, as if she'd given him a great gift. "Thank you, sweetheart." He placed his lips on Becky's head and kept them there for a minute. Baby silk hair, tiny fingers squeezing his heart without touching him. If he didn't get a grip, he was gonna bawl all over this beautiful child Claudette had left him.

Aiden straightened, feeling as if he didn't deserve Becky and had never deserved Claudette. If only he could make up to Claudette for being such an arrogant jerk.

"Da Da. Loops," Becky said, showing him the loop impaled on her baby finger. Then she popped the finger into her mouth and giggled when it came away clean.

"I can't believe I fathered a morning person."

Claudette's mother brought a plate of fresh pancakes to the table, though Storm had been munching on dry Froot Loops.

"Ginny," Aiden said, "can you tell me where Claudette is buried, so Storm and I can pay our respects?"

Ginny dropped her fork, her expression disbelieving.

"What's wrong?" Aiden asked.

"They're not removing Claudette's life support until noon today. That's why Social Services isn't coming until later."

Aiden shot from his chair. "Claudette's alive?"

"Yes and no. She's been in a coma since the accident."

"I have to see her," Aiden said. "I have to tell her that I'll take care of Becky."

"She won't know you're there, son."

"I don't care. I have to go. I have . . . unfinished business to take care of."

Chapter Thirty-nine

STORM stood stone cold and unmoving.

Life . . . or death . . . had just taken a new turn.

"Where's the nursing home?" Aiden asked, and after Ginny gave him directions, he practically ran out the door. Storm heard him unhooking the camper and starting the engine. She stood to look out the bay window as he backed the coach out of the driveway.

"He's in shock," Storm said when Ginny rolled her chair over and put a comforting hand on her arm.

"He's filled with guilt," the old lady said.

Storm agreed. "That, too." He was running again, but he was running *toward* something for a change—no, toward *someone*—the most significant sign she'd seen that Claudette mattered to him . . . a great deal.

While she tried not to feel deserted, Storm played with Becky, which was a treat, and yet . . .

For heaven's sake, Aiden had gone to say good-bye to the mother of his child, and he would, of course, stay with Claudette until after she passed, but later he'd need someone to comfort him, and Storm promised herself that she'd be there for him when he did.

She also realized that he might not actually come back for *her*, but he would be back for his daughter.

She simply hadn't realized how much Aiden loved Claudette until she saw the way he'd reacted.

The wall phone in the kitchen rang, startling her, which made Becky laugh. Ginny answered it, spoke for a minute, then dropped the phone, leaving it to swing from its cord and hit the wall.

"What is it?" Storm asked.

"She's awake. Claudette came out of her coma." Ginny wept unrestrainedly, and though her tears should have been of joy, Storm thought they sounded more like a soul-deep sorrow. Talk about mixed messages.

They had to be tears of joy, and so they should be. Becky would have her mother, and Aiden . . . Storm didn't know what he would do when Claudette got well—stay in Cape May or return to Salem—but wherever he went, he would probably have Claudette and Becky with him.

She suddenly felt like a fifth wheel, and how horrible was she to be thinking of herself when someone who'd been dying was now going to live? Which meant that she no longer belonged here. "I should go," Storm said.

"No!" Ginny said again, taking her hand. "You can't abandon Aiden. He'll need you more than ever, now."

"No, Ginny. You saw him. It's Claudette he needs."

"Here. Here are the keys to my car. Go to the nursing home and see what's really going on. Talk to Aiden. Meet Claudette."

"Don't you want to come?" Storm asked, confused.

The old lady shivered. "Maybe later when you come back . . . if . . . everything's all right, I might go, but I don't have a good feeling about this."

"Ginny, you're getting your daughter back. Becky's getting her mother."

The old lady patted her hand. "I'm old. I've seen a lot of

death in my day. I've been watching my Claudette die for a year, you understand. I can't watch anymore."

"That's just it. She's going to live."

Ginny shook her head and stared out the window.

Storm washed her face and put on the little bit of makeup she kept in her purse. Thank goodness she'd brought her purse inside for her cell phone, or her driver's license would have been gone with the motor coach.

Warlock curled himself around her legs.

Oh gosh, her kitten might be gone, too, if not for Becky's infatuation with him. "Once again, we don't have food or kitty litter for you, do we, Warlock? I'll have to run to the store before I go to the nursing home. Given this change of events, I think a new carrier is in order as well."

Back in the living room, Storm couldn't fathom the torment in Ginny's expression.

"Claudette's out of her coma," Storm repeated. "She'll get better now."

"You keep thinking that, sweetheart. God knows somebody should."

Storm didn't know why she had to go to the nursing home. She just knew, deep down, that she did.

Chapter Farty

AIDEN hit the brakes in the nursing home parking lot, surprised that every cupboard door didn't pop open and spill its contents. He hit the tarmac at a run.

The first floor nurse sent him to the fourth floor.

At the nurses' station there, they gave him Claudette's room number. He wasn't sure he was prepared to see her, especially in a coma.

When he got to the door, he felt dizzy, thought he might pass out.

He blinked to clear the hallucination.

"Hello, Aiden," Claudette said. "I've been waiting for you."

Okay. Not a hallucination. A miracle.

"You . . . you've been in a coma."

"So they tell me."

"I thought . . . I'm so glad you're okay." She looked pasty, the skin beneath her fingernails purple.

"You can't be as happy to see me as I am to see you," she said, her breathing pattern alarming. "I know this is a shock."

He hadn't even touched her. Aiden stepped closer to the bed, took Claudette's hand, and kissed it. "I've never been happier about anything in my life." He tried not to focus on the bones beneath the thin veneer of waxy skin on her hand.

"You found our baby," she said, joy on her features—features he barely recognized, except for the light in her eyes.

"How do you know I found her?"

"I've been trying to get you here."

"Wait." Aiden held up a staying hand. "I'm confused." He bent over the bed rail and kissed her, then he had the rails taken down by a nurse so he could sit beside her. "How do you feel?"

"Pretty good, considering."

"What do you mean, you've been trying to get me here?"

"Have you ever had an out-of-body experience?" Claudette asked. "I think I've had a few. I watched them performing the C-section on me. I floated above myself and saw them take our baby out of my body. I stayed near the incubator and watched her grow strong. She was a pre-emie, so I talked to her, hoping she could hear or sense me on some level, until she was able to go home with my mother."

Claudette drifted off—back into her coma, Aiden thought, and he shouted for help, but she opened her eyes. "Hey, easy. People are trying to die around here."

"That's not funny." But the disinfectants failed to hide the odor of death.

"I left my body often when I was in the coma," Claudette said.

Before Storm, he would have doubted those words. Maybe he still did on some level. "I know someone you should meet. You two could exchange stories."

"You were stubborn about coming. I nudged the sea horse necklace from the top cupboard to the counter for you to find—which was very hard to do and took days' worth of energy—and you put it in that drawer, so deep down, there was no way for me to dig it out."

Yes, damn it. He had done that, but Storm had dug it out later and started wearing it. "Seeing it on the counter spooked me, Claudette. I'd just heard about your accident. What the hell am I talking about? How could you have spooked me? You were in a coma. That must have been a dream."

"For both of us?" She smiled. "But I finally found somebody who heard my call."

"What are you saying?"

"You were in a place with enough spiritual energy for me to tap into for strength. I tried to leave clues for you there."

"What clues?"

"I wrote my name in the steam on a mirror, and when that didn't work, I wrote it in the dust on a table."

"*You* did that? I thought our resident ghost was playing mind games."

"Someone there was very receptive."

"Claudette, shouldn't you be resting? Or maybe you're hungry?"

She shook her head to both suggestions.

"Maybe your meds gave you those dreams."

"You just admitted that you were in a place with a ghost."

"I did. I was."

"Someone there," Claudette said, "heard Becky crying when you were near her."

Aiden loosened his collar. "*You* put the sound of the baby in Storm's head when I was nearby?"

"Storm? Is that her name? She has a gift. She didn't need much from me. She got you here, right? Though I got the sense that it wasn't easy for her, even dangerous at one point."

"Wait, what could you see?"

"I didn't see in the sense that you mean, I felt, sensed . . . objects, people . . . their feelings. Why?"

"Storm and I, we've been . . . seeing . . . each other."

"Well, I didn't see you 'seeing' each other when I went mind to mind with Storm. I'm not Superwoman. What I did takes energy. I used our baby's cry to bring you to her, however I could. Aiden, don't look so guilty. You never loved me. I knew that. But between you and Storm, I've sometimes felt love—which *you* haven't faced yet. No surprise."

"Claudette, this is insane."

"Don't worry about it then. Pretend I dreamed it, if you want."

"I'll do that while you concentrate on getting better."

"I'm tired, Aiden."

"Rest, then, but before you take a nap, we have to talk." Just this morning he'd wished he could make up to Claudette for everything he'd put her through. "Marry me, Claudette. Marry me and make me Becky's stepfather. You'll get well, and we'll be a family."

"I don't think I have time to get married," Claudette said.

"Nonsense, we don't need a fancy church wedding." He asked the floor nurse to call a priest. The poor old guy expected the last rites in this place, not a wedding, but he seemed up for the challenge once he spoke to Claudette's doctor. That made Aiden nervous, because the doctor wouldn't tell *him* anything, but if his conversation with the priest moved the wedding forward, so much the better.

The priest rubbed his chin. "I know a judge, no two, who owe me, and . . . today's a business day," he said, thinking out loud. "Mr. McCloud, I'll arrange for you to get your blood test here while I make a few phone calls."

A nurse came in to give him his blood test while Claudette napped.

Later, one of the judges called, the priest told them, also to speak to Claudette's doctor. Within the hour, a messenger arrived with a marriage license. The priest found a doctor and nurse who would stand up for them when everything was in place.

The impossible became possible almost too easily. There were circumstances at work here that Aiden didn't understand, and maybe it was best that he didn't.

Preparing for their wedding became surreal in that sterile hospital room, especially so soon after King and Harmony's lavish affair, and considering the fact that Aiden felt as if he was marrying the wrong woman.

His life was passing before his eyes. To keep from losing Becky, he needed to marry Claudette. By marrying Claudette, he'd lose Storm. If he stayed with Storm instead of Claudette, he'd lose Becky.

Only one choice.

He'd do anything in his power to keep Becky.

"You're doing this for our daughter," Claudette said. "I know that, Aiden."

He sighed. "And for you, Claudette. You shouldn't have gone through your pregnancy without me. It's past time I made it up to you—"

"Time has run out for that."

"But not for me to become our child's father. My name's not on Becky's birth certificate."

"Becky? Is that what my mother named her?" Claudette smiled, the rattle in her breathing making Aiden nervous.

"I named my favorite doll Becky when I was a kid. Is she pretty?"

"Becky's gorgeous. But Social Services is about to take her away and put her in foster care, because your mother's in a wheelchair. I'll take care of your mom. That'll be the easy part. Keeping Becky will be the hard part. Social Services needs proof that I'm her father."

"I can put it in writing, while I have the strength."

"Why didn't I think of that?" Because he was rattled out of his mind, that's why. A daughter he hadn't known about. His ex back from the dead. "Let's have you do that now and get it notarized."

Aiden spoke to a nurse, got paper and a pen, and before long, a hospital worker arrived to notarize Claudette's statement naming him Becky's biological father.

When the priest finally opened his book for the ceremony, Claudette's smile outshone her pallor. She looked almost radiant. He'd be a good husband. A good father, and they'd all take care of Ginny.

Storm—he couldn't think about Storm. He'd failed her . . . except that, because he'd come here with her, she'd fulfilled her psychic mandate. This was good then. Good, he told himself.

Claudette squeezed his hand.

He could do this.

He could.

Chapter Forty-one

STORM went shopping for cat supplies first, and brought everything back to Ginny's. Yes, she was putting off the inevitable, and she knew it.

She got lost on the way to the nursing home twice, whether by mistake or on purpose, hard to know, but she did finally find the right place.

She rode the elevator up to the fourth floor, but she couldn't bring herself to get out, so she rode back down again. On the second trip, she got out on Claudette's floor.

"Can you direct me to Claudette Langley's room?" she asked at the nurses' station.

When she heard people talking in the room, Storm stopped outside the door and stood at an angle so she could see in but not be seen. Aiden stood beside Claudette's bed, her hand in his, his other hand covering hers, cherishing her.

Claudette looked like a cadaver—well, maybe that was being kind. She looked like a skeleton, her skin stretched tightly over her bones. Being in a coma for a year had changed her dramatically from the woman in the pictures at Ginny's to an emaciated being with gray streaks in her red hair, but that could easily be fixed.

Aiden gazed down at Claudette as if she was the only woman in the world. Storm knew the gaze well, and she mourned its loss.

Claudette looked up at him with so much love and adoration that Storm might have doubled over in pain, if she weren't in such a public place. As it was, she held a hand to her mouth, to keep her grief from overflowing.

Someone else in the room spoke, and Storm stretched her neck to see a . . . priest, book open, stole around his neck, standing on the opposite side of the bed with a doctor and nurse. "Will you, Claudette Marie Langley, take Aiden Archer McCloud . . . ?"

Claudette's "I do" was heartfelt.

When it was Aiden's turn, he didn't answer . . . until the priest asked him a second time.

Storm backed away, but not before she heard Aiden's soft, "I do."

She felt a mind-numbing paralysis.

The man she loved—Aiden, the independent, no-commitment type—was committing.

Storm turned and began to walk aimlessly.

She picked up speed when she saw a door marked Stairs, and took it. In the stairwell, she shut the door behind her and doubled over as she leaned against it.

Married. Aiden was married.

She'd led him to his daughter, which led him to the woman he loved.

Insight and self-awareness hit her, a recognition of selfishness. She'd told herself all along that she was looking for Aiden's baby *for him*, but deep down, she'd wanted that baby for herself. For them.

She and Aiden had had nothing but a fling. No commitments; she'd known it from the beginning. Just because she broke her promise and fell in love with him didn't mean he'd fallen in love with her.

She'd tried not to. He'd annoyed the hell out of her with

his quick-flight response. She'd managed pretty well to keep it just sex, she thought . . . until she watched him falling for his daughter.

She'd been managing to fight that final tumble into love, until she woke in the middle of the night to find him watching Becky sleep, worrying about all the things a good dad should. That's when she'd faced the truth. She loved him.

"Damn me for an idiot!" She shook herself from her misery and took the stairs to the parking lot.

She managed to find Ginny's house without getting lost, a surprise, considering. Driving there was as close as she'd ever come to walking in her sleep. "Let me take you to the nursing home," she said to Ginny as she entered the house. "Claudette is awake and talking to Aiden."

She wouldn't tell Ginny they were married. That was their news to share.

"No," Ginny said. "I'm not ready." She looked heartsore, terribly so.

"Then I have no need to stay," Storm said. "I'm going to call for a car rental and see if they'll bring it here."

"For goodness sakes," Ginny said. "Take my car. I haven't had a license in more than a year."

Storm came out of her fog with Ginny's words. "The car's registered, right? I mean I just drove it."

"Of course."

"I'll buy it from you then. How much do you want?" Storm took out her checkbook.

Ginny put her hand on Storm's. "It's supposed to be towed away later today. Here's the paperwork the towing company asked for. I signed everything to turn it over to the new owner. I just needed to fill in the owner's name, but I didn't know the used car dealer's legal title. I'd rather put your name there."

Storm hugged the frail old woman. She was a sweetie, even if Storm didn't understand why she wouldn't see her daughter. "Listen to me, Ginny. If you ever need anything, here's my number, and you call me."

"I'll be fine, but you should stay. Aiden will need you when he gets back."

"Aiden will be too busy taking care of Claudette, Becky, and you. He won't let you go to assisted living, but if for some reason you end up in a home somewhere down the road, and you don't like it, call me, and I'll come and break you out. My sisters and I have a big house in Salem. You can have our grandmother's room. We didn't get to know her very well, and we missed that. She would have liked you. My sisters would, too."

"Aren't you sweet? I didn't know you had sisters."

"Hah. I came in a three-pack. There are two more *exactly* like me, as in identical. One's married and no longer lives with us. I also have two half sisters. One is my father's only legitimate child. The other . . . I believe . . . needs to be rescued. Did I tell you that we have a big house? The walls stretch, and we like it best when it's bulging at the seams. Call me. Now, do you still want me to take the rest of Claudette's jewelry to sell in my shop?"

Once Storm packed everything, including the jewelry, she went into the nursery for a long, cuddly good-bye with Becky, who called her Mama with a whimper as she walked out the door. Storm could only hope that when her real mother came home, Becky would forget her.

Driving away from the Langley house was almost as hard as driving away from Aiden at the nursing home had been.

She'd had no idea that finding Aiden's baby could change her life so radically. She hoped Ginny called. She hadn't been able to help Nana at the end, and she'd like a chance to make up for that with Ginny.

Besides, Aiden would return to his job at the castle, and he'd probably have Becky and Claudette with him, so if Ginny was living in Salem, she'd be near them.

Who was she kidding? Ginny would be with Claudette and Aiden.

Never mind how their nearness would affect her.

Ready or not, she was moving on.

She didn't have a choice.

Chapter Forty-two

AIDEN found Ginny sitting on her porch almost like the first time he'd seen her, though Becky wasn't with her.

Ginny's radar went up the minute she saw him.

Hard to believe he'd only known her for twenty-four hours.

Aiden stooped down in front of her wheelchair.

"She's gone, isn't she?" Ginny said before he had a chance to speak.

Aiden gave a half nod. "I married her, Ginny, and she passed peacefully in my arms not long after."

Ginny shuddered. "Always early, that girl. She was born early, and she died early. It's not even noon." Ginny ran a gnarled hand over his hair, and Aiden felt comforted. "I lost Claudette a long time ago," she said, "but I'm sorry for what you must be going through. You didn't come here expecting to have your world turned upside down like this, did you?"

"I pretty much did—once I started believing Storm— though I only expected an unknown baby. I didn't expect to fall in love with the whole family."

"Nobody should have a marriage certificate and a death certificate dated the same day," Ginny said.

"I don't deserve your sympathy. I was nearly too late. I should have been there for Claudette from the beginning. She'd be alive today, if—"

"Don't do that to yourself. Claudette made her own decisions. She *chose* not to tell you about the baby."

"Nah. I should have sensed something was up with her. I should be shot."

"Never. Becky needs you. And, frankly, selfish as it sounds on this of all days, I'm glad you're my son, glad you're Becky's father."

His parents had never been glad to have him as a son. Aiden wanted to share this moment with Storm, this feeling of being wanted, but it felt wrong to ask for her right now.

"Thank you for being there with Claudette at the end," Ginny said. "It would have killed me to lose her all over again. I said my good-byes a long time ago. Maybe it was a cop-out, not going, but I figured I had Becky to think about."

"Claudette hung on for you and Becky," Aiden told her. "She was too stubborn to let go until she was sure you were settled."

"That's my girl."

"I sent my lawyers to Social Services," Aiden said, "with Claudette's notarized statement that I'm Becky's father, a copy of our marriage license, and . . . everything." A copy of her death certificate would follow. "I'd like to take care of you both, if that's okay with you. Think you can live with your son-in-law and forgo that assisted-living place you've had your eye on?"

"I'll make the sacrifice." Ginny cupped his face and kissed his brow. "I can see why she loved you."

This must be what it felt like to have a mother, Aiden thought, clearing his throat at the childish notion. "Since Claudette donated her body to science, we don't have a funeral to deal with. She thought that was best. She sent you her love and her thanks. She knew she had yours, and she knew you had Becky. She said she went looking for me and used Storm as a conduit to bring me here."

Ginny smiled, but tears streamed silently down her cheeks. "Sounds like something Claudette would do. Very spiritual that one, like your Storm, I think. But how did Claudette do all that?" Ginny asked. "Was she spying on us?"

"Sort of."

Ginny militantly resettled her shawl. "She might have let me know."

"Did you ever see Claudette's name in the steam on your bathroom mirror?"

Ginny held a hand to her chest. "She didn't. I thought—"

Aiden nodded. "She did it to me, too, but I wiped it off. Aren't we dense?"

Ginny shook her head. "No, I think it was a matter of self-preservation."

"I have to agree. Hey, it's too quiet. Where's Becky? Playing with Storm?"

"Becky's napping inside. Storm . . . she went to the nursing home a few hours after you, Aiden, but she didn't stay long. Didn't you see her? She told me you were with Claudette."

Aiden ran a hand over his face, all the possibilities coming at him like prickling sleet in an ice storm. What could she have seen? Heard? If anything. "No, I . . . didn't." *But if Storm saw the wedding ceremony . . .*

When Aiden focused on Ginny, she seemed to understand his preoccupation.

"You're not a superhero, Aiden. There are only so many women you can save in one day. I'd say three out of four is a pretty good record."

"Storm left, didn't she?"

Ginny firmed her lips, and Aiden placed his head in her lap and let his tears fall.

He'd hardly had time to sort his grief when the front doorbell rang.

His knees nearly buckled when he realized that a man

and woman from Social Services had arrived to take Becky away.

"But my lawyers were supposed to take care of that!" Aiden shouted, more at the man than the woman. "I married her mother today. Besides being her biological father, I'm now her stepfather. Your office has the paperwork."

"Nobody told us not to come. We're sorry," the man said. "We have a job to do. Is the baby ready?"

"Of course not," Ginny snapped, her fury greater than her sorrow. "We didn't think she was going. Call your office to be sure. Please."

The male social worker instructed the woman to call. They exchanged speaking glances. She rolled her eyes, flipped open her cell, and called, but their orders hadn't changed.

Aiden called the foundation's lawyers again to tell them what was happening, and then he held Becky, who cried as if she knew something was terribly wrong, while Ginny packed her things. He felt as if he'd been stabbed, and his heart was bleeding.

The couple from Social Services waited patiently to complete their assignment.

Aiden refused to let either of them carry Becky to their car. He about broke as he strapped his daughter into a car seat in which she would be taken away from him.

"Da," she said, touching his lips. He held that tiny hand against his mouth and closed his eyes.

"We have to go," the male social worker said.

It was all Aiden could do not to deck the bastard. "Rip out my heart, why don't you?"

"If everything you said is true, you could have her back in a few days."

"Days! She doesn't belong in the system for a minute."

The male social worker tried to get him to step away from the car, but Aiden stuck his head inside again and gave Becky one last kiss on her cheek. "Bye, baby girl. Daddy loves you. You'll be back soon."

Becky cried and called "Da Da" as the man shut her door, and Aiden was forced to step aside.

He stood in the road watching the car disappear down the street, the echo of Becky's cry, the lump in his throat, and the ache in his chest about bringing him to his knees.

He'd lost a year of her life before he realized she existed, and now he'd lost her, again, within a day of finding her.

Chapter Forty-three

STORM began getting pictures in her mind's eye of Claudette's jewelry as she left Cape May's Victorian shops and seaside cottages behind, but the jewelry images dimmed to sepia tones until they turned gray and disappeared altogether.

In their place came a whisper in the voice of the woman who'd spoken her vows with Aiden: "Thank you. I'm ready."

Storm touched her sea horse necklace, an oddly treasured reminder of the handsome and beloved knight she'd lost to a damsel in true distress . . . the damsel who'd crafted the sea horse.

"Merry part," Storm said, wishing Claudette a safe journey—not to the afterlife or the Summerland as a Celtic sea horse totem would suggest—but in her marriage to Aiden.

Since Aiden's wife—heart-stopping words—since . . . Claudette had made so many Celtic totem symbols of the sea, Storm figured she understood the significance of the sea horse.

Storm wondered how Claudette felt about dragons. She didn't remember seeing a single one in her jewelry collection, but that was heartless. She didn't want them unhappy. She simply coveted a family, like Claudette's, for herself.

Except . . . there would never be another Aiden.

Pepper. She had to think about Pepper. Storm filled Ginny's gas tank then pulled into a drive-through for a burger, remembering what Aiden liked on his, and how they'd squished it when their dragons got naughty on the picnic table.

She took a bite of her sawdust burger and wondered what kind of junk food Pepper liked. Taking the Garden State Parkway, she saw the sign: Atlantic City—45 miles.

"Pay attention to the signs," she said as she turned on the radio to "Big Girls Don't Cry."

Signs on top of signs.

She took the Atlantic City Expressway. Dragon's blood, she missed Aiden. "Oh!" She hiccupped—a half sob and half laugh. *No more dragon anything for you, girl. You really do need to get yourself a new expletive, and you need to find a new focus.*

She *needed* to stop feeling sorry for herself.

She did allow herself to feel cheated, though, by fate. Difficult to be gracious about something you did for love—even if you didn't understand why you were doing it—when the recipient of your love married someone else, good reason or not.

She missed Aiden something fierce. Tears-in-her-eyes fierce. Never-wanting-another-man's-touch fierce. Pulling-over-for-a-rip-roaring-pity-party fierce. Storm let it all out until there was nothing left in her but a sniffle and a scratchy throat. She blew her nose, repaired her smudged makeup, and started the car.

She missed Becky. Hard to believe how fast she'd fallen for that little girl. But she had Pepper. Maybe. Her instincts were more than a little skewed today. She believed Pepper needed her, but she couldn't hear Pepper crying. Maybe, like her, Pepper never—well, rarely—cried.

Maybe Pepper just got sarcastic or silent.

Storm drove around Atlantic City several times looking for Pepper's school, wishing she remembered the roads Aiden had taken to get there. Hard to believe that so much neon glitz and high-stakes flash could live beside such abject poverty. This city had it all.

She finally found the brick school trimmed in granite with teal doors—retro meets new millennium—and recognized the elaborate escutcheon at its peak. Out front, buses made a never-ending line. Storm checked her watch. Only two o'clock, but it felt like ten at night. What a long day: getting up at Becky time, losing the man she loved, and now, after all that, here she was about to stage another rescue. She hoped.

Storm parked behind the buses and waited for the end-of-day school bell.

The first rush of students separated into bus lines like ants at a picnic. One by one, the buses pulled away.

The rest of the students came out in a second assault, racing in every direction. Pepper was, clearly, the odd girl out, a misfit like her, trailing behind the wild legions, alone, dragging her heels and her backpack, as if she dreaded the thought of going home. Or maybe that was wishful thinking. Storm lowered the power window on the passenger side. "Pepper?" she called. "Need a ride home?"

Pepper's bright red head came up fast. "I didn't dare believe it, but you did come!" She came to the window and leaned against the car door, not so much the sulky kid with attitude that she'd been a couple of days before.

"I take it you're glad I came back?" Storm asked.

Caught with the electric fence around her feelings unplugged, Pepper checked her enthusiasm and worked up a little attitude. "I could care less." She shrugged. "Why did you?"

"I wanted to spend some time with my baby sister."

"Cut the baby crap." Pepper slung her bag over her shoulder and stepped away from the car.

"Okay," Storm said. "I'll come clean, though we

shouldn't be having this conversation until I talk to your mother—"

"*Your* mother."

"Right, her. I hoped you might want to come home with me . . . for a trial visit."

"Not interested." Pepper walked slowly down the sidewalk, and Storm drove the car as slowly beside her.

"Why not?"

Pepper huffed. "No thanks. I'm always on trial. I'd be afraid to burp wrong and get shipped back."

Storm keyed into Pepper's negative vibes, and they spelled insecurity in caps. "What's the usual threat?" she asked, playing a hunch.

"Boarding school."

"Forget the trial, then. Vickie didn't try us out when she took us in. She just kept us and set down some rules."

Pepper stopped, opened the car door, got in, and heaved her backpack over her head into the backseat.

Warlock yowled.

"Hey, you have a cat!"

"You mean, he's not dead or concussed?"

Chapter Forty-four

"HEY, he's in a cat carrier, and I didn't know he was there. Sorry, Storm kitty."

"Warlock. His name is Warlock, because he's black."

"Great name for a Storm cat." Pepper crossed her arms. "What kind of rules?"

"Be nice to our cats. Go to school."

"I love cats, and I'm too young to argue about school, except . . ."

"Except?"

"Can I go to public school?"

Storm thought about the possible pitfalls for a rebel like Pepper. "I'll trade you private school for public school with rules."

Pepper slapped her plaid skirt. "I knew it. Let me out."

Storm hit the childproof locks. "Here's the thing: The minute you start using the skills you learned at your mother's knee, like theft, deceit, or any I haven't yet discovered—"

"Like treachery, extortion, and blackmail?" Pepper asked.

"Yeah . . . like those." Storm did a double take and hoped she was joking. "Felonies, misdemeanors—or any behavior inappropriate to a ten-year-old," Storm said, "and I'll transfer you from public to private school, but not to a boarding school."

"Deal," Pepper said.

"I'm not done. No goth in junior high. In high school, if goth is your thing, you'll have my support."

"Sounds like we're thinking long-term here," Pepper said.

Storm guessed she was, which surprised her, but she was impulsive, and stubborn, and as tentatively pleased as Pepper. "If you like Salem."

"I will. Let's go."

"Whoa. We need your mother's permission first. I'm never kidnapping anybody again."

"Marvelanne wouldn't care if you did. Again?"

"She's your mother," Storm said. "She needs to okay this."

"She's *your* mother, too. Again?" Pepper said. "You'll never kidnap anybody *again*?"

Storm rolled her eyes. "It was more of an abduction than a kidnapping, and he was a consenting adult, more or less, and I *know* that you and I have the same mother."

"Sucks doesn't it?"

"The word *sucks*, among other peppery curses, will also be put in cold storage until high school."

"Tell me about the abduction."

"Sure, when you're twenty-one." Maybe by then she'd be able to talk about it without getting choked up. "How about I take you to your house, then I'll drive over to see Marvelanne at the casino, and if she says it's okay, I'll come back and take you home with me?"

Pepper turned to face her in the seat. "For how long, precisely?" She picked up Storm's purse.

"That's up to your mother. How long would you like to stay? We have two other sisters, Harmony and Destiny, and a half sister on my father's side, Vickie, who'll adopt you, too."

"Adopt?" Pepper looked up from ransacking Storm's purse.

"We're getting ahead of ourselves. Is that what you want? You want out of here that bad? For good? How old are you?"

"Thirteen."

"Pepper . . ."

"Okay, twelve."

"Pepper?"

Her sister huffed. "Eleven. Exactly. Tomorrow. I didn't mean to be pushy. If you really wanted to take me home with you, you would have asked your mother first."

Storm took her birth control pills from Pepper's hand, dropped them in her bag, and put it behind her seat. "You mean I would have asked *your* mother."

"No," Pepper said. "This sister stuff has its perks. I'll never have to think of Marvelanne as *my* mother again. I'll be happy to think of her only as *yours*."

Storm couldn't blame her. "I came here first because I wanted to know how you felt before I asked Marvelanne, but I guess you just answered my question."

"So now you know. How long can I stay?"

"I thought I'd take you home and we'd see if you like it. If you don't, I'll bring you back. By the way, you can come visit your mother anytime."

"*Your* mother. No thanks."

Storm hadn't thought that a kind of peace would settle in so soon after losing Aiden, but she and Pepper seemed to belong to each other. Pepper needed her, and she'd discovered that she liked being needed. She was tired of being the third twin with little purpose besides shock value.

Maybe Pepper was the reason she'd been lured to Atlantic City in the first place. Not to find her mother, but her sister. "Let's go. Direct me to your house."

It was little more than a shack. The view: a parking lot of stretch limos surrounded by more shacks. Pepper started the chores on her list, then she showed Storm around the winterized old summer house. The decor: early dump, except for Marvelanne's bedroom, and all the gorgeous clothes stuffed in her closet.

"I don't think your mother would like it if she knew we were rifling through her things." *Her expensive things,* Storm thought.

"She wouldn't, because she wouldn't want anybody to know how much child support she spends on herself."

Storm and her sisters had lived in dumps growing up, but their father had been a better mother than Pepper's, and he'd spent less money on himself than on them, even with the booze. "I'm off to see your mother."

"*Your* mother."

"*Yours!*" Storm said. "I know. Let's call her Destiny's mother?"

"Works for me. I'll pack while I wait."

"You'll have to unpack if Marvelanne won't give you up."

"Storm, let me give you some advice," Pepper said. "Tell her she can keep her lucrative child support scam, and she'll ship me out so fast your head will spin."

"You're ten years old, Pepper, not thirty."

"I'll be eleven tomorrow."

Storm ruffled her paprika screw curls. "Let's see if we can make it a good birthday."

The minute Storm walked up to the cocktail waitress in the cool, noisy casino, Marvelanne looked up at her and said, "No. Absolutely not!"

Chapter Farty-five

"YOU don't even know what I want," Storm told the mother she almost wished she hadn't found, except for the fact that she found Pepper as a result . . . at Marvelanne's instigation, come to think of it.

"I know *who* you want," Marvelanne said. "Pepper, and you can't have her. The answer is still no."

"Why not?" Storm asked. "You won't miss her. And if you didn't want me to take her, why did you introduce me to Pepper in the first place? This was a setup. We both know it."

"I need to talk to a lawyer," Marvelanne said.

"Good idea." Storm fished her cell phone from her messy purse and called Destiny. "Des, let me talk to Reggie. I need the name of the lawyer handling her custody suit."

Marvelanne reached over and flipped Storm's phone shut. "Don't you understand? Pepper's father is stinking rich!"

"And you don't care that Pepper is stinking miserable?"

They were gathering an audience among the high-stakes

slot players, so Marvelanne took Storm's arm and propelled her outside.

Storm found the contact surreal. Her mother had just touched her for the first time since the day she was born, and she felt . . . *nothing* . . . except the heat of the July sun on her head and the cool rush of air-conditioning escaping out the casino doors.

"Where would you take Pepper?" Marvelanne asked. "*If* I let you take her."

"Salem, Massachusetts. We have a house on Pickering Wharf."

"The house your father grew up in, you mean?"

"Yeah, it's Vickie's house now. I'd give you the address and telephone number. If Pepper wanted to come back, I'd bring her."

"She wouldn't."

"If *you* wanted her back, I'd bring her."

Marvelanne raised a skeptical brow. "You'd have to hog-tie her, shove a gag in her mouth, and put her in your trunk to transport her. What about school?"

"I wouldn't let her quit school."

Marvelanne bit her lip. "If her school returns his tuition checks, he'll know something is up, and he'll get nosy, or worse, he'll stop sending child support."

Storm wished—"Marvelanne, what name did you use to sign our birth certificates?"

"I was in hiding. I used M. Anne Buford."

Storm sighed in resignation. Marvelanne was, indeed, for good or ill, her biological mother. "For all the support you shower on Pepper, you're already taking money under false pretenses. You're not raising her. She's raising you. That place is a sty."

"Pepper lies."

"She took me home with her. Showed me her room, *your* room, and your big screen TV. She put in a batch of laundry and vacuumed while we talked, the first in a list of chores with her name on them. When does Pepper play?"

The mother of the year huffed.

"Look," Storm said, "if you keep taking child support, it's on your karmic credit card. All I want is Pepper."

"Why, in God's name?"

"Nice thing to say about your own kid. She's my sister, and I love my sisters. I want her to grow up better than we did."

"What will Harmony and Destiny think about the brat gumming up their lives?"

"They'll take Pepper in and love her the same way Vickie took us in and loved us."

"Pepper is exactly like you," Marvelanne snapped. "I knew it the first time I held her. She looked right at me, and she defied me to screw up, as if she knew I would."

Telepathic communication at birth? "Which one of you is psychic?" Storm asked. "You or Pepper?"

"Both of us, I think. You and your sisters are, too, right?"

Hmm. They must get their magick from their father's side of the family and their psychic abilities from their mother's side. Who knew? "All three of us."

Marvelanne snuffed her cigarette and placed the flat of her hand on the casino door. "Then you already know that I'm keeping Pepper. End of discussion."

Chapter Forty-six

WHEN Storm returned to Marvelanne's house, Pepper was sitting on the curb, with a stuffed dog under her arm, drawing in the dirt beside her backpack, a blue suitcase with a broken handle, a radio box, and two grocery bags.

When Storm got out of the car and Pepper looked up, she was furious. "She thinks she's going to stop me from going, doesn't she?"

Uh-oh, Storm thought. She knew that confrontational look. She'd worn it plenty in her day.

"Come inside," Pepper said. "Marvelanne's got a surprise in store." Her sister ran into the house and left all her earthly possessions on the curb, except for the stuffed dog, and Storm followed her.

She found Pepper in Marvelanne's room dragging a cardboard box of what looked to be bookkeeping records from the bottom of her mother's closet. She hefted the box and dumped the contents on Marvelanne's bed.

Storm cringed. "Pepper, I don't think this is a good—"

Pepper pulled out a folder and stopped her scold with a practiced cheer, her body forming the letters. Give me an

E . . . Give me an X . . . By the time she ended on the floor in a full split, she'd spelled the word *extortion* with a cat-ate-the-canary grin.

Storm pretended not to be charmed. "Have you lost your mind?"

"Nope. Here's my ticket out." Pepper handed Storm a folder of canceled child support checks, different colors, different addresses, and different signatures. Four sets. "I have four fathers," Pepper said proudly. "Kind of makes me a medical marvel, don't you think?"

For a minute, Storm lost her ability to speak.

Her mother was a con artist.

A thief.

Pepper really did need her.

"What exactly do you think I should do with these?" Storm asked, slapping a wad of checks against her palm.

"Tell Marvelanne that you know about her scam, and if she doesn't let you take me, you'll tell my fathers about . . . my other fathers."

"Okay, let me get this straight," Storm said. "Your mother is an extortionist—"

"*Your* mother, and, yes, big time."

"And you're a blackmailer?"

"No," Pepper said. "You'd be the blackmailer. I've been picking my battles and waiting to use this info for something big, like a car when I was old enough to drive, but now I'm giving it to you."

"How very generous of you." Flying foxglove, she and her sisters had played the system, Storm thought, but this kid was ready for juvenile hall. "I'm gonna have sooooo much to unteach you, young lady, starting with the fact that I'm *not* blackmailing your mother."

"*Your* mother."

"I wish you'd stop reminding me of that."

"What's going on here?" Marvelanne asked, making Storm and Pepper jump, and scream, and scare each other . . . and when they realized it, they fell over each other laughing.

Marvelanne was not amused by this sign of sibling bonding. She grabbed Pepper by the shirt collar and shook her, choking her, until Marvelanne yelped and let go to grab her arm.

"You!" she said turning on Storm. "I only get zapped when that brat's pissing the hell out of me and *you're* around."

"So stop manhandling her." She needed to get her sister out of here.

Pepper stepped in front of Storm as if to protect *her*, and Storm got the warm fuzzies. "Okay, here's the thing, Mommie Dearest," Pepper said. "I've known for some time that I have four fathers, and I've talked to all of them on the phone in the last year. The first time I called them, I said you wanted us to connect. Short talks. Nice guys. I think they like me better than you do."

"Yeah, well they don't have to live with you." Marvelanne lit a cigarette and took a long drag.

Storm called in the big wings.

> *Guardian angels,*
> *Hear my plea.*
> *Set Pepper free*
> *To her sisters, three.*
>
> *Childhood hard won,*
> *Hurt be undone.*
> *So mote it be done,*
> *With harm to none.*

"I could get one of my fathers to take me," Pepper said. "Ralph, I think, but he'd probably want to tell the others they're not my fathers. On the other hand, I could go quietly and live with my sisters."

Pepper raided Marvelanne's makeup stash and stuffed her pockets with goodies while her mother watched. "Think about how nice life would be for you, if you didn't have to live with me," Pepper added, as if to emphasize her little demonstration. "You wouldn't have to pay for my food, clothes, doctor, dentist, or send me to a movie every time you bring a man home."

Pepper turned to Storm and rolled her eyes. "Different loser every week."

Chapter Forty-seven

MARVELANNE took another puff on her cigarette, her face impassive, but Storm saw that her nicotine-brown fingers were no longer as steady as they'd been outside the casino.

"I'll do you a favor before I go," Pepper added with an enticing lilt to her voice. "I'll call the 'dad' who pays my tuition and tell him to send the check to you every month, instead of the school. I'll tell him you don't want to ask, but the school isn't respecting your rights as my mother, and they would if *you* wrote the checks."

"Call him," Marvelanne said, with the confidence of someone calling a bluff.

Pepper knew the number by heart. "Ralph, Dad, it's Pepper . . ."

Storm wanted to put a stop to the deception, but she thought about the day she and her sisters were thrown out of college for nonpayment of tuition. She remembered driving their battered van home to find that their father had sold the house and taken off for parts unknown.

She remembered their fear while driving toward the

home of the grandmother they hardly knew, praying she'd take them in. She would have pulled a con for a place to sleep that night. Lucky for them, they found Vickie, who had inherited Nana's house and her big heart.

Now it was time for Pepper to have that kind of good luck, even if she took a slightly skewed proactive stand. She was only doing what came naturally, biting the crooked hand that resented feeding her.

Pepper was, in essence, buying her way out of hell, and who could blame her for trying? She completed her call while Marvelanne's face turned the color of stripped drywall.

"Storm won't blackmail you," Pepper said, "because you didn't raise her to be devious the way you raised me, so negotiations are up to me. But look on the bright side, this is our last battle. I wanna go home with Storm, and I'll forget everything I know."

"Suppose one of your dads comes looking to meet you?"

"Flying foxglove," Storm said. "For a con, you're pretty slow on the uptake, Marvelanne. You tell the truth. She's staying with her sisters. Which reminds me, I need a copy of her birth certificate, before we go."

"Why, to prove she's your sister?" Marvelanne raised a knowing brow. "Not so generous after all, are you?"

"I need it to put her in school," Storm said, placing a hand on Pepper's shoulder. "I have a gift for rescuing kids, Marvelanne, but this one, I'm keeping, whoever's name is on her birth certificate."

Pepper stamped her foot. "Marvelanne Buford, did you steal me to get all that child support money?"

"There isn't enough money in the world that could force me to raise a kid, especially you, if I didn't have to." Marvelanne snorted, went to the mess of papers on her bed, and shuffled through until she handed Storm Pepper's birth certificate and medical records.

"Then why have you been fighting us?" Storm asked.

"Storm," Pepper said. "For a rescuer, *you're* pretty slow

on the uptake. She was looking to make a profit on the deal. Leaping lizards, are you naive."

Storm's cell phone rang. It was King's lawyer, the one handling his custody battle for Reggie.

Storm went outside to talk to him, grateful that Reggie had called the man on her behalf. He gave her some good advice.

"Are we ready to go?" Storm asked going back inside. "Marvelanne, that was my lawyer. You have to write and sign a letter saying that I'm taking Pepper with your permission. To protect me from kidnapping charges."

"Or else?" Marvelanne crossed her arms in satisfaction. For an extortionist, she was no poker player.

"Or else?" Storm repeated, using her cell phone to snap a picture of the assorted support checks.

"Okay, okay."

Marvelanne made a grab for Storm's cell, but she shoved it in her pocket. "Write the note."

Marvelanne did, and signed it, a cigarette dangling from her mouth the whole time. "I sure hope Harmony's rich husband can afford this kid."

Okay, so she was gonna hit King up for money later. They'd cross that bridge . . . later. Permanent custody, however, they would deal with sooner than later.

"Okay, Pepper. Let's go home."

"Yay!" Pepper Snoopy-danced her way out the door, not even saying good-bye to Marvelanne. When she stopped and ran back inside, Storm watched, but all Pepper did was grab her stuffed dog. "Almost forgot Freckles!" At the car door, she looked earnestly up at Storm. "She's gonna ask for money at some point. You know that, right?"

"I figured."

"I thought you should know."

"Our castle-owning brother-in-law has some great lawyers. I think we'll be okay."

"Yes!" Pepper cheered as if the Sox had won the World Series again.

"You sure you don't want to run back in and say good-bye to your mother?" Storm asked Pepper.

"That's a joke, right?"

They packed the car together and got on the road.

For a few minutes, Pepper sang, "I Gotta Go My Own Way," and suddenly she stopped and turned Storm's way. "Are you the boss of me?"

"Absolutely. Buckle up."

"Are Harmony and Destiny the bosses of me, too?"

"Absolutely."

"Who gets final say in the event of a disagreement or a . . . three-way split?"

"Vickie?"

"My halfish sister? Okay. She could be impartial."

More thoughtful silence as they left slums, casinos, and board game street signs behind.

"Storm? Where's home?"

"I didn't tell you? Salem, Massachusetts. Ever heard of it?"

"Sure. I love to read about Salem. Are there really witches there?"

Uh-oh. "Yeah, there are. Does that bother you?"

"You wanna know the truth?"

"Always."

Storm watched Pepper brace herself for a reprimand. "I kinda like to read books about witchcraft, and I try spells in secret."

Oh yeah, she was their sister. "It can be dangerous to practice magick, if you don't know what you're doing," Storm said, "and did you know that whatever you send out into the universe comes back to you times three, good or bad? We'll teach you to do it right so you don't get hurt, okay?"

"We?"

"My sisters and I. I should have told you up-front, I guess, but it's like announcing your religion, which nobody thinks to do. I'm a witch. We all are. And we're psychic, too."

"Gnarly! I think I might be psychic, too."

"Destiny's mother thinks you might be. Is Pepper your real name?"

"Afraid so."

"Did Destiny's mother ever say why?"

"Sure. She said that when she held me for the first time, she knew I was going to spoil the taste of life forever."

"She's—" Storm clamped her mouth shut.

"Yeah," Pepper said, "she sure is. Throw a little water on her and watch her melt. Her name is *not* Glinda."

Chapter Forty-eight

WATCHING Pepper in the passenger seat, out of the corner of her eye, Storm could practically see her unclenching and becoming a little girl again. Storm only hoped that she could live up to this new sister's expectations

Pepper looked at her as if she could sense her insecurity. "Where's that great-looking guy you had with you the last time you came to Atlantic City?"

"We broke up."

"Too bad. I thought you'd keep him around for a while. Great eye candy."

"We have to turn you back into an eleven-year-old," Storm said, "and I know exactly where to start."

"Where?"

"For tonight, we'll stay in a hotel, order room service, and watch a movie of your choice . . . not porn. And tomorrow morning, I'll treat you to a birthday surprise at a destination of my choice."

Storm couldn't afford a suite like Aiden, but they found a nice hotel with a room service menu to satisfy their junk food palates. Pepper chose to watch *Practical Magic*, a favorite of Storm's, too, and when the midnight margaritas song came on, they got up to dance.

The following morning, on the way to her surprise, Pepper looked a little down, and it broke Storm's heart. "Do you miss her, Pepper?"

"Nah, I just wish she'd miss me. I can feel how happy she is now that I'm gone."

Storm put a hand on Pepper's arm and squeezed. "Be happy. It's your birthday!"

They got to the elephant poop carnival by eleven. Winkie the Clown recognized her and Warlock, on his leash, right away, and came over to say hello. Winkie didn't mention their first meeting.

Pepper was impressed, and Storm was grateful.

"I love the music at carnivals," Pepper said. "I used to hang out around the rides in Atlantic City just to hear the music."

First thing they did was get their faces painted. Storm got a cat face, and Pepper became a Dalmatian puppy, spots and all, some of which came off as she ate corn dogs, pizza, cotton candy, and funnel cakes, two of them.

"You're gonna turn into a funnel cake," Storm said.

"Can we go on every ride?"

That was the real reason Storm hadn't taken her to a gigundous amusement park. She'd hate for Pepper see her throw up on a roller coaster. Besides, this place had called to her as much now, maybe more, as when it was an open field. Now happy family vibes marched beside some amazingly warm and erotic memories. Boy, did it.

She'd been blissfully, ignorantly happy that day. She must be nuts to have come back, and yet this is where her heart had led her.

As if to prove her point, she heard a little one cry, a frightened, "I'm scared," that came with the scent of candy apples. "Let's go find the candy apple stand," Storm said.

"Yes!" Pepper did a mini cheer, but thankfully, the word *extortion* was not mentioned. "I never had a candy apple. Gotta try one."

"Of course you do. Remind me to buy you a barf bag for the drive home."

Pepper stopped when Storm got on all fours beside the stand. "Storm, you're embarrassing me."

"And it's gonna get worse. Get down here and crawl through this small space. I don't fit."

Pepper looked at her as if she'd sprouted a second head. "Did I leave one fruitcake behind to go home with another?"

"Kinda, but I think there's a little boy stuck back there. He needs to be led out."

"You just *know* this, right?" Pepper said. "Like I *knew* you belonged to me the minute I met you?"

"Did you?" Storm's heart expanded. "Yes, sweetheart, that's how I know."

"Okay." Pepper crawled through a tiny space between a generator and the side of the candy apple booth until Storm lost sight of her.

"Is he in there?" she called.

"I don't—oh, yeah, he's really little and he's afraid of me, Sis."

Fine time for Pepper to claim kinship, when she couldn't hug her. "Will he let you take him back through the crawl space?"

"No. He keeps moving away from me, shaking his head."

Probably around two, Storm thought. "Stay with him."

Storm asked the owner of the candy apple stand to make an announcement that they'd found a little boy by the stand, which he did. She tried to buy a large lollypop for bait and he waved away her money. Back on all fours— though she'd attracted a crowd—Storm reached into the space with the lollypop. "Pepper, take this and see if you can lure him out with it."

"I don't have to," Pepper said. "*You're* luring him out with it."

"Okay." Storm wiggled the pop as she drew her arm back slowly, until she saw the blond toddler crawling through the space on his knees. When she could reach him, she gave him the lollypop, and while he got busy trying to unwrap it, Storm pulled him the rest of the way out. Pepper came out two seconds later, in time to get her share of the applause.

A man came breaking through the crowd and whisked the little boy out of her arms. "Jeffrey! Thank God," he said, hugging the boy, whose only interest was the lollypop. "How can I thank you?" he asked Storm.

"Thank my sister. I didn't fit in the space Jeffrey had crawled into. Hello, Jeffrey."

The stand owner came around and blocked the dangerous opening and gave her and Pepper their choice of candy apples. Pepper chose a chocolate-and-caramel-covered apple, and Storm wondered where she was going to put it.

As the crowd dissipated, Winkie high-fived her.

"That was cool," Pepper said. "You're like Super Psychic."

She was more like superstupid, because now she heard another baby crying, except that it sounded like Becky, with baby powder, apricot scents, and all, and suddenly she was looking for Aiden around every corner. Wow, she had it bad. Did people wither away and die from the disappointment of terminally hopeless lovesickness?

As they walked, Pepper bounced around, eating her candy apple, recounting her own psychic experiences, and they were significant. "This is my best birthday ever. Well, it's the first I've ever celebrated. Let's go on the Ferris wheel. I've never been on one. It looks scary."

"You never went on the Ferris wheel in Atlantic City?"

"Get real," Pepper said.

"Okay, but if we're going on rides, we have to put Warlock in the car. We'll buy her a cup of vanilla ice cream, get a bottle of water to replenish hers, and leave the windows cracked so she can catch a breeze."

Later, on the Ferris wheel, Storm managed to make Pepper laugh, but when they got to the top, her emotions got the better of her, though she tried not to let it show.

She'd been here last with Aiden, after all. But Pepper's psychic sensitivity must have kicked in, because she leaned into her and pretended to yawn.

Storm put an arm around her shoulder. "I never cry," she said, wiping her cheeks.

"Me either," Pepper said, wiping her own. "Though I almost did the morning I met you when I stood inside the door of the school and watched you drive away."

"You did? Why didn't I sense that? I usually sense children crying."

"I told you. I never cry. I get bratty or silent. Very silent."

"Aha, and that's all I could hear as we left, a heavy silence."

"That was me!"

"I was so shocked that Marvelanne was my mother, and surprised that I couldn't hear Aiden's baby crying anymore, that I never thought . . . I'm sorry I didn't understand right away what you needed."

"No problem. Heck, I can't believe you came back."

"I couldn't get you out of my mind, silence or not."

Pepper took another bite of her apple. "Would you have come if you were still with the eye candy guy?"

"Aiden? Absolutely. It was his idea to drive around and see if you were okay before we left."

"That's because I—"

"You what?"

"I . . . watched you leave the restaurant. I think he spotted me. You really miss him, don't you?"

"I really do."

"Maybe he'll come find you."

"With his wife?"

"The two-timer!"

"He wasn't married when we stopped to see you. It's a long story."

"Tell me in the car then, 'kay? Can we go on the teacups after this?"

"I'll throw up," Storm threatened.

"Nah, only sissies barf on the teacups, but it's okay to puke on roller coasters. That's what I do. Hey," Pepper said, "eye candy alert, one o'clock."

Storm looked down from three-quarters up the Ferris wheel to see Aiden pushing Ginny in her wheelchair with Becky on her lap. "Oh my Goddess. What is *he* doing here? I can't take this now. I'm not ready to see him and Claudette together. Pepper, stay with me, okay? Pretend you're sick, so we have to leave."

Pepper patted her hand. "I'll take care of everything."

Aiden and Ginny had spotted them and were waiting when she and Pepper got off the Ferris wheel. Storm homed in on Aiden and couldn't take her gaze from his, because he seemed to have eyes only for her.

"Good to see you, Storm," he said. "Cute cat face."

"Meow." She'd *had* to get a painted kitty face. "What are you all doing here?"

"I . . . wanted to show Becky our . . . carnival," he said, something in his voice more personal than was comfortable, under the circumstances. "When we drove into the parking lot, Ginny recognized your car, so we knew you were here, and we came looking for you."

Storm put her hands on Pepper's shoulders, as much for support as anything. "You remember Pepper?"

"I'm a Dalmatian." Pepper barked, making Becky giggle. "Storm rescued me."

Aiden looked up at her. "She rescued me, too."

Storm broke eye contact first to run her hand through a thatch of paprika screw curls. "It's Pepper's birthday. She's eleven today."

"Happy birthday, Pepper," Aiden said, and cleared his throat. "I'm glad Storm went back for you. It wasn't my imagination, then, that you mouthed the words, 'Take me with you,' before we left?"

Pepper stiffened beneath Storm's hands. "I never—" She looked up at Storm, then down at her sneakers, and kicked a clump of dirt. "Yeah, I did."

Storm really looked at Aiden then, ate him up with her

gaze, while she tried to survive a buckling in her knees and heart. "Why didn't you tell me she wanted to come with us?"

"Your heart was already broken, Storm. I thought you needed to come to terms with meeting your mother first, and I didn't think Marvelanne would let Pepper go lightly. I planned to tell you, but when we got to Cape May, everything went haywire, and we never got a chance to talk. You rescue kids. I *knew* you'd rescue your own sister when the time was right. Pepper, this is my mother-in-law, Mrs. Langley—"

"Call me Ginny, sweetheart."

"Hi, Ginny."

"And this dumpling is my daughter, Becky," Aiden added, lifting Becky in his arms. "I still find the words a shock. My daughter. Storm helped me find Becky, Pepper. I didn't know she existed."

"So Storm rescued Becky, too," Pepper said.

"And me, too," Ginny added.

"Mama?" Becky raised her arms to Storm.

Storm didn't know where to turn, but she wished she could find a hole to crawl into. Where the hell was Claudette? How could Aiden leave his sick wife at a nursing home to come to a carnival several hours down the pike? "We have to go now," Storm said. "Pepper is feeling sick."

Pepper made a ridiculous attempt at fake gagging.

Storm rolled her eyes and pulled Pepper against her with an affectionate squeeze. "Forget it, Princess Funnel Cake, we'll cross *actress* off that list of things you want to be when you grow up."

Chapter Forty-nine

GINNY winked at Pepper, but she took Storm's hand. "Don't run, Storm. Aiden is a widower. Claudette died shortly after the ceremony. I know you were trying to make me believe she'd get well, but people rally before they die. It's something I've seen often. I knew that's what was happening. I'm sure Claudette knew, too."

"Oh, Ginny." Storm kissed her cheek. "I'm so sorry. Claudette was a good woman." Storm looked up. "Aiden, what can I say?"

"Mama?" Becky whimpered, and Storm picked her up, her heart full of love for this little girl she barely knew. Aiden's little girl. Maybe that's why she loved her.

Becky touched her black kitty nose. "Nose," she said. Then she examined the black face paint on her finger and smeared it on her own nose. She turned to show her father and smear some on him. "Nose," she repeated, amusing them. "Mama," she said, turning back to Storm. "Mama." Becky nodded, circled Storm's neck with her little arms, and hugged her so tight, she grunted.

"She missed you," Aiden said. "Your absence was difficult to explain."

"She's been clingy like that since Social Services took her," Ginny added.

"They took her!" Storm clasped Becky tighter. "What happened? How did you get her back?"

"After they came to the house with their paperwork," Ginny said, "and after Aiden kept from beating the male social worker to a pulp, they took Becky and drove away. I don't know which one of us was more broken. But Aiden rose to the occasion. He called his lawyers, and together they stormed Social Services with his marriage license, and Claudette's notarized statement that Aiden was Becky's father. One department already had the paperwork, of course, because Aiden had dropped it off earlier, while a different department had Becky."

"They're overworked, Ginny," Aiden said. "That was easy to see. And they didn't hurt her. One worker confessed that it might have taken a day or so for the paperwork to be processed, which isn't unreasonable. Hell, I sometimes take days to get my paperwork done. They'd tried to console Becky, but we were scared to death, in the meantime."

"I'll bet you were," Storm said.

"She didn't stop sobbing for an hour after they handed her back to me." Aiden stroked his daughter's head on Storm's shoulder so his knuckles grazed Storm's cheek with every stroke. The awareness between them was alive, the communication almost as strong as when she spoke telepathically with her sisters. He wanted them to be a family, and he was trying to show her how it could be.

Storm's emotions were in turmoil. Actually, she was scared to death. He'd just lost his wife. How could he possibly be thinking clearly?

His touch was torture, wonderful bad, as was the feel of Becky filling her arms. Then that giggle as Becky smudged her face paint with obviously amusing results. Storm wallowed in the silk of Becky's skin, her dark flyaway curls, and the sweet, familiar scent of baby powder.

It hurt so much knowing their reunion would end that Storm tried to give Becky back to Aiden sooner, rather than later, but Becky refused to leave her, not even for Ginny. "Want Mama," she said, snuggling in, and a bittersweet lump formed in Storm's throat as she cupped that little head close.

Selfish, selfish, selfish.

Claudette should be holding her own baby, and *she* should not be grateful that Becky was calling her Mama. "We do have to go," Storm said. "You need time to grieve, you and Ginny, and Pepper and I need to . . . go."

"Drive back to Salem with us in the coach," Aiden said, the need rolling off him palpable, but who did he need? His dead wife or his lover?

Yes, that's what they'd been. Lovers. Storm shook her head. She couldn't bear to be this close to him without touching him. "I have the car," she said. "Thanks anyway."

"I can tow the car."

"I can drive."

"It'll be more comfortable in the coach. We should be back on Paxton Island by six. Destiny knows that Ginny and I are on our way, and she went to tell Vickie, who's planning to feed us all. Did you tell Destiny that you're on your way home? At least I assume that's where you're going?"

"You assume right." Storm sighed, seeing no way out. "No, Destiny doesn't know we're on our way. I wanted to surprise her, let her meet Pepper before I told her we had another sister."

"The thing is," Aiden confessed, "I'm driving the coach, so Ginny has to tend Becky, who gets restless in her car seat that long. Having you and Pepper along would give Ginny a break, which I think she's ready for. And it's obvious that Becky wants you."

Low blow, Storm thought.

Becky hugged her tighter, choking tight, as if she understood the conversation.

"We'll go with you, if you drop us off at the house in Salem. I'm not up to the island tonight." She needed as quick an escape as she could get from Aiden, and from her yearning for this beautiful baby girl.

"Please come to the island with us. Humor me," Aiden said so softly and with such a raw look of yearning, that Storm felt a shiver, as if he'd stroked her with his gaze.

Disarmed, there was nothing she could do but turn and make her way toward the car, carrying Becky, while Pepper and Ginny chatted behind her, which meant that Aiden was pushing the wheelchair along the uneven terrain, his gaze warming her back.

A shiver of awareness radiated inward to all her welcoming parts—parts that should have known better than to shiver in anticipation of something . . . someone . . . they could no longer have.

His wife had died *yesterday*, for heaven's sake.

Storm stopped when she saw his coach parked beside her car, the dragon's tail mostly on the grass. Memories rushed her at the sight. *Forget both dragons, missy,* she told herself. *No more dragon games for you.*

A few people looked twice as they passed the coach, but nobody stopped. No crowd had formed. She guessed their notoriety had finally breathed its last, thank the angelic protector of all fools in merry widows who carry hand-cuffs.

Before Aiden set up the makeshift ramp he'd impro-vised for Ginny's wheelchair, Storm took Becky and Pep-per inside and gave them drinks. Lemonade for Pepper, and juice for Becky's sippy cup.

Aiden got Ginny up the ramp and into the coach, then he took her straight to the big bedroom at the back so she could lie down.

Storm changed Becky's diaper, then she put her in her car seat on the sofa nearest the driver and passenger seats up front. Pepper buckled herself in beside Becky.

Pepper was the only reason Becky removed her arms from around Storm's neck. Thank the Goddess for the unexpected gift of sisters who attracted toddlers. When Becky started stealing Pepper's face paint, Storm took wipes from her purse and handed one to Pepper, then she used the other on Becky.

Aiden shut the bedroom door and came down the hall with a bag of books and toys for Becky, and Pepper dove right in.

"Storm," Aiden said. "You might want to use one of those on your own face."

Pepper giggled.

Storm went to the bathroom mirror to see nightmare cat staring back at her. Face clean, she returned to find the girls laughing. It occurred to her that Becky had perhaps not seen too many small people in her short life. She'd been rather isolated in Ginny's cottage. Pepper would be good for her.

"Pepper, do you mind watching Becky while I unpack the car?" Storm asked.

Pepper looked surprised. "Thank you for trusting me. I'll take good care of her."

Storm kissed her sister's brow. "Thank you for watching her."

Becky raised her little heart-shaped mouth for a kiss, too. Storm chuckled, kissed her, and cupped her cheek. "Be good for Pepper."

"Pep," Becky said, and nodded.

Storm rescued Warlock first and left him in his carrier in the air-conditioned coach. Then she went for Pepper's things.

"You lost your clothes a second time, didn't you?" Aiden said.

Startled, Storm jumped. "Someone took off in his motor coach with them."

"Bet you didn't buy that saucy sundress at a mall. If you did, it'd be black. But it looks too good to be yard sale fare. Turquoise, Snapdragon?"

"Don't call me that!"

Aiden stepped back. "I'm sorry. Time warp."

Their eyes met, and Storm felt hers fill, damn it. She blinked and raised her chin.

Aiden's arms fell to his sides. "I apologize . . . for everything."

"Let's move it," Storm said. "Those two aren't going to sit and play quietly for very long."

"Right." Aiden took Pepper's broken suitcase, radio box, and backpack, leaving Storm with the paper bags.

After everything was inside, Aiden drove her car around behind the coach, and Storm watched him hook it up to be towed, the silence between them deafening. "This dress has a designer label," Storm said to break the tension. "Pepper 'acquired' it, among other things, from Marvelanne's closet when she packed."

Aiden shook his head, looking almost proud. "The cheeky little thief."

"She learned from the best."

"You have to give Pepper points for thinking of you."

"Hah. You think she took it for me? Turns out we wear the same size. To quote Pepper, 'We just stretch and fill it out differently.' And it's longer on her. Pepper took this dress for herself."

"Stealing a dress like that isn't the same as stealing a sugar packet," Aiden said. "Do you have a little delinquent on your hands?"

"The sugar packets were the tip of Marvelanne's vice-berg," Storm said. "I hope with all my heart to turn Pepper in a new direction. After this dress has been cleaned, it's going back to Marvelanne with anything else the chip off the old klepto took. I'm gonna have Pepper work off the cost of cleaning and postage at the Immortal Classic."

"You're gonna be good for her," he said. "Already, she's wearing less makeup. So are you, come to think of it."

"Maybe that's because most of my makeup is in your coach."

"Ah, right." He wiped his hands on his jeans. "You told Ginny she could call you if she wasn't happy at assisted living. That was nice, Storm."

"Withering witch balls, don't go telling anybody."

"Scout's honor. Here you go, all hitched and ready to roll."

"As far as looking less goth," Storm said, "now that I've got Pepper, I made her promise not to go goth until high school, so I intend to tone it down myself, for a while.

"Keep the blue hair," Aiden said. "I really love—"

"Awkward moment," Storm said, and walked away.

Chapter Fifty

WHEN Storm returned to the coach, Pepper had opened the carrier, and Warlock was now sitting on Becky's lap licking her hand and giving her a fit of the giggles.

Aiden went into the bathroom to wash his hands from hitching up the tow, and Storm spotted the kitchen drawer where she'd found the sea horse. She removed the necklace and put it back where she found it. After all, it belonged to Claudette when she and Aiden were together. It must mean something to him, if he'd kept it for a year and a half.

When she heard him coming, she shut the drawer and headed for the passenger seat.

"Are we leaving catastrocat loose while we drive?" Aiden asked.

"I'll hold him in my lap," Pepper said.

Storm turned in her seat. "He might scratch you. He goes a little bonkers when we start driving."

"Me and Becky wanna see him go bonkers."

Becky nodded. "Bonks."

Aiden tilted his head as he focused on her, like he didn't know what was missing, and Storm kept herself from covering the spot where the sea horse had rested. "Pepper can hold Warlock while we take off," he said, heading toward the kitchen area behind her, as Storm faced forward.

"If it turns out psycho cat needs to be crated," Aiden said, "we'll stop and crate him. How's that for a compromise?"

"Great," Storm said. "Everybody ready to roll?" she asked, still facing forward.

After some rustling, and some Aiden-type footsteps that stopped behind her, the copper sea horse slipped between her breasts.

Aiden took forever hooking it, as if he were stroking her on purpose in a place that yearned for his touch.

Storm remembered the feel of him stroking her there, and wondered if he did, too. "I'll get it," she said, pushing his hands aside and hooking the clasp. "According to Celtic myth," she said, "the sea horse is the transporter to the afterlife, or Summerland, as we call it."

Aiden gave her a double take. "As in . . . Claudette chose you to help her cross over?"

"I've been wondering about that myself. I believe I was the last person she spoke to. In my mind, I heard her say, 'Thank you,' and 'I'm ready.' And I bade her merry part, and wished her a safe journey . . . into your marriage . . . I thought."

Aiden lowered himself to the driver's seat.

"Are you all right?" Storm asked.

"My belief system has been scrambled," Aiden said, "but other than that, I think I'm okay to drive."

"I'll drive if you want."

His smile was weak. "I'm not up for getting seasick."

"I'd drive straight down the highway this time."

"So you say, but we never know what'll pop into your head, now do we?"

"No," Storm said, only just realizing it, "and we never will." The prospect pleased her.

Aiden hooked his seat belt. "Ready, Becky? Ready, Pepper?"

"Ready," Pepper said, and Becky nodded.

Pepper held Warlock in her lap while Aiden pulled out of the parking lot. "This is not as much fun as the first time," he said. "Something's missing."

Storm looked at him. "What?"

"Elephant poop." He winked. "We need at least a foot to stage a good getaway."

Storm found herself smiling until Becky screeched and Pepper giggled.

Aiden looked in the rearview, and Storm turned in her seat.

Warlock hung from the ceiling-fan paddles.

"That's *his* favorite carnival ride," Aiden said.

Storm pointed to her cat. "Is that what he was doing that night?"

"Yes, except that there's no trampoline with bruisable parts beneath him this time."

Aiden drove toward the interstate. "North to Salem, right?"

"Now you ask?"

"Chalk it up to . . . a journey of discovery."

"Who discovered what?"

Aiden looked in the rearview.

Storm looked, too. Pepper was reading Becky to sleep.

"Triton discovered Elektra," Aiden said, "and before you zap me, remember that aliases are necessary within range of kiddos and kleptos, okay?"

Storm gave a nod of consent. "Go on."

Aiden nodded as well. "Triton and Elektra discovered they were both misfits who belonged nowhere. They were the same in those ways. Triton wept in loneliness, and only Elektra heard."

Storm shrugged, not totally agreeing. "I'll grant you that once Elektra realized Triton was as flawed as her, she didn't feel as compelled to hide. So, yes, in that way, they were the same."

"And yet," Aiden said, "they're a study in contrasts."

"Explain," Storm said.

Aiden changed lanes. "Triton grew up alone and lonely.

Elektra and her sisters raised each other, not lonely, but alone. Elektra rebelled against what she missed. Triton accepted his aloneness."

"He embraced it."

Aiden tilted his head in concession. "Triton was popular and a good athlete, a member of the in crowd, a class officer, while Elektra was a self-appointed outcast—a rebel with attitude who dressed different and looked different, the only way to prove she didn't care what anyone thought."

"I'll bet Triton had plenty of girlfriends," Storm said.

Aiden shrugged. "While Elektra had the wrong kinds of boyfriends . . . on purpose?"

Storm sighed. "Something like that."

"When Triton and Elektra met," Aiden said, "they shared an instant attraction—on every level, shall we say?" He checked the rearview mirror again. "They shared a love of art and antiquities and a gift for rebellion—she of the quieter sort, whereas he was never shy about his rebellion. Triton stands testament to that."

Storm looked at him over her sunglasses. "Triton had better stand down. Elektra has gone into hibernation."

"Elektra doesn't react well to emotion, because she doesn't know how to react. The fact that she slipped into hibernation at the first sign of an emotional upheaval doesn't surprise me. Elektra hides, you see, like Triton's turtle used to—"

"Used to?"

"You'll see, but no subject-changing. Back to Elektra. Now here's Triton telling her he wants to reveal something about her, and peel away her protective layers, to bare her loving soul, which scares her half to death."

"It's called prudence. Triton has moved on. He's in mourning."

"He is, but in more ways than Elektra can imagine. He was caught in a . . . tempest and set magnificently free of his turtlelike idiosyncrasies, until an old ghost—bearing a host of responsibilities—caught him in a . . . cyclone, let's say . . . not unkindly, but in desperate need, and gave him a gift of rare and unimagined joy."

"Becky," Storm said.

"Becky," Aiden admitted. "Both tempest and cyclone gave Triton something he thought never to receive: acceptance, flaws and all; unqualified trust; and the unconditional love of a child, which forged a new kind of independence. Triton is nearly content, and more than up for making a life, but something vital is missing."

"I don't think so," Storm said. "I think Triton has everything under control. Look, Pepper," Storm called. "We're getting close to Salem. Aiden, when you get there, drive by the house and show Pepper her new home."

A short, silent while later, Aiden parked in front of the house on Pickering Wharf, so Pepper could unhook her seat belt to get a good look.

"It's so beautiful," Pepper said. "I can't believe I'm gonna live there."

"And work there, occasionally," Storm added. "The shop out front is ours."

"What kind is it?"

"It's a vintage clothing and curio shop."

"Retro!" Pepper said.

"Exactly."

"Can we see it now?"

"Your other sisters are waiting for us on the island," Aiden said. "Buckle up. Let's go."

Her conversation with Aiden had blown Storm's mind. Maybe he was right. She really didn't know how to react to emotion.

Helluva time to find out.

Chapter Fifty-one

PEPPER stood on the Salem dock shaking her head in disbelief. "I get my first boat ride, today, too?"

"Having a good birthday?" Storm asked as she helped her into the water taxi.

"Are you kidding? It totally made up for the other ten. Holy crackers," she said when she saw the castle. "Are we going there?"

"Harmony lives there."

Vickie was waiting on the dock to meet them. "I saw you coming."

"Vickie," Aiden said, "this is my daughter, Becky, and her grandmother, Ginny."

"Storm!" Vickie shouted, hugging her. "You *did* hear a baby crying!"

"More than one baby," Aiden said. "But we'll save that story for later."

Before Storm had a chance to introduce Pepper, Destiny came running over. "Well, if it isn't the Silver Fox and the nymphomaniac."

"Who's a nymphomaniac?" Pepper asked.

"It's a joke," Storm told her.

Destiny took Pepper by the chin to examine her with the eye of an artist. "Who *is* this beautiful child? Aiden, you didn't tell us you were bringing Storm *and* a mystery guest. Did you find you had two children?"

"I'd be honored if Pepper was my daughter," Aiden said, and if he hadn't already won her heart, that would have done it, Storm thought.

"Vickie and Destiny," Storm said, squeezing Pepper's shoulders. "This is Pepper. She's our half sister. I found her mother first, then I found her."

Destiny's head came up. "You don't mean that you found *our* mother?"

"Actually, Destiny, Pepper and I have agreed to call her *your* mother from now on."

"What does that mean? I get the feeling it's not a good thing."

"We lost the dice toss on the mother roll, Sis, but I found Pepper, and she's better than what we thought we wanted. Pepper's eleven today."

"Happy birthday, Pepper," Destiny said, pulling her against her skirts. "Storm, could we call the woman you found *Harmony's* mother?"

When introduced to Becky and Ginny, Destiny hooted. "Storm! You did hear a baby crying!"

"Don't be so shocked. I, my dear sister, have a gift for finding lost children, and I believe that finding them is my psychic mandate. I can't wait to tell Harmony."

Destiny elbowed Aiden. "Hey, how does it feel to be a father?"

"Wonderful," Aiden said.

"So what are you two doing together?" Destiny asked Storm. "Aiden gave us the impression you had split—"

Storm cringed. "He picked us up along the way, like *he* had psychic powers, or something," Storm said, a little miffed that Aiden had told her sister what should have been hers to tell.

Aiden shrugged. "I went to a carnival that meant

something to both of us, and so did you. We could call it fate. Who are you to argue with fate?" He gave Storm and Pepper pointed looks. "And speaking of fate, I'd like to be the first to clarify a long-held misconception. Destiny, Storm wasn't the straw that broke the camel's back. The camel didn't want any of you, one, two, or three. Period. You owe the unexpected twin an apology, and I'd appreciate it if you'd pass the word on to Harmony."

Storm stood there dumbfounded and humbled.

"We were kids," Destiny said. "We teased her, but we didn't mean it."

"She was a kid, too, and childhood scars rarely heal," Aiden said.

"Sheesh, when did you become her knight in shining armor?"

"Some wounds need to be opened to heal, and this is one of them."

Destiny huffed and turned back to Storm. "You will explain everything Cranky Pants just said in detail, later, right?"

"She will." Vickie chuckled. "Or I won't let her off the island."

"Wow, you two really look alike," Pepper said, looking from Destiny to Storm, "except for Storm's blue hair."

"Storm, did you neglect to tell her something?" Destiny asked.

"You know we're triplets. Guess you didn't know we're identical. Harmony gets home from her honeymoon next week; then you'll see."

Storm hooked her arm through Vickie's. "The preggers one, here, is Vickie, our half sister on our father's side."

Rory opened the castle door. "Ach, are you gonna stand bletherin' on the stoop all night?"

Vickie hooked an arm through his. "Pepper, this strapping Scot is Rory, my husband, and your brother-in-law. Rory, Pepper is a triplet half sister on their mother's side."

Rory took Pepper's hand, bowed, and kissed her fingers. "Ach, and aren't you a comely lass?"

Pepper giggled, first-crush style, as they went inside, where she walked in a circle to take in the great hall.

"Pepper, this is Reggie, Harmony's stepdaughter, and that little guy flirting with Becky is Reggie's son, Jake."

"You have a big family," Pepper told Storm.

"No, Pepper, *we* have a big family."

Pepper covered her blush with her hands. "I love big families."

"Mama," Becky said, reaching for Storm, and as she accepted Aiden's daughter, Storm saw Vickie and Destiny exchange glances.

"I'm starved," Storm said.

After dinner, Vickie brought out a birthday cake that the cook had improvised during dinner, and they sang happy birthday to Pepper, who needed instructions on how and why to blow out her candles.

Their applause surprised her, as did the wrapped gifts they each put in front of her.

"How did you do this? You didn't know I was coming."

"We're into vintage and antiques, as you know," Storm said. "Nothing is new, but everything is from the heart."

Pepper put on Destiny's colorful bangle bracelets, slipped into the retro slides with kitten heels from Storm, and got up to parade around in her first pair of girl shoes. They had to lure her back to the table to open her bell-bottoms from Reggie. Then Vickie and Rory gave her a kilt pin and invited her to Scotland with her sisters in the fall for the baby's christening.

Pepper burst into tears, and only Storm could comfort her.

"You're so great. I can't believe you're my family. Marvelanne never celebrated birthdays or Christmas. I'm mad at myself for missing her, but I'm madder at her for being . . . her."

"If it's any consolation, my sisters and I have been mad at her for twenty-seven years," Storm said.

"Can I stay with you for twenty-seven years?"

"You just said you missed your mother."

"No, I said I missed *Harmony's* mother, but with you, I feel . . . like I'm home."

"Lass," Rory said, taking Pepper's hand. "Come see Harmony's castle, and maybe we can give you your giggle back."

On cue, Pepper giggled.

Storm started to follow, but Aiden caught her hand. "Take a walk with me across the island?"

She didn't want to be alone with him. Her feelings were all mixed up with Becky and motherhood. Too confusing. "Not right now," Storm said, worried also about what Ginny would think.

"Oh go for a walk," Vickie said. "Have a talk. It's a great night. It's still light. In the air, there isn't a bite."

"She's rhyming again," Storm said.

"Ach, she's worse than ever," Rory said. "She can rhyme me into rowing to the mainland in the middle of the night for chunky doodle ice cream."

Vickie grabbed Rory by his shirt collar with both hands and pulled him so close, they went nose to nose. "I can rhyme you into having morning sickness for me, Hopscotch."

Rory groaned. "Aye, and that's the bloody horrid truth," he admitted.

"Enough," Storm said. "You've talked me into going just so I don't have to listen to you two lovebirds."

"Vickie, Rory, I owe you one," Aiden said.

"Wait," Vickie said. "Here's the plate of dinner I promised Morgan. He was too busy to stop and eat with us."

Storm started walking ahead, while Aiden took the plate of food, but he caught up with her.

"You need time to grieve," she said. "Why don't I take Morgan his food, and you go back to the castle. I'll take a rain check. Maybe in the fall or winter, we can take a walk."

"I'm definitely up for some fall and winter walks with you," Aiden said, "but I'm up for one on this fine July night, as well. Accept it. Besides, Morgan's working on a project he wants to show you."

"Why me?"

Aiden took her hand, and though she tried to pull free, he held it tight.

"What's Ginny gonna think?" Storm whispered, imagining her watching them.

"Ginny is your cheering section," Aiden said.

"I have no idea what you're talking about."

"I realize that, and you don't want to know, either."

"Do not get snippy with me, Aiden McCloud."

"*Do* get sassy with me, Storm Cartwright. I like your sass."

Storm huffed and freed her hand from his grip to fold her arms across her chest.

"There's no use in trying to protect yourself, either, from your own emotions or from my intentions," Aiden said. "That horse has already left the barn, and he's running at a full gallop."

Storm looked down at her crossed arms and lowered them to her sides. She realized that she hadn't told her sisters what happened with Aiden, but she wasn't ready to talk about it, anyway. They knew something from Aiden, or they wouldn't have thought they'd split. Besides, Ginny would fill them in.

Storm was surprised to find a construction crew working on an addition to the windmill. Morgan stood outside at a sawhorse table going over architectural drawings.

Her favorite Paxton Island property, the five-story tower windmill—where she and Aiden used to come to make out—was made of stone like the castle and built on the island's highest point. She loved its sails turning in the wind and its periwinkle blue shutters and doors.

Around the windmill, wildflowers grew helter-skelter, except on the well-worn paths to and from the island castle and lighthouse. In the distance, a breathtaking field of peach-colored poppies danced in the breeze rolling over the island.

"What's Morgan up to?" Storm asked. "Is King making this into a guesthouse?"

"No," Morgan said, getting up to greet her. "King sold it. It's being turned into a private residence."

Storm couldn't believe her ears. "King sold an island property to a stranger?"

"The new owner's not *terribly* strange." Morgan grinned.

Storm turned to see Aiden watching her.

"What's going on here?" she asked.

Chapter Fifty-two

STORM'S heart pounded, and she didn't know why.

Aiden drew her toward the windmill, the extra current tossed by the sails playing with that lock of his hair that kept falling on his forehead. A sunbeam picked him out like an earth god—the god of the physical. Big surprise.

Storm cleared her throat and stepped inside the windmill, only to come face-to-face with the memories of all the times she and Aiden had spent playing sexual chicken here.

Aiden blocked the doorway so she couldn't leave.

"Aiden, you have to get past what happened with Claudette."

"No, Storm, you have to get past what happened with Claudette." He placed his hands on her arms, but Storm pulled from his touch, slid passed him, and went back outside into the moving shade made by the windmill's sails.

She went and sat on a rock not far away. "You're a widower. You have to grieve."

Aiden sat on the rock beside her, so close, it was necessary for him to put an arm around her waist, his hand splayed there, and a little bit on her bottom, not an unpleasant or unwelcome feeling, but perhaps inappropriate under the circumstances. Yet she stayed exactly where she was.

"It was the damnedest thing, Storm. I ran into that nursing home to apologize for being a jerk before she passed away, my heart racing, my mind full of all the things I needed to say, even if she couldn't hear me. But when I got to her room, she was sitting up in bed, as if she'd been expecting me, when she'd just come out of her coma a few minutes before."

Aiden took a deep, shuddering breath, while Storm's heart broke into smaller pieces. He really loved his wife.

"I knew what I had to do, Storm. I owed Claudette, and I needed to keep Becky."

"I'm sorry you lost her, Aiden. She looked so happy during the ceremony. Her love for you was written all over her face."

"You *were* there. God, I'm sorry." Aiden touched his head to hers, and it was all Storm could do not to pull him close and press her lips to his.

He pulled away first, and she chided herself for her weakness in clinging.

"While the nursing home chaplain pulled in some judicial type debts of the big-brass variety, Claudette said she'd always loved me, but she knew I didn't love her, and that's why she left. It wasn't because I wouldn't put down roots. She knew I was marrying her to become Becky's stepfather. She knew you'd brought me to Becky, and I told her that you and I were seeing each other."

Seeing. Not exactly a commitment, but she hadn't expected him to tell Claudette about her at all.

Aiden took her hands, a touch Storm should reject, but in light of what he'd just said, she didn't pull away.

"She told me the most amazing story about what happened while she was in her coma, how she came looking for me and used you to help me find Becky."

"It sounds like Claudette was a great lady."

"And a good mother," Aiden said. "She refused to cross over until Becky was with me, but she was more than ready once everything was settled. At the end, before she passed, she said when I found you at the carnival to thank you for her. That's why I stopped at the carnival. Fate, with a helping hand."

Storm melted into Aiden's embrace, their need for consolation was mutual and desperate, neither of them quite steady. Aiden's grief became hers, one occasion where sensing the present nearly broke her. He'd cared deeply about his wife. It would take him a long time to heal.

"If Claudette could astral project," Storm said, taking them away from emotion, "Becky might have some psychic power of her own."

"I wonder if that's why she thinks you're her mother. Maybe she can sense the future. If she is psychic, I'll really need your help raising her."

"That's it?" Storm asked. "She's yours, no question?"

"I have Claudette's signed, notarized statement that I'm Becky's biological father."

A jolt, Storm felt. Shock. Awareness. Claudette was Becky's biological mother. You couldn't argue with biology. Becky wasn't hers. Claudette and Aiden's love had created Becky.

She'd been deluding herself about her and Aiden. Lust was not love. Sex for pleasure was not commitment. Self-conscious to find herself in his arms, Storm made the first move to pull away, but she shivered when Aiden let her go.

He placed his jacket over her shoulders. "After Claudette passed, I went back to Ginny's, and I needed you, Storm, but I understood why you left."

"I went to the nursing home to be there for you, but what I found was a happily ever after. I saw love in Claudette's gaze when she looked at you, so I left. I had to move on and, now, so do you." Storm stood. "When do you have to go back for the funeral?"

"Claudette donated her body to science. It's done, Storm."

"Not by a long shot, Aiden. You have a lot of healing to do."

"I know what I want," Aiden snapped, angrier than when she'd cuffed him to his bed.

Storm shook her head, telling herself not to go there. "You can't know what you want after everything you've been through. It's too soon. You have to make peace with Claudette's coma, your guilt, her return to your life, and your marriage . . . then you have to deal with her death all over again."

Storm rubbed her arms against a sudden chill. "Call me when you come out the other side, whole, and you can think straight again. No decision you make now will stand on solid ground . . . which probably doesn't matter to you, because you'd rather have wheels beneath you anyway." Storm turned to make her way back to the castle.

"Effin' A," she heard him say. "Now who's running? Not me. Wait, I'll give you the code to the keyless entry system on my shell, since you're the one acting like a turtle, now."

Yes, he was angry, but he didn't try to follow her.

He didn't run her way like he'd run toward Claudette. Granted, she hadn't risen from the dead, though in walking away from him, she felt a lot like she was dying inside.

At the castle, Storm kissed Ginny good-bye, and damned near broke down when she kissed Becky, and she gathered her household together to go back to the mainland. Vickie would take good care of Aiden and his family.

BACK in Salem, Destiny and Reggie offered to take Pepper out for a late movie as a final birthday gift.

Storm offered to stay with Jake. After he fell asleep, she did a lot of pacing, until she went into her bedroom for her herbal dream pillow and her dream catcher. She lit ritual candles for peace and love and took out Nana's aquamarine necklace. She gazed at it, concentrating on her emotions over Aiden and Becky.

She drank in the gems' pale aqua color and let herself relax into the energy of the crystals.

When she got sleepy, she snuffed the ritual candles and placed the aquamarines around her neck. She hung the dream catcher over a bedpost and hugged the dream pillow as she closed her eyes. In the fertile solitude of her mind she allowed herself to acknowledge each emotion claiming her, each secret desire, while she fingered the aquamarines.

Spells were considered a form of prayer, so Storm poured her dreams into prayer:

> *I amend my behest;*
> *A love bond is my quest.*
> *This former wild child*
> *Begs to nurture and guide*
> *Aiden's babe who was lost*
> *To fortune's gruff toss.*
>
> *Love as the price,*
> *I send my plea twice.*
> *With the man of my heart,*
> *May our goals never part.*
> *On wheels or roots*
> *Wherever love suits.*
>
> *Though one babe I keep*
> *And one child I reap,*
> *I'll open my mind*
> *To additional cries*
> *And follow cry's guide*
> *Till each child I find.*
>
> *This I will*
> *My fate to fulfill*
> *With harm to none*
> *So mote it be done.*

Storm stood at the bottom of a tall, curving Victorian stairway in a huge, wondrous place—a palace or cathedral—its ceiling too high to be seen, its nebulous walls bathed in pale blue light filtering in from every direction.

Claudette stood at the top of that curving stairway looking down at her. She had given birth to a baby girl, the baby Storm held, but Claudette held a baby, as well, one wrapped in blue.

Claudette was too sick to care for the baby girl, so Storm had come to take it into her own care. As she dressed the girl in her tiny clothes for the long journey to her home, Storm couldn't stop crying, because her house seemed so far away from this place where Claudette would live.

Storm's heart was breaking just thinking about how sad Claudette must feel to be losing her daughter to the care of another.

Guilt filled her over taking Claudette's little girl away from her, even though it was her only choice. A man stood beside Storm, waiting for her, but his image was vague, a strong, supporting presence, but not the point of this emotional exchange between her and Claudette.

Storm took the baby girl in her arms, ready to leave but unable to move, hating to take that last monumental step of walking out the door and separating Claudette from her little girl forever.

"I'm sorry." Tears streamed down Storm's face. "Claudette, I'm so sorry that I have to take her away from you, but it's the only way that I can care for her."

"Storm, stop!" Claudette said with patient authority. "This is the way it was always meant to be." She spoke with surety and serenity. She looked peaceful, accepting, young, vibrant, and healthy in a long white gown, the baby wrapped in blue held close to her heart.

She no longer looked like the dying woman in the nursing home, yet she accepted her fate, while Storm could not.

"This is the way it was always meant to be," Claudette repeated.

"No guilt.

"Only love.

"The way it was meant to be.
"Always."

"I don't understand!" Storm shouted and opened her eyes.

Disoriented to find herself in bed, she sat up, lowered her legs to the floor, and sat on the edge of her bed, hands shaking, heart pounding, expecting Claudette to be there.

She'd just been talking to her. It had all seemed so real . . . as if Claudette had . . . visited her . . . to take away her guilt for loving Becky, her guilt for the joy, hugs, kisses, and smiles Becky gave her. For the way Becky filled her heart with laughter and love.

Storm now understood that her turbulent emotions rested on one issue: her guilty love for Claudette's child.

Her love for Aiden wasn't the problem. Her love for Becky was.

The way it was always meant to be.

Storm felt guilty for the joy she experienced in loving Becky, especially when Becky called her Mama and returned her love.

Had Claudette just given her permission to be Becky's mother, and whose baby had Claudette been holding?

Storm sat straighter, an impossible thought filling her mind. Could Claudette have been holding the baby she miscarried?

The way it was always meant to be.

It was time to relinquish her guilt over losing her own child, Storm understood, as well as her guilt over loving Becky. Claudette and Becky had been as important a part of her psychic destiny as Aiden.

Aiden, the strong, supporting presence. Aiden, waiting patiently for her to go with him. Standing by her. Waiting for her to walk beside him.

In the dream, yes.

But what about in real life?

How long would his denied grief take to heal?

If she'd learned anything on her psychic journey, it was

to trust her instincts, to accept herself and be true to herself, because in doing so, she was free to love and trust another . . . Aiden.

The way it was always meant to be.

He did need time to grieve, but now that she had accepted Claudette's blessing, her permission, Storm wondered how long she would be able to stay away from the man and child . . . both meant to be hers.

Chapter Fifty-three

WHILE Aiden had given every indication of wanting her in his life, Storm decided to stay away from the island for a week to give him time to grieve and to realize—likely for the first time—that he was dealing with a long-term decision that would affect the rest of his life.

For a nomad, that was pretty serious business.

She was also trying not to distract him, pleased to remember that she had quite the distracting effect on him.

Still, he'd been through an emotional wringer, and his life had taken a U-turn in a dark tunnel with no headlights . . . and no wheels. Not that his coach was gone—she checked the Salem dock daily to make sure. But he had so much adjusting to do, and she had no right to further complicate issues.

While she could stay away from Aiden, she could not responsibly stay away from Becky, so she asked Destiny to bring Becky and Ginny to Salem. Storm was certain, after Claudette's visitation—and it was a visitation, not a dream—that she couldn't disappear from Becky's life for even a day.

After that, since she'd practically kidnapped Aiden's

daughter, part of her hoped he'd come—for Becky, at least. She was that starved for the sight of him. He'd gone to Claudette, after all, but he'd been running toward what he perceived to be an ending, not a beginning, and that was a very different cauldron of emotions. He'd also said that Claudette knew he didn't love her, but he never once said that Claudette was wrong. The realization strengthened Storm's resolve to do this right.

After three days of playing with Becky and hoping to find Aiden on her doorstep, Storm suddenly sensed that it was time to go to him. She dressed in the full-length royal blue jersey halter dress she chose with Aiden in mind and matching flats for an island walk. Her sea horse necklace looked great with the matching earrings she'd bought from Claudette's stock.

With Ginny, Becky, and Pepper, Storm returned to the island.

She left Ginny and the little ones with Vickie and went to find Aiden at the windmill. But he didn't exactly come running when he saw her. If anything, he took a step back . . . as if he'd been gut-punched.

Aiden stood . . . rooted—an unusual description for him—with a hammer in one hand, the other going to his tool belt. Their gazes locked, and she wondered if he'd been as tortured by what might have been a mutually self-imposed separation.

The work crew exchanged looks with each other before their gazes wandered from Aiden to her and back.

"Morgan," Storm said, afraid to make a fool of herself by running into Aiden's arms. "You never told me who bought the place."

"I bought it," Aiden said, slipping the hammer in the tool belt with an attention to his actions that called her to take note . . . of the tool belt she'd worn to seduce him.

Hammer in place, he came toward her, and again she held herself steady, so as not to run into his arms. "*You* bought the windmill? As an investment?"

"I bought it to live in."

"For *who* to live in?"

Aiden frowned. "Me, for one . . ."

"But . . . you're a nomad."

"I liked being a nomad better when I was with you. Go figure. I've been thinking—"

"About damned time."

His lips quirked. "I'm beginning to believe that I have been searching for home." His eye crinkles about buckled her knees. Not a smile, but the hope of one. He didn't look the least resentful for having his wheels severed when there was a time she was certain he would have considered the notion nothing short of castration.

"I guess you've had time to think in the past few days," she said.

"I have, because somebody kidnapped my daughter."

"Like father, like daughter?" Storm quipped, biting her lip at the light in his eyes. "Show me what your new house is going to look like."

"I guess you've been thinking, too," he said, stroking the sea horse necklace and setting an earring to swinging. "Nice dress. Great *color*." He cleared his throat and showed her Morgan's gorgeous windmill design.

The focal point and entry to Windmill Cottage—according to the name on the plan—would be the tower itself, but the living quarters would take up several graduated levels behind the tall structure.

Morgan had echoed its structural design by capping the upper levels with a topmost tower, containing the master suite with a circular stairway to the sitting room above, a widow's walk around it, the fence mimicking the windmill's sail design.

"It's absolutely gorgeous," Storm said. "A view of the sea from the master suite. It's so romantic."

"You watched the sea from the hotel penthouse," he said. "And yes, it was romantic."

"You were paying attention."

His look about singed her eyelashes. "Like I've never paid attention in my life."

In the spa, during the fireworks, she'd felt as if they were making love. Now she wondered if he'd felt it, too. The heat in his gaze spoke simmering volumes. Storm swallowed a rush of hope as she tried to stay practical. She'd be no fool rushing in only to be turned away with a broken heart.

"I recognize your construction crew," she said. "I thought they were on vacation."

"Vacation with pay and, now, double time pay on top of that, until the job is done. They're happy."

Storm walked the perimeter of the cottage, shocked at how far construction had progressed. "You got this much work done in a few days?"

"Almost a week, actually. I made King an offer for the windmill when I called him from the penthouse in Atlantic City while you were sleeping. Then I called Morgan at his place in Boston to tell him to fish out our old idea for the design and get started. Between us, we added the new changes to the master suite."

"What possessed you, on that particular night, to make such a bold move?" she dared ask.

Aiden walked her away from the crew, so far away that as they crossed the field of poppies, construction sounds echoed in the distance. "Part of my reasoning was your story about the turtle and the dragon raising a family near the sea."

"But we hadn't found Becky yet."

"No, but I'd found you."

Storm's limbs nearly failed her.

"I fell in love with the windmill when I was a kid," Aiden said, "which is probably why I brought you here when we were looking for a place to—"

"Taunt the dragon?" she suggested. "Though I didn't know the dragon existed back then." The memories of their time at the windmill warmed her, and judging by the glint in Aiden's eye—and the stirring of his dragon—it warmed him, too.

She looked up quickly and hoped she hadn't been caught checking Triton out, but she had.

Aiden let it pass, on his best behavior, apparently. "When Morgan was studying architecture, he wanted a project to practice on. I told him about my idea for the windmill. The final design is close to the original, except for the sitting room and widow's walk, and the porch around back with a view of the sea for Ginny."

"She'll like that."

"Like it? She suggested it." Aiden smiled. "The fact that you and I adopted the windmill for a while makes it more special, so Windmill Cottage is what came to mind when I thought about . . . us . . . and a few days later, I knew it was where I'd like to raise Becky. I'll keep the coach, of course. A man doesn't give up his wheels cold turkey."

She finger-combed that lock of hair from his brow. "Boys and their toys—"

"Are nowhere without someone beside them." He took her hand.

She took it back and fisted it. "I'm worried it's too soon."

"I'll always love Claudette for giving me Becky, but I was never *in love* with her."

"Well, you wouldn't be, would you? You never fall in love. It's the rule. You're the independent sort."

"Every rule has an exception," Aiden said, standing so close now that Storm could hardly breathe. "Storm, you caught me with that peek of you playing dress-up. I want to see you as happy as your inner child, but I yearn, I ache, for Storm the woman, a rare one, who enchants and beguiles, who invades my dreams, and whose absence in my bed when I open my eyes in the morning about breaks me. The way I was lost before is nothing to the way I'm lost now."

He led her toward an outcropping of rocks with a sandy path between them that led to a private beach on a part of the island she'd thought nothing but rocks.

"This place is beautiful."

"I think so."

Storm grabbed a branch and sat in the sand to envision a

circle of light surrounding her. She drew a wide clockwise spiral around herself, five rows deep, like the one she and her sisters had drawn the night of Harmony's wedding.

"Aiden," she said. "Find five smooth beach stones and place them equidistant on the outer circle."

In silence, he did as she asked, as if he understood and respected her actions.

Five stones—one for Aiden, one for her, Ginny, Becky, and Pepper, together on a new journey of discovery.

"Come and sit in the circle with me."

Aiden sat without question and took her hands.

Storm wove their fingers together and raised them toward the sun. She imagined a line of light coming from the pebbles and tenting toward their clasped hands in the center of the spiral encircling them. She imagined the light spinning at increasing speeds while she laid firm claim to this man, this land, and the family she hoped they would raise there. She let her needs be known to the universe, but not to Aiden. Not yet. The decision had to be his, freely made, no magick involved.

> *My lover beside*
> *The Goddess to guide.*
> *Hear my behest;*
> *Our family, my quest.*
>
> *More children I pray*
> *To bless many days;*
> *His blood, my blood*
> *A joining of ways.*
>
> *Take heed, I pray,*
> *Aiden's heart*
> *Lead the way.*
> *I spell not to sway.*

Aiden kissed her, their interwoven hands raised, the sun god smiling down.

"When you hurt, I hurt," Aiden said. "Unless your heart heals, mine never will."

His words brought a knot to her throat and a rush to her heart.

"Your rebellion," he said, "your psychic sense of the present, your brilliant abductions, and bruising telekinetic ability, the children crying in your head, all add to your fascination. Storm Cartwright, you are one of the most easily lovable people I have ever come across, though I know you may never believe it."

"I *don't* believe it. Not for a minute. And you don't know *how* to love. Your words."

"You and Becky taught me how to love. Why did you come back, if you didn't think I'd changed?"

Storm squeezed his hands tight but set them at arm's length without breaking contact. "I knew I needed to be here today, in the same way I knew which mall, which campground, which casino."

Aiden shook his head. "Why would a smart and beautiful woman like you want a Scruffleupagus?"

"I think the Scruffleupagus is lovable. Your parents taught you abandonment. Military school taught you a man has to be strong, unemotional. You learned you shouldn't want home, though you do, which makes you doubt your inner strength. If a military man's inner strength is in question, his worth is in question."

She clasped his hands tighter. "You're strong, Aiden, in a thousand ways. You're a white knight, which you won't admit, who'll do whatever he must to stage a rescue. So strong, I believe—and I think I'm right, considering when you bought the windmill—that you were willing to sacrifice your happiness with one woman for the sake of another, and for the sake of the child you love. That's strength, Aiden. You even reveal your strength in words—scary for any man, except for the strongest of the strong. You use soft words, emotional, beguiling words, as enticing as a stroke or a touch, though I like those, as well."

"I can't believe that you find my words enticing."

"I can't believe that you found your home on Paxton Island."

"Yes . . . and no. I found my home in you. Wherever you are, I'm home."

"What are you saying?"

He hesitated. "I don't have anybody to play dragon with?"

Storm broke their connection, rose, and ran up the path.

Chapter Fifty-four

AIDEN knew exactly where he'd gone wrong. He wondered if witches knew how to roll back time.

Storm had run up the sand path between the rocks so fast, he had a hard time keeping up.

"Storm Cartwright?" asked a stranger in a pinstripe suit who seemed to have been waiting for her.

"I've told you," Storm said. "No story. He wasn't my sex slave. It was a joke. A bad joke. Who let you on the island? This is private property."

"While I'd like to hear that particular story, that's not why I'm here. As to how I got this far, about twenty of your closest relatives grilled me so hard, I was sweating as if it was a tax audit."

Storm smiled. "What is it, then?"

Aiden stood beside her to lend his silent support, silence being his best friend, after the gaffe he'd just made.

"My name is Zach Ward, and your sister Vickie told me where to find you." Ward showed her what appeared to be an ID badge.

After Storm looked at it, Aiden took it to examine it. "PAC?" Aiden asked. "Never heard of it."

"That's good. It means we're doing our job. Psychic Aid to Children. We work anonymously. We're a nonprofit organization of psychics who help find missing children. We've gotten reports of four children being found by someone with blue hair traveling in a dragon motor coach. When my supervisor saw the story in the newspaper with a picture of the coach, including the license plate, we followed the clues, and I came looking for you, Miss Cartwright."

"What makes you think *I'm* the person with blue hair? It could have been Winkie."

"Excuse me?" Ward said.

Storm shook her head. "I didn't find four. I found two, no three."

Ward opened his BlackBerry and hit a few keys. "Kelsey Harrington, age two, mall rescue, Massachusetts. Leslie Vallancourt, age nine, campground rescue, Connecticut. Becky Langley, age one, Social Services rescue, New Jersey. And Pepper Buford, age eleven, wicked mother rescue, New Jersey."

Aiden chuckled at Pepper's obvious word choice.

"We both missed one," Storm said. "I found a toddler before he was reported missing, Jeffrey . . . something . . . at a carnival last week. And the last two rescues you mentioned don't count, because they're *our* children," Storm said, pointing to the two of them . . . as a couple. Aiden's heart beat faster. *Our* children, she'd said, and she meant it collectively.

Maybe he *did* have a shot, big mouth, bad timing, and all.

Ward grinned. "Pepper told us about the way you rescued her, and Becky's grandmother told us—"

"That's my mother-in-law," Aiden said. "I'm Becky's father."

Ward grinned. "Aiden McCloud, I know, but you didn't know that you were Becky's father until Miss Cartwright led you to her."

"Is this some kind of rescue reality show?" Storm asked.

"I apologize for not making myself clear. I had coffee and cheesecake at the house before I came to find you. Ginny and Pepper gave me an earful. I'm a PAC agent, and I'm here to offer you a job, Miss Cartwright, with PAC, doing what you do so well, finding children in trouble. Except that you can't always be in the right place at the right time, unless you spend your life in that motor coach. Though maybe you'd like that, since the motor coach is registered to you, Mr. McCloud, which must mean—"

"You're toast, if you finish that sentence," Aiden snapped.

Ward raised a hand. "I apologize."

"Did you come to our home to insult us?" Aiden asked.

Storm elbowed him. "Aiden, you said *home*." Storm's giggle punctured a hole in his fury—*pffftt*—like a balloon. Oh, the things they'd never be able to tell their children.

This is what life with Snapdragon McGee would be like, if she ever let him catch her. "I said *our* home, but do you catch that? No."

Ward looked from one to the other and cleared his throat. "Storm, think about working with PAC. You can work from here, or on site, if you feel the need. We'll send you the leads."

"There's no contact to, or from, the island, right now," Aiden said. "No landlines and no cell phone towers close enough."

"King is working to fix both," Storm said.

"We can work around that." Ward turned to Storm. "The work is sporadic. Our psychics have different talents for different situations. Sometimes they work in groups, sometimes alone. I'd like a chance to sit down with you, now, if you're willing, and talk about your specialties. The pay isn't great, because we never charge the missing children's families, but finding children in peril is quite rewarding."

"Because it gives psychics an opportunity to use their gifts!" Storm said, beaming. "I *do* have a gift for finding missing children. I've always known it on some level, but never for sure until . . . well, you, Aiden, and Becky. I felt I had a purpose in life, but I couldn't put my finger on what, until you mentioned getting together with Mel to— Wait!"

Storm rounded on him. "Aiden McCloud, if you set this up . . . I needed to earn this on my own. I don't need your charity."

Aiden honestly didn't know what she was talking about. "What do you think I did?"

"You said that you and Mel should put something together for some kind of child-find funding."

"Storm, believe me, I didn't," Aiden said. "Ward, how old is PAC?"

"Six years in September."

"There you go," Aiden indicated Ward. "I asked my people to call Mel's people yesterday when I went to the mainland, but I have no idea if they connected yet, and I've never heard of PAC."

"If I may," Ward said. "What people are you talking about connecting with, Mr. McCloud?"

"I was looking to connect the McCloud Foundation with the Keep Me Foundation."

Ward whistled, and Storm looked fit to kill. "I'm telling you, Aiden, if you promised to fund them so they'd take me on . . ."

Ward shook his head. "Miss Cartwright, I left the West Coast to come east on business and find you three days ago. Mr. McCloud couldn't have had anything to do with our offer." He turned to Aiden. "So you're a McCloud of the McCloud Foundation?"

"Sweet summer savory, he's *the* McCloud of the McCloud Foundation."

Aiden sighed. "So much for anonymity."

Storm gave him a "payback" face.

So she'd outed him, because of his badly timed dragon play remark, the witch. That must mean she cared about what he had to say.

"Sir," Ward said. "We'd be honored if you kept an eye

on PAC over the next year, check out the good we do. With your approval, we could send semiannual reports. And if you have the ear of Ms. Seabright from the Keep Me Foundation, we wouldn't mind her keeping a lookout, either."

"I'm impressed," Aiden said. "You didn't hit me up for money on the spot."

"Please understand that I didn't come looking for *you*. I came looking for Miss Cartwright. Also understand that our development director's head would be spinning if she knew I hadn't solicited you. Let's just pray that she doesn't make the connection between you and Miss Cartwright."

"Okay, okay," Storm said. "You convinced me. You're not connected."

She must have realized that the job was hers and honestly earned, because Aiden saw her eyes go bright and her demeanor radiate joy, as if from the inside out. God, he was hooked. "Storm, can you juggle PAC with your job at the Immortal Classic?"

"Actually, I think Reggie wouldn't mind becoming a full-time employee at the Classic. Destiny said Reggie did my job all the time we were gone, and she did it well. I'd still be part owner."

Aiden realized that Storm's involvement with PAC would mean more wild rides like the one they'd just taken. Then again, wild was one of the things he loved most about her. The goth rebel who'd cuffed him to the bed and listened for crying children was the Storm he'd fallen in love with.

He didn't care how much using her psychic gifts would impact them, having a wife who found missing children would be an honor. He'd be happy as long as they had a life together.

"So, what do you say, Miss Cartwright?" Ward asked. "Want to sit down and talk about your association with PAC?"

Storm hooked her arm through Aiden's and threw his heartbeat into overdrive.

"Mr. Ward," she said. "Meet me at the Immortal Classic in Salem tomorrow at noon, and we can talk over lunch. Your treat."

"I hoped we could talk now," Ward said.

"Not now," Storm said, squeezing Aiden's arm and sending hope sluicing through him. "I have a previous engagement."

Chapter Fifty-five

AIDEN watched Ward leave. An engagement, she'd said. God, he hoped she'd chosen the word carefully. "Where were we?" he asked, unsettled and exhilarated.

Storm gave him her feline look and stance. "You don't have anybody to play dragon with . . . and I'm taking that position."

Aiden curled a lock of hair around her ear. "That was a Storm statement if ever I've heard one. You're taking which? The PAC position . . . or the dragon position?"

"Yes." Storm said. "But I'm still mad at you."

"Zapping mad?"

"Don't worry. The family jewels are safe, but at that moment on the beach, playing dragon was *not* the point."

"I now realize that." He pulled her into his arms so she couldn't run. "But you have to admit that it's a hell of a perk."

Her chin came up. "Granted." She looked toward the crew and urged him behind an ancient oak.

He liked where this was going. "God, you look great in that dress. What did you say about me in that tux? You could eat me up with a spoon? Well, Snapdragon, I'm looking for a spoon."

She tried to hide her smile as she looked down to play with the snap on his jeans, his dragon rising in hope. "You accused me of running when I left a few days ago," she said.

"I was frustrated," he admitted.

"I was running," she admitted. "But not really. I was trying to do the best thing for you—well, for the both of us in the long run—and maybe, deep down, I was trying to protect myself. It made me kind of 'get' the whole turtle syndrome."

"I have an idea," Aiden said. "In the future, when either of us is unsure, and we get the urge to run, let's run *toward* each other, and let it all out, and by that, I don't mean the dragon—though he does want out, you tease—I mean let's share our fears with each other."

"That could work," Storm said.

"Our strengths and weaknesses play off each other, so much so, that your needs become my challenge—my reason for living. You were the first to allow me in when you played dress-up. You welcomed the real me, showed me what home could be, and then you *became* my home.

"Storm, I can't live without you. I love you."

"You can't love *me*."

"Why can't I?"

"I'm not lovable. I'm a bratty pain in the ass."

"You *are* lovable, and you can take that to the bank, to quote a famous dragon man."

"But I've been my worst self with you. I kidnapped you. Cuffed you. Humiliated you—unintentionally—but you stuck by me and disarmed me, until I let down my guard . . . and—" She shrugged.

"And?" he said trying to read her.

"And wha'd'ya know? I guess . . . I love you, too."

"You guess? I was hoping for something less vague."

She led him down to the beach again and brought him into the center of the spiral, and he felt as if something magickal was about to happen.

"I *know* I love you," she admitted.

"That's the best magick I've ever heard." He took her in his arms, kissed her, and waltzed with her, there, on the beach, holding her close and singing, "Can I have this dance for the rest of my life . . ."

Storm sighed in contentment.

"What does the spiral stand for?" he asked.

"It represents a journey of discovery." She cupped his cheek. "I can live in a motor coach, as long as I'm with you. I'll journey with you wherever you want to go."

"And I can live in one place, as long as I'm with you."

"You'd do that? Stop wandering? For me?"

"I'd do anything for you, but I'm part of a package, now, so you'd better think this through."

"I don't know," Storm said. "I think you're sunk. I'm afraid I'm in love with the whole package, but *you'd* better do some hard thinking. I have baggage of my own now. An eleven-year-old who knows all the tricks of the extortion trade. I need someone to help raise her right. A father with a strong sense of family. For Pepper, I'm asking for more than a home, Aiden. I'm asking for roots."

Aiden nodded. "When you walked away from me the other day, I swear that I felt my roots curling into the earth, and instead of running, like my old instincts called for, I settled in and let my roots grow. I stayed here and waited for you to come home to me."

"Aiden McCloud, you threw roots into the earth when I gave you the best excuse in the world not to?"

"I'm rooted, but I'd still like you to get in that coach with me once in a while and go off on a jaunt, not all the time, and not necessarily alone. I want our family with us, whether we're on wheels, sailing into the sunset, or staying right here. Maybe I have windmills in my head, but Windmill Cottage won't be home until you move in."

"Did I ever tell you that I love you, despite your flaws, quirks, and hungry man dragon?"

"You love my hungry man dragon," he bragged, "but lust aside, you have some flaws, quirks, and a lady dragon of your own."

"But you love me anyway."

"Go ahead, get cocky," he said. "Turns me on."

She shook her head. "When turtles flip on their backs, they use their heads to right themselves. You used your instincts to right yourself when your world went more topsy-turvy than any of us could have imagined. You did good, turtle."

They heard Pepper calling, so they left the spiral to the mercy of the tide and climbed the hill. Pepper stood in the poppy field with Becky in her arms, Morgan watching over them. When Becky pointed their way, Morgan saluted and walked back to the windmill.

"Rory walked us to Morgan," Pepper said, "and Morgan walked us here. Becky was calling you both, so Vickie said I could bring her to you."

Aiden kissed Becky's and Pepper's cheeks. "Did you ever want a little sister?" he asked Pepper.

"I never thought much about it. With a mother like mine, siblings seemed pretty much a toss of the dice."

"Well, think about it," Aiden said. "First order of business, learn to be a babysitter. We'll be near that tree, if you need us."

Pepper winked. "Sure thing."

"She's too smart for an eleven-year-old," Storm said as they walked the short distance away, hand in hand.

"Let's teach her to be a kid again."

"She's got a lot of kid in her yet. I told her the elephant poop story when we first got on the Ferris wheel, and she nearly giggled us out of our seats."

Near the tree, they stepped into each other's arms. "Remember what I said about the link between water and land being significant for the purpose of reproduction?" Storm asked.

"I do," Aiden said.

Storm smiled. "Since you can't live without me, and the island is home, can we stop sheathing the dragon?"

"Excuse me?"

She got all feline flirty on him, again. "You know, play naked dragon games, and see what develops?"

"Hey, Morgan," Aiden called, his grin growing.

Morgan looked up from his work.

"Add a middle floor," Aiden shouted. "All bedrooms."

Morgan gave them a thumbs-up.

"So," Aiden said, turning back to her, "Storm Cartwright, will you marry me?"

"Only if you accept me in hail, thunder, lightning, hurricanes, and storm surges."

"Rain gear and all."

Storm kissed him. "I'll happily commit myself to you and our family, but I will never lose who I really am."

"Because you're too stubborn."

"I certainly am."

"I wouldn't have you any other way. Who you really are *is* who I love. I think I knew the first time I saw you that if anybody could tame my dragon, it would be you."

"Hey, you're not the knight," she said. "I am. I get to slay the dragon over and over again."

Aiden pulled her into his arms. "I'm in love with a dragon slayer."

She nipped at his ear. "I think I might just be able to work up the telekinetic passion to make your dragon dance," she whispered, and when she grinned, he kissed her with all the emotions he'd felt when he thought he'd lost her, and with all the joy he felt now that she was his.

Becky threw herself against their legs with a giggle, and Storm picked her up.

"Mama," their daughter said.

Aiden extended his free arm to include Pepper and caught her up in his arms.

Pepper squealed in surprise. "I might be a little heavy for this."

"It's not every day you become part of a new family. We're celebrating."

Storm sighed. "A family. *We* are a family."

"Is that a yes, Cartwright?"

"I'd rather be a McCloud, if you please."

"I most certainly do please. Four McClouds coming up."

"Four? Really? Me, too?" Pepper asked.

"Of course, you," Aiden said.

"But it could be more than four," Pepper said, "if you have babies."

Storm gave him a cryptic look. "I'm partial to the sound of babies."

"So am I," Aiden agreed. "It's the sound that brought our family together."

Turn the page for a preview of
Annette Blair's next novel

Never Been Witched

Coming soon from Berkley Sensation!

DESTINY Cartwright sought peace in her ritual circle but found censure instead. Drat the Goddess of mischievous matchmaking pranks. How could a psychic witch lust after a paranormal debunker? What were the odds?

Talk about a lousy loser chooser.

Morgan Jarvis—six feet of baditude, in torn jeans and open shirts, with burnished bronze hair, wide shoulders, and a five o'clock shadow—would debunk her psychic goal in a blink, if she ever discovered what it was.

That's why she'd come to the lighthouse.

Alone in its dark parlor, she sat surrounded by votives for earth, air, fire, and water, situated north, south, east, and west, with one in the center for spirit. The crystals between each cinnamon candle refracted the flames like stars, the ageless echo of breaking waves at high tide adding an earthy rhythm to her magick.

Though her clairvoyance allowed her to see the future of others, never her own, she had envisioned the Paxton Island lighthouse—as lost in a fog, and as much in need of comfort as she—as the place to find her future. Here, she hoped to find her psychic path, her reason for being, and then she'd spell her perverse attraction for Morgan the Miserable into the sea.

Fine, he might well be hiding Morgan the Mystic deep inside, as she suspected, but since the night of her sister Harmony's wedding, he would always be Morgan the Mistake to her.

Destiny shivered as regret threatened to swamp her, until the moon slipped from the clouds and its beams pierced the windows to fall across her shoulders like a shawl, warm, protective, and forgiving, a welcome and affirming caress.

Shadows danced in her circle, leaving the room's edges in darkness, including the stairs along the outside wall that she faced but could no longer see. Her flashlight had picked them out on arrival a short while ago, and her possessions now sat at the bottom, in large, wheeled carts awaiting transport to a bedroom upstairs.

Relief improved Destiny's spirits. She was here, not in Scotland with her well-meaning family automatically pairing her with Morgan Jarvis, who was so much a friend, he felt like family . . . to everyone except her.

Peace, Destiny sensed . . . just out of reach.

Serenity . . . if only she could grasp it.

Her hyperactive cat's purring contentment attested to the tranquility surrounding them. She petted her caramel-and-marshmallow-swirl tabby. "You like the lighthouse, don't you, Caramello? I like it, too. I think it wants us here."

Destiny centered herself, a first step on this journey of discovery fired by a profusion of confusion over her illusive psychic goal and a riot of romantic fantasies over one maddening man.

Breathe. Release. Breathe. Release.

Perhaps she should have saved her ritual for morning, but . . .

"Now feels right.
In the dead of night

I dare to invite . . .
Profound insight."

A tentative calm settled over her, obscurity filling the dark edges of her consciousness the way it claimed the periphery of the room. Destiny closed her eyes and searched the recesses of her mind before letting her words pour forth:

"Earth, water, fire, air,
Angel guardians hear my prayer.
Help define my psychic brand,
For those who seek a helping hand.

"Moon, stars, high, bright sun,
Light my way to souls undone.
My psychic goal with speed, reveal.
Harm it naught, I seek to heal."

Destiny opened her eyes . . . and she lost her breath.

In her circle stood a man dressed as if for a centennial sail. Beside him, an apple-cheeked young girl sat in a grotto of bright white angel wings. Standing tall behind her: an angel . . .

Destiny's heartbeat trebled. Fear stole her breath, prickling her from the roots of her hair to the tips of her toes. She shivered and clutched her cat so tightly that Cara meowed and jumped from her grasp to circle, examine, and "talk" to the little girl.

Destiny had never seen her cat try so hard to communicate.

The child held her hand flat, well above Caramello, and the cat purred loudly, and arched as if into an actual caress.

The girl smiled and the angel said, "Be not afraid."

Destiny about choked. Wait a minute. She tried to regain her composure. "The last time an angel spoke those words, a virgin got pregnant!"

The angel remained passive, its lucent amber eyes

deeply probing, while centennial man's eyes widened. "I don't think that's the issue, here."

"I resent that!" Destiny snapped, fighting a warm shot of embarrassment at her knee-jerk reaction.

Despite the entities' lack of apparent threat, Destiny stood and pointed a large green fluorite crystal their way like a negative-energy stun gun, because she knew—*she knew*—they were ghosts.

> *"Negative entities away.*
> *Protection come to stay.*
> *White light, elliptical in flight,*
> *Surround me in a sphere so bright*
> *As to sever threat and sight,*
> *Of visions in the night."*

Adrenaline pumped through her as she stepped back.

Her visitors remained.

Normally, she'd feel safe in her ritual circle, except that *they* shared the circle with her.

Destiny gasped, knelt, and with a sweep of her arms, pulled the candles and crystals closer, to form a smaller, safer circle.

The ghost child's lips quirked upward on one side, bringing Morgan's rare smile to mind.

Centennial man shook his head, as if in warning. "We're not negative," he whispered and pointed behind his hand. "That really *is* an angel."

Destiny rose and straightened, preferring to tower over them, though no one could stand taller than that angel, and she chanted her spell again, this time loud enough to wake the dead.

A light appeared at the top of the stairs.

Another icy rush of fear. An involuntary catch in her breath. "Don't tell me there are more of you!"

She heard footsteps, running on the floor above. A crash. A curse.

Another male ghost? Destiny stamped her foot. "Enough already," she whispered.

A hair-raising stair creak. Two. Three.

Very heavy footsteps . . . slowly descending the blacked-out staircase.

Words of inquiry stuck in Destiny's paralyzed throat as she stood frozen in her protective circle. *Beast or ghost, he could not harm her, here.*

She aimed the fluorite crystal high and at the next creak—thank the Goddess for teen softball—she threw it in a deadly pitch.

A grunt. A tumble down the stairs.

A horrendous crash against wheeled carts, her cater-wauling cat leaping into the fray, and her personal belong-ings flying into view, turned her mind from ghosts to a flesh-and-blood man . . . about the size of Bigfoot . . . wrecking everything she'd—"My things!"

Silence . . .

Her heart beat a wild tattoo, yet shame for her first selfish thought claimed her. A ghost would not have disturbed her carts or landed with a thud and a shivering head crack. Un-able to reach a light switch without stepping near Sasquatch, Destiny set her athame on the floor to open the sacred circle and allow for her escape. Then she grabbed a large potted geranium off a nearby table. "Anyone hurt?" she called.

Silence reigned.

As she tiptoed forward, her intruder groaned, sat up, and breached the light. Sasquatch indeed, judging by the size of his chest and the bright of his eyes in shadow.

With trembling hands, Destiny lowered the clay pot and crowned him.

Like a tree trunk in a hurricane he fell, judging by the sound, taking at least one of her carts down with him, his torso in darkness, hairy legs and gigundous feet in candle-light.

Sasquatch in the flesh, moaning like he'd been shot.

She skirted the interloper and flipped on the light.

Curled in the fetal position, his back to her, he'd caught her purple bra on his wrist, and her cart in the crotch.

"Uh-oh."

Blood from cat scratches dripped down his arm and landed on his red boxers. "Balls . . . busted," he said.

At the sound of his voice, Destiny's fear morphed to horror. "Morgan?"

For **Annette Blair,** writing comedy started with a root canal and a reluctant trip to Salem, Massachusetts. Though she had once said she'd never write a contemporary, she stumbled into the serendipitous role of "Accidental Witch Writer" on that trip. Funny how she managed to eat her words, even with an aching jaw. After she turned to writing bewitching romantic comedies, a magic new world opened up to her. She loves her new home at Berkley Sensation.

Contact her through her website at
www.annetteblair.com.